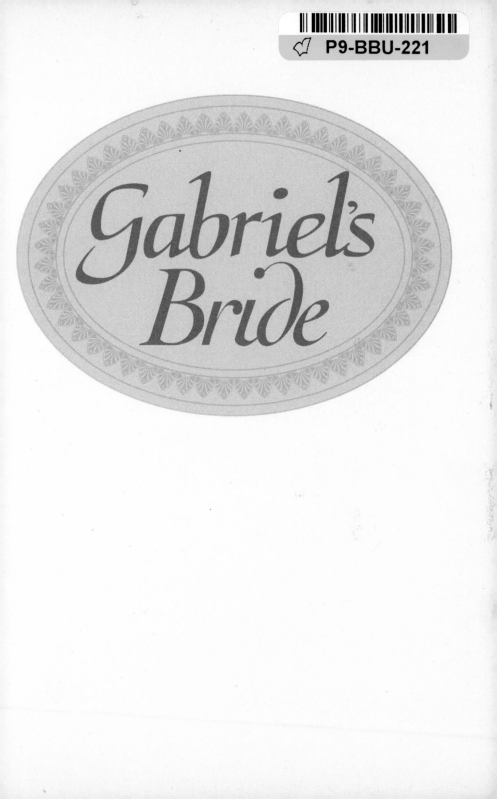

Gabriel's Bride

A CLOVER RIDGE NOVEL

AMY LILLARD

Gabriel's Bride

B&H
PUBLISHING GROUP

Nashville, Tennessee

978-1-4336-7754-0

Published by B&H Publishing Group
Nashville, Tennessee

Dewey Decimal Classification: F
Subject Heading: AMISH—FICTION \ LOVE STORIES \
ROMANTIC SUSPENSE NOVELS

Scripture is taken from the Holman Christian Standard Bible®
(HCSB). Copyright © 1999, 2000, 2002, 2003, 2009 by Holman
Bible Publishers. Used by permission.

1 2 3 4 5 6 7 8 • 18 17 16 15 14

To my father, Stanley Davis. I love you. And I miss you.

"My sheep hear My voice, I know them, and they follow me.
I give them eternal life, and they shall never perish—ever!
No one will snatch them out of My hand." (John 10:27–28)

Acknowledgments

The making of a book is never an easy task. There are always bumps along the road, and some journeys are harder than others. This book had one of those tough routes. Shortly after starting *Gabriel's Bride*, my father passed away. He'd been in poor health for a few years and watching him decline was hard, even from five hundred miles away. I was still reeling from losing him when my eighteen-and-a-half-year-old cat died. Not the best time to write a whimsical romance.

My kind editor told me I could have extra time if I needed it, but all I could see was my daddy's disappointment that I didn't uphold my end of the bargain. "Baby girl, get it done" was all I could hear him say. So I plunged ahead with *Gabriel's Bride*, determined to finish it on schedule.

So many times I have heard authors say that they didn't like a particular book of theirs because they suffered a personal tragedy while writing it. I suppose the book becomes a reminder of times that are impossible to forget and hard to deal with all at once. I did not want *Gabriel's Bride* to be that story for me.

I'm not going to tell you that it was easy, but I knew my daddy would be upset if I didn't give it my all. So I worked hard, I cried, I rewrote, and I prayed. And I'm proud to say that I finished the book on time and I don't hate it. I love it. In fact, it may be my favorite of the Clover Ridge books.

I need to say thanks to my husband and son for putting up with my mood swings and grief as we all mourned the loss of our "poppaw" and beloved Ch'ing Cheng. My "boys" are the best, and I love you.

Another thanks goes out to my agent, Mary Sue Seymour, and everyone at The Seymour Agency—agents and clients alike. I'm so thankful to be a part of such a wonderful group.

Thank you to my editors Julie Gwinn and Julie Carobini and the entire team at B&H Publishing. As always, you make me look "good." And to my dear friends Amy Clipston and Sarah Grimm, thank you for reading and rereading and keeping me sane.

And of course, I thank our awesome God who extends His patience and love in troubled times, and gives me wonderful stories to share with you.

T he Lord was testing him. It was as plain as that.
Gabriel Fisher sat down on the bed, its quilt pulled up and neatly tucked in. She hadn't even slept in it.

He looked at the note in his hands as if seeing it for the first time. From downstairs, he could hear the sounds of the boys stirring around, arguing over who was going to eat what, too impatient in their hunger to wonder where their sister was.

Gone.

He crumpled the paper, not needing to read the words again. Not able to read them through the tears welling in his eyes. His daughter was gone. She had left, wanting to see what the *Englisch* world could offer her. She wanted to go to school, help animals, make more of herself than she could if she stayed in Clover Ridge.

Gabriel raised his eyes toward heaven. "Where did I go wrong, Becca?" He dipped his chin and shook his head. "I did the best I could."

He rose, his joints popping, his heart breaking. He felt old.

His baby girl was gone.

He tossed her good-bye note onto the bed, then retrieved it again, smoothing it back flat. He'd keep it. It might be the last he heard from her. At least for a while.

Quietly, he shut the door behind him when he really wanted to slam it to expel the growing remorse, regret, hurt, and anger that boiled in his gut.

He wanted to run after her, get in his buggy and scour the county. But she was long gone. Probably already in Tulsa. Staying with strangers. Or at least with people she knew but who were strangers to him. *Englischers*. Too many places she could go in a car. He'd never find her.

He took a deep breath at the head of the stairs, held it in. Let it go. Then started down.

His oldest *bu*, Matthew, stood in the middle of the kitchen, hands propped on his hips. He surveyed his brothers as if he wasn't sure if he should intervene or walk away.

In that moment, Gabriel realized that Matthew was next. Steady and true, Matthew would turn sixteen next year and get his taste of the *Englisch* freedoms.

"*Halt!*"

He hadn't meant to raise his voice quite so much, but there it was, and it was effective. Simon, who had been holding the remains of last night's pie above his head to keep it away from leaping David and bouncing Joseph, stopped his own jumping and stared at his father. All three of them turned as if only just now aware that their father was anywhere near.

Samuel quietly sat at the table waiting on someone to stop their nonsense and feed him. Poor child. He hadn't been the same since his sister, Katie Rose, had moved back in with their folks, but that was customary while she and Zane Carson were courtin'. But this . . . this would set Samuel back even more.

Gabriel took a couple more steps into the room, his boys still watching him closely. They knew something was wrong. Their sister had not been about this morning, cooking and laying out their clothes. There was no coffee brewing, no boiled eggs to eat on the way to the barn to jumpstart their morning chores. No Mary Elizabeth.

"Sit down." He nodded toward the table. There were chores that needed doing. Cows to milk, eggs to gather, horses to feed, but they needed to know first.

He waited until they had all settled themselves into their seats before he started. He took a deep breath. Carefully avoiding the empty seat where his *dochder* should have been, he looked at each of them in turn. "Mary Elizabeth has gone."

Matthew's eyes widened as if he understood, yet could hardly believe that what he had heard was true. He alone remained silent; the other *buwe* began speaking at once, talking over each other, but asking the same questions: "Where has she gone?" and "When will she be back?"

Gabriel shook his head, refusing to answer. "Now, go do your chores. I will make breakfast, and we will not speak of this again."

They hesitated, but only for a heartbeat, then the sound of their chairs scraping the floor filled the room. They trudged out the back door, their faces reflecting their unasked questions. But they all knew better than to push him.

All but Matthew.

His oldest *sohn* remained seated, his green eyes so like Gabriel's own filled with concern and dismay. "*Dat?*" His voice was barely above a whisper.

"There are horses to feed, Matthew."

"She's not coming back, is she?"

Hearing the words spoken out loud nearly broke his heart in two. But he had to push the pain aside. He had to remain strong for all of them. "The horses, Matthew." His voice came out gruff, not at all like it had the day before.

"*Jah, Vatter.*"

Gabriel dipped his head as Matthew pushed his chair back and rose from the table. He didn't watch as his son reluctantly followed his brothers outside to complete the morning chores. Instead, he closed his eyes and uttered a small prayer for her safety and well-being. His Mary Elizabeth was smart, but unaccustomed to the ways of the *Englisch*. He could only hope wherever she was that she was safe and protected from the temptations which made up the outside world.

With an *aemen* and a sigh, he rose from the table and started breakfast.

≈ ≈ ≈

About noon time, Gabriel came out of the barn, drawn back into the sun by the jingle of a horse bridle and the creak of a buggy. He blinked a couple of times to right his vision as Zane Carson, the fancy reporter who was bound to marry Katie Rose, pulled his buggy to a stop.

"*Goedemiddag,*" the *Englisch*-man-turned-Amish greeted, jumping down from the buggy and smacking his horse affectionately on the rump.

For a fancy city boy, Zane Carson had adapted to the Plain ways as if he had been born to them. Yet the bishop had his reservations about allowing him in, making him wait over a year before he could begin classes to join the church. Amish folk leaving the district was more likely than the fancy joining up. With Gideon marrying his own *Englisch* bride . . . well, two *Englisch* asking to join in the same year had the bishop as wary as a fox.

Thoughts of leaving brought Mary Elizabeth's desertion

back to the front of his mind. He sighed and pushed back those thoughts. She was in *rumspringa*. That didn't mean she wouldn't return. She hadn't joined the church. She wouldn't be shunned for testing *Englisch* waters, but she was his little girl, and he worried about her. Hadn't known that she was so unhappy with the lot God had provided for her that she felt there was more to be found in the world.

"*Wie geht?*" he asked his sister's intended.

"*Gut, gut,*" Zane Carson said, with a dip of his chin. "Deacon Esh sent me. Katherine Yoder passed in the night."

Gabriel tsked and shook his head. What was it about the night that so many things turned for the bad? "Terrible sad, that. Katherine was a *gut* woman."

"That she was. Uh, the deacon wants you to accompany him to the funeral."

"Me?"

Zane Carson shrugged. "I'm just the messenger."

Unsaid was the truth that Old Ezekiel Esh, for all his obedience to God and heavenly aspirations, was something of an odd duck. A little like Katherine herself. It would do no good to question him on the matter. Compliance was the surest way to discover the method of the old man's thoughts.

The more logical choice would have been Zane Carson himself, since he had moved in with the deacon, seeing after his farm while waiting for permission to become a part of the community.

No doubt Old Zeke had a motive, but Gabriel would only find out when the old man wanted him to know. Even though Katherine Yoder's house was no longer in their district, the deacon would naturally attend the services to pay his respects to the family.

"The funeral will be next Tuesday."

"Is there anything else he needs from me?" There was a mighty lot to do when a body went on to the Lord. With the woman's niece Rachel being her only kinfolk around, Gabriel expected the responsibility of the district would be far greater than normal.

"That's all he said."

Gabriel nodded, his mouth pulling down into a thoughtful frown.

Zane's deep brown eyes studied him closely. "You alright?" The man was shrewd to a fault.

He didn't want to talk about it, but soon everyone would know, and there would be no hiding from it. Gabriel sighed. "Mary Elizabeth left last night."

"Left?"

"*Jah.*"

Zane blinked once as the meaning sunk in. "She left."

"That's what I said." Gabriel hated the harshness of his tone, but Zane Carson didn't seem to notice.

"I would have never thought she would—"

He was a *gut* man, his sister's intended. With any luck and the Good Lord's grace, Zane and Katie Rose would be allowed to marry soon, maybe even as early as June. Though most Amish waited until after the harvest to speak vows, the couple was understandably anxious to start their life together.

"Nor did I." Gabriel shook his head and stared out over the pasture. "I'd appreciate it if you didn't say anything to *Mam* and *Dat* just now. I need to be the one to tell them."

Zane gave an understanding nod of his head. "Should I tell them you'll be around for supper?"

With five kids to feed and acres of wheat to tend to . . . "*Jah.* Supper sounds like a fine idea."

~⊘ ⊘~

There was just so much to do.

Rachel Yoder looked around her, eyes darting from one chore to the next. The supper dishes still needed to be put away, her bed needed to be made, *Aenti's* bed needed to be stripped, sheets and bed clothes washed and hung outside to dry in the fresh spring sunshine. There were funeral clothes to ready.

The thought of the funeral brought tears to her eyes, tears that she fought with all of her being. She didn't have time to cry; there was too much to do. *Aenti* surely wouldn't want her crying. Katherine Yoder believed her life had been lived for the Lord and peace awaited her on the other side. She was happy and joyous at the transition, and Rachel knew that she would want her to be as well.

Rachel sniffed back the tears and smoothed her hands down her black everyday apron.

There was just so much to do.

She turned toward the stairs, thinking of stripping the beds and washing all the sheets. But the house would need to be scrubbed from top to bottom. *Aenti* may have been a different sort, but she had lived in these parts since she was a child. Her kind-hearted neighbors and members of the surrounding districts would surely come say a final farewell. It was the Amish way.

Maybe she should get the clothes ready first.

Rachel placed her hand on the banister thinking of her aunt's dresses. What dress should she pick for her aunt to wear? There was nothing white in her closet as far as Rachel knew. Katherine Yoder had never been married. Still she would have a *fer gut* apron somewhere about. Maybe something made especially for the occasion.

Chills slid down her spine. She hoped not. How sad for her *aenti* to stitch a garment knowing that it would be the last thing she would wear.

"Miss Yoder?"

She stilled her footsteps, spinning around at the call of the voice.

The nice Mr. Evans stood near the front door with his *Englisch* haircut and kind smile. Rachel wondered if that was what got him this job of driving around and retrieving the dead, for his smile alone was sweet enough to calm a family's grief.

"Jah?"

He flashed her that gentle smile. "We're ready to go now."

Rachel dipped her chin, her throat too clogged to speak.

"We'll have her back by Monday."

Hopefully by then she would find someone to dig the grave. Maybe locate help in sewing the necessary white funeral clothes. Round up a few willing souls to assist her cleaning efforts. *"Danki,"* she whispered.

"You're welcome." Mr. Evans smiled again.

Rachel turned away unable to watch as they loaded her only relative in Clover Ridge into the fancy hearse-car. They would bring her back soon enough, embalmed, though not entirely necessary by state law, but needed just the same. The process would buy Rachel a few more days' time to gather her resources and lay her aunt to her final rest.

She wiped the tears from her eyes with the back of her hand and continued up the stairs.

2

Gabriel loaded Samuel into the buggy bright and early Tuesday morning. Though he lived outside of Katherine Yoder's district and had not been chosen as a pallbearer for the service, he knew Old Zeke would want to get there in enough time to visit and make sure everything was in place for the simple Amish funeral.

Matthew and the other boys were coming in a separate buggy closer to time. Gabriel had just purchased his eldest *sohn* a buggy of his own, and Matthew was rarin' to show it off. They had talked about the perils of pride when they'd commissioned the buggy, but Gabriel himself remembered his first conveyance and how anxious he'd been to drive Rebecca home in it. *Buwe* and their buggies. Some things would never change.

"We're going over to get Deacon Esh," Gabriel told Samuel as he clucked the horses into motion.

"I like Deacon," Samuel replied. "He smells like peppermint."

"Indeed he does." Gabriel laughed. Old Zeke had something of a sweet tooth and usually had a pocket full of peppermints to share with willing children.

For the first time in a long while, maybe even years, Gabriel was alone with his youngest. Not that he hadn't spent any time with him, just that he didn't often find the two of them together without a woman tagging behind making sure that Samuel didn't want or need for anything. He supposed that his sister and his daughter both doted on the young *bu*, but it seemed the knowledge that he was loved and cared for had made him confident beyond his years. He seemed to take his sister's desertion well enough. He'd given Gabriel a sad smile and said, "She'll be back." He hoped his *sohn* was right.

"The woman who died, did she have any peppermint?"

Gabriel shook his head. "I do not know. Perhaps her niece has some."

"Is she old?"

He remembered another time, a couple years back when he had seen Rachel Yoder. She had been young then, not more than twenty-two or three. Wouldn't be much older than that now. "I don't think so."

Samuel sighed in only the way a six-year-old can. "Then she ain't got no peppermint. Only old people got peppermint."

Gabriel tried not to laugh as he turned his buggy down the drive toward the Esh place.

The last couple of years had brought great changes to the once rundown property. Shortly after coming to Clover Ridge, Zane Carson had found favor in Old Zeke's eyes and the man had sort of adopted the reporter from the city. When Zane had decided to stay in Oklahoma and marry Katie Rose Fisher, Esh had taken him in and given him a place to stay in the community as Zane worked toward lessons and winning over the bishop. In return, Zane had cleaned up the place, made it sparkle like new.

Gabriel set the brake and climbed down from the buggy. "Samuel, you need to get into the back and stay there while I help the deacon."

He nodded his head and reached for his door to comply.

Gabriel started toward the house as the screen swung open and Esh came hobbling out, Zane Carson right behind him.

"*Guder mariye,*" he called with a wave.

Old Zeke returned the gesture with a flick of one gnarled hand.

Gabriel hadn't realized how slow the deacon was getting around these days. He looked to Zane, who shook his head and shrugged as if to say, "What's a man to do?"

Sure enough, only Ezekiel himself could determine when he was ready to give up some of the more strenuous aspects of his position. It wasn't normal for a chosen one to stand down before death, but not every man selected to serve God had the health issues that Esh faced. That would surely have bearing in the event that the deacon decided to turn over his station. Gabriel hoped for Old Zeke's sake that he made that decision sooner rather than later. But there was no sense in talking to the man about it. He was as stubborn as they came.

"Fine day for a funeral," Esh said once he had been settled into the buggy. He took a deep breath, sucking in the warm spring air.

Gabriel supposed that since funerals were a necessary part of life, that today was as good a day as any to lay a loved one to rest.

Memories of his Rebecca's funeral came to the front of his mind. He pushed those thoughts away. Too many hard memories had been surfacing lately. Memories he didn't want to recount.

"Eh?" Esh said, turning around in his seat enough to look at Samuel behind him.

Gabriel gave a small smile, knowing already what Samuel wanted.

"I did not know we had a third man with us today." Esh gave an important nod of his head while Samuel beamed at being called a man.

Down syndrome had put him considerably behind his peers. Samuel would perhaps live on his own one day, but it was doubtful, and the idea that one day he would marry was a dream as far away as the moon. Still, Gabriel considered him a gift, a vessel for all the sweet disposition of a normal child mixed with all that his mother had possessed as well.

"Let me see what I have here." From seemingly nowhere, Old Zeke produced a peppermint.

Samuel laughed out loud as Gabriel hid his own smile.

"*Danki*," Samuel said, before looking to Gabriel.

He gave his son a quick nod, then the child tore open the wrapper and pushed the treat into his mouth.

"One for later, *jah*?" Esh handed the child another candy, then with a satisfied smile turned back to watch the road with his wise blue eyes. "You want to talk about it, boy?"

Gabriel almost jumped out of his skin. "Talk about it?"

"*Jah*." Esh nodded. "Your Mary Elizabeth jumping the fence."

No, he didn't want to talk about it, but Esh wasn't really asking. "There's nothing much to talk about." He shrugged trying to appear as if every day his only daughter left in the middle of the night, as if his heart was accustomed to being broken in half.

"She won't stay gone for long."

Gabriel wished he had that kind of confidence in the matter. Every night he prayed for his child to find her way back home. But he wouldn't let any of the *buwe* speak her name. It was too painful to hear it said when he knew she wasn't there.

"You can mark my words on that."

Gabriel wished he could.

They rode in silence for a few minutes, the only sounds the creak of the buggy and the smack of enjoyment as Samuel ate the tasty candy.

"I'm stepping down." Old Zeke's words were such a surprise Gabriel almost pulled the buggy to a complete stop.

Instead, he nodded and searched his mind for the proper response. Finding none, he simply nodded once more.

"I'm telling you because I want you to be prepared."

Prepared?

"The district will have to choose a new deacon, and I'm putting your name in."

A dozen conflicting emotions swamped Gabriel. He wasn't worthy. He was a widower. He didn't need the responsibility while he was alone now and struggling to raise his children.

"I'll say that I'd rather you didn't." Being a deacon, or any of the chosen leaders, was no easy job. Aside from feeling like he wasn't worthy, he simply wasn't up for it.

"It'll do you good, son."

Gabriel took a deep breath, slowing the mad thump of his heart. Just because his name went into the lot wouldn't mean he would be chosen. Only God knew the outcome.

"Course'n it'd be better if you were married."

He had no intention of getting married again. He'd been so blessed before, marrying a woman he loved with all his heart. Then the Lord had seen fit to take her home at the same time He gave them Samuel. Gabriel would never love like that again. Having experienced it once before, it wasn't fair to ask another to enter into a relationship that was not as wondrous. Oh, he knew that he'd had something so special with Rebecca, he couldn't settle for less. He'd make do in his life, knowing that once he had held the world in his arms.

But, the little voice whispered in his head. He no longer had a woman partner, someone—anyone—to help with chores and teaching the boys the ways of women. Katie Rose was getting ready to get married and Mary Elizabeth was gone, her love of animals and desire for an education pushing her into the *Englisch* world. His mother was doing well after her cancer treatments a couple of years back, but she was not as strong as she used to be. Gideon's Annie was going to deliver their first child soon. No, all the women in his life were busy living their own lives. Oh, they would help if he asked, but he didn't feel that was fair, nor was getting married again. He'd just have to manage.

"I don't think—"

Esh shushed him with a wave of one hand. "You just be open to whatever God has in store for you."

There was no way to argue with that. "*Jah*, Deacon. I will at that."

⚜

Rachel's heart pounded in her chest. So many people in the house. She wasn't used to so many people. The large church services every other Sunday didn't seem to bother her, but this . . . today was about to be her undoing.

There had to be at least five hundred people milling around, spilling out into the yard, her barn, and all the way to the pasture. She just couldn't imagine where they had all come from. Her aunt had been something of a recluse, at least by Amish standards. She never attended quilting bees or barn raisings, barely stayed after the worship services to eat, much less socialize. Rachel had no idea that her *aenti* even knew this many people. She had not been prepared for them to show up to bid Katherine Yoder a final farewell.

She wound her way through the crush of bodies. She needed to get out, away. She needed air. She felt trapped.

Thankfully she could see the light shining in from the uncovered front window. Just a few more steps and she could escape, maybe climb up in the barn loft and not come down again until everyone was gone.

"Rachel, there you are." Warm fingers clasped her arm and halted her progress mere steps from the door.

Her body nearly crumpled with disappointment. She would have loved to relax for a moment, shed a few tears, and pull herself together. Now she would have to do that without the break. She pasted a polite smile on her face and turned back to her captor.

Ellen Byler. She should have known.

"Rachel, these are the men I was telling you about." She gestured toward the men behind her. One was tall, built like a bull, with a broad chest and small eyes. The other was thin and lanky like the scarecrow her father used to have in the corn field. Neither man was Amish.

"I'm sorry I—" She wanted to shout her protest loud enough to rattle the ceiling, but her voice was more like the squeak of her bicycle chain.

Ellen's expression hardened, but her polite smile stayed in place. "The men who are interested in buying your property. Well, your aunt's property."

Her aunt's? It was hers now. Wasn't it? "I'm sorry. I don't—"

"Rachel, they came all this way to be here today. The least you could do is hear them."

Rachel nodded numbly. She remembered Ellen mentioning something about some friends of hers who wanted to move into the district and were looking for property. At the time, she hadn't thought the conversation was any more than idle chitchat to pass the time while they sewed her aunt's funeral clothes. But now . . .

It couldn't be these men she had been talking about. They weren't even Plain, though neither one seemed uncomfortable surrounded as they were by the entire community.

Ellen steered her around and nudged her toward the front corner of the living room. The patch of sunlight glittered like certain treasure and beckoned to Rachel. She longed to excuse herself and run out the door as fast as her shaking legs would carry her. But for now she had to listen to what the men had to say. *Then* she would politely thank them, refuse their offer, and make her blessed escape.

"Frank Dowd," the bull man said, giving her a nod of greeting instead of reaching for her hand to shake.

"I'm Robert Davies." At least the scarecrow clasped her hand in both of his. He gave it a small pump before releasing it. "I'm very sorry to hear of your loss."

Rachel nodded, fighting the tears. Something told her she was about to lose so much more.

"Normally I—" He stopped just short of actually saying it, but Rachel knew what he had been about to say. Normally he didn't do business with a woman. But he had to this time, because she owned the house. "Normally I don't come in situations such as these, but this is a unique state of affairs."

"I appreciate you coming all the way out here," Rachel started, sucking in a deep breath and pulling up all her courage. "But I'm not selling my house. *Gut* day to you." She started to push past them and finally make her way into the warm sunshine, but Ellen Byler caught her arm before she could succeed.

"Rachel, dear, you don't own the house."

The buzz that started in her head nearly blocked out the loud drone of the crowd surrounding them. "I don't?" Of course she did. Who else would own the house but her?

"I do," Frank Dowd said in his rumbling voice. Or maybe the sound was distorted like the waves of her vision. Her head pounded. Her heart ached.

"That is to say," Robert Davies added, "our bank does."

Rachel shook her head, strangely aware of the strings of her prayer *kapp* brushing across her shoulders while her fingers tingled like they had no blood in them. "No."

"I'm afraid so." Robert Davies, she decided, was a nice man. Almost as kind as the smiling Mr. Evans. "See, your aunt needed some money . . ."

How could that be? She worked so hard to bring in what they needed.

Ellen Byler took one of Rachel's frozen hands into her own. "There were medical bills, dear."

Wasn't it enough that they had laid her aunt to rest this morning? Did they have to talk about such things right now? "But my cheese and milk." What about all the hours she worked selling her products at the market?

"Apparently that wasn't enough to control the debt." This from Frank Dowd. It was a sin to hate someone, even worse to hate them on sight, but she'd pray about it later. Right now she wanted to refute his claim, cross her arms over her chest, and lift her chin in the air.

Ellen squeezed her hand. "Your aunt took out what is known as a reverse mortgage."

Robert Davies gave a quick nod. "Basically, the house and the land it sits on belong to the bank." He started talking about equity and loan payoffs and other things she couldn't understand.

"So I don't own the house?"

Robert Davies gave her a smile, the same kind she received from Mr. Evans. A smile of pity and remorse mixed in with a small bit of guilt. "I'm sorry."

She turned to Ellen Byler. "You knew this the whole time?"

"Dear, your aunt had to tell someone."

She could have told Rachel.

"You're not entirely broke," Frank Dowd added. "There are some monies left after the sale. You'll have a small dowry."

"Or enough to take you to the nearest relative," Mr. Davies threw in.

She didn't have any relatives.

"Your aunt told me about her cousin in Ohio. All the way to Holmes County." Ellen Byler sounded falsely upbeat, like her news was the most wonderful in the world. "She felt confident that he would take you in. His wife has been ill lately and what with eleven children still living at home, he could use a bit of help around the house."

Ohio? She didn't want to move to Ohio. What would she do with her goats? Eleven children? Her head swam.

"Your aunt left you this letter. Maybe it will explain everything a bit clearer." She held out a plain white envelope.

Rachel took it and shoved it into her apron pocket. She would look at it later. Much later. She rubbed her fingers across the pain in her forehead. "I don't have to decide this right now."

Mr. Davies gave her that same kind look. "It'll have to be determined soon."

Somehow she managed to keep herself together until they exchanged the good-byes, the "nice to meet yous" and the "so sorry for your losses." Once Mr. Dowd's big form disappeared into the throng of people, Rachel wrapped her arms around herself and ran for the door.

If anyone gave her a second look, she didn't pause to acknowledge it. She ran, her skirt swishing around her legs, the wind tangling the ties on her *kapp*. She ran past her pen full of silky white-faced goats and on until she reached the big oak tree at the edge of the back yard.

There she collapsed into a heap at its roots and let her tears have control. Gone. Everything was gone. No more *Aenti* Katherine, no more house, no more security.

Ohio.

So far away. But there was no one here that would take her in. No one who would help without needing something in return. For her to care for their children or cook their meals. No one who would understand how important it was for her to keep her goats and make her cheese. To understand how important it was for her to make her own way.

Once again she was adrift. Alone in the world. Except this time she was twenty-six, not ten. This time she was an adult, though she still felt like the frightened child who had come here all the way from Florida to live with a maiden aunt after her parents had died in that awful accident.

Rachel touched the thin scar that cut across her face, just under her eye. It started at her cheek bone and disappeared under the edge of her prayer *kapp*. A constant reminder that while her family had died, she had lived. She had told herself for years that she had been spared for some reason, but she had yet to discover the notion. All she could see was that her family was gone, her mother, father, both of her brothers, all dead in the buggy accident that should have killed her too.

A warm hand settled on her shoulder. Rachel jumped at the touch, her breath hitched on a sob. A little boy stood next to her. He couldn't have been more than five or six with a slew of freckles across his flattened nose. His emerald green eyes tilted up at the corners behind his wire-rimmed glasses. The spectacles looked too old for the rest of him, like he'd taken them from his *daadi's* pocket as a lark. The little bit of hair that stuck out from under his worn straw hat was as bright red as a new penny.

"Don't cry." His voice was sweet, pure and innocent.

Was he a figment of her imagination? An angel come to help her through the hardest day of her life? Maybe so. She had never seen him before. Maybe he wasn't really there even now.

He extended one chubby, angelic hand and held it out palm up. A red and white peppermint candy dotted the middle of his palm. "I was saving this for later, but I think you need it more."

She looked from the candy to his incredible eyes. "Why is that?"

"Because you're not old. Only old people gots peppermint."

His words brought a smile to her lips, even as the last of her tears rolled down her cheeks.

He moved his hand closer to her. "Take it."

She shook her head. "It looks like your last one."

He shrugged. "I came with the deacon. He always has more."

"*Danki*." Rachel accepted the candy, unwrapped it, and popped it between her lips as the child watched her every move.

The sweet taste filled her mouth and nearly brought her tears flowing once more. How long had it been since she'd had a peppermint? Too long. Her *daadi* had always kept a pocket full of them to share with his *kinder*. But that had been so long ago.

"What's your name?" she asked, hoping to keep the tears at bay now that they had subsided.

"Samuel."

"Nice to meet you, Samuel. I'm Rachel."

He gave her a solemn nod. "I know." He plopped down onto the ground next to her and starting plucking the grass from the earth. "I'm sorry that she died. My *mamm* died too."

Rachel didn't bother to tell him that Katherine Yoder was her aunt and not her mother. The wrinkles of concentration lining his brow and the downward turn of his mouth were enough to have her hold her tongue. How sad for him to have lost his mother so young, even younger than she had been.

He shrugged again as if it was no matter. Rachel wanted to pull him into her lap and smooth down his shiny hair.

"Samuel."

He turned as a big, dark-haired man came striding toward them. "The deacon's ready to go."

He stood and brushed the grass from the seat of his pants. "*Dat*, this is Rachel."

She wiped the last of her tears from her cheeks and pushed herself to her feet. She'd had her cry. Now it was time to march back up to the house and deal with this problem head-on.

The big man dipped his chin in her direction, but didn't smile. "I'm sorry about your *aenti*."

With him standing over her, she felt like a child, no bigger than Samuel. A shiver ran down her spine at the thought, and she nodded in return to ease the uncomfortable tingling. "*Danki*."

"Let's go." He reached out one of his big hands and gathered Samuel close.

She watched them grow smaller as they made their way to the house. She decided that she didn't like the frowning father of her little angel. He was so big and stern. The man didn't look like he ever smiled.

"Lord, forgive me," she whispered. That was two men she had decided she didn't like just based on their looks and a very short conversation.

That was so unlike her. Given her choice, she would rather go up against the unfeeling Mr. Dowd from the bank rather than the unsmiling dad. At least with the banker she knew what she was up against. She knew what he wanted and why.

It was only then that she realized the fancy *Englisch* bankers had talked about the sale as if it had already occurred.

3

Gabriel had just rounded the last turn that would take him by the deacon's house when the old man spoke again.

"That Rachel Yoder is a handsome woman."

He wouldn't call her handsome, and he certainly wouldn't call her a woman. Slip of a girl was more like it. She had light brown hair and big brown eyes that somehow seemed bottomless and lost when they looked at him. She was easy enough on the eyes, he supposed.

"It's a shame. Don't know what she will do now."

He shouldn't be so suspicious, but something told him that he was being set up for something bigger than he could imagine. "*Jah?*"

Esh gave a quick nod. "Her aunt had mortgaged the property and now the bank will take over. Poor Rachel will have to move."

"That so."

"Course'n her next kin lives on up in Holmes County."

"Hmm . . ."

"In Ohio."

Gabriel gave a swift nod. "That's where Holmes County is."

"I hate to see her go. Never been married, that Rachel Yoder."

Just what was the deacon hinting toward?

"Make a good wife for someone who needs a partner. Hard working. God loving. *Gut* Amish woman."

Ah-ha. So that's what he was getting at.

"I'm sure she'd make a man a *gut* wife," Gabriel said. *Just not me.*

"You say the words, Gabriel Fisher, but you don't have your heart behind them. When the time comes, you will see."

Gabriel pulled the buggy to a stop in front of the deacon's house. Nothing much stirred except the chickens and the dogs, and Gabriel figured Zane Carson was still with Katie Rose.

"A man should have a good woman behind him when he stands up for the Lord."

How was he supposed to answer that? Esh hadn't even stepped down yet, and Gabriel as surely hadn't been chosen. God knew that he had enough on his plate raisin' his family. The Good Lord wouldn't lay this burden on him too.

"If you marry her, you'll get the goats." Esh opened the door and started to get down from the buggy while Gabriel stared at him gape-mouthed.

Gabriel roused himself with a shake of his head. "Marry her?" He climbed down, hustling around the front of the horses in order to brace the deacon as he stepped to the ground. It was well known that the Amish were an old-fashioned lot as it were, but he wasn't about to barter a bride for a passel of goats. "I do believe you have been in the sun too long. Perhaps a wider brim on your hat is in order."

"You know the bishop's stand on that," Deacon Esh said. "The wider a man's hat brim, the more he has to hide."

Gabriel laughed, hoping the deacon would let the subject drop. But it seemed that fortune was not on his side today.

"I saw you looking at them. They are fine goats. Many a marriage has been started with less."

Gabriel sighed. The deacon meant well, but it seemed his good sense was as failing as his body these days. "I don't need a wife."

"But there's where you're wrong, boy. You need help with the *kinder* and the farm. A *gut* woman to cook and clean for you and help you raise your family. Rebecca would have wanted it that way."

The deacon's words cut him like a knife across his heart. It had been over six years, and he missed her like it had only been yesterday that she had gone to the Lord. He and his Rebecca, they had shared a love like the *Englisch* talked about, a once-in-a-lifetime bond that even death could not break. It wasn't right for him to marry another knowing what he had with her could never be repeated.

"Now that Katie Rose and Mary Elizabeth have found their paths, you can't put it off any longer. There comes a time in every man's life when he must put aside his needs for the good of his family. In this case, you will benefit too. Stop acting like an old mule and hear what I'm telling you."

Gabriel guided Ezekiel up the steps to his front door, opening the screen with one hand while still grasping the old man's elbow in the other.

The deacon stepped into his house. Then he turned, his blue eyes as sharp as the blade on a hunting knife, and pointed a gnarled finger at Gabriel. "The Lord sees a need, and He provides for it. It is a sin to waste opportunities as surely as it is to defy God Himself."

⚹⚹⚹

The deacon's words kept repeating in his head over and over for the rest of the day and all of the following one. His house was slowly falling to disarray. Dirt piled up on the floor. Dishes stacked in the sink. He himself had been plowing all day.

After scrounging through the refrigerator for all the leftovers he could find, he managed to present the boys with a meal. Although it was odd in content, it was filling, and they wouldn't go to bed hungry. He couldn't say the same about the next day.

Gabriel sent the children to bed and eased his tired body into the rocking chair. He would read for a while, then get some rest himself. The dishes and such could wait. Plowing and planting were more important today.

He took his Bible from the knitting basket next to his chair and pulled on his wire-rimmed reading glasses. Yet the Lord's verses could not hold his attention this night. It was the deacon's words that kept coming back to him.

Maybe Esh was right. Maybe Gabriel did need a woman to help care for his brood, cook and clean, and otherwise handle the womanly chores. He had made it all these years without a wife. At first he'd had his sister, Katie Rose, and then Mary Elizabeth had grown and taken over more and more of the work load. Except for the cooking.

The thought brought a sad smile to his face. His Mary Elizabeth had never mastered the art of cooking. Her mother had been one of the finest in the county, but the skill had not been passed on.

Jah, he needed womanly help at his farm, but that didn't mean he had to take a wife. There was more than one way to skin a cat.

Decision made, he climbed the stairs to his room, the weight of the day a little easier knowing there was help in sight.

"Guder mariye, Rachel Yoder."

At the *Deutsch* greeting, Rachel smiled at the postmaster behind the big wooden counter. For her it was always so special when the *Englisch* members of Clover Ridge welcomed the Plain folk so openly. She had read about the troubles others had in different communities all over the country. Why, there was even a group of Swartzentruber Amish who were being forced from their land in Pennsylvania. The group of nine families would have to move to another state where they would be allowed to carry on with their ultra-conservative ways. 'Course, she wasn't sure that not allowing caution triangles on the back of their buggies was safe, and it did make a home look better to everyone if the owners were allowed to plant grass and pretty flowers, but it wasn't hers to judge. She was just thankful that she lived in a community where such luxuries were approved.

Not for much longer, the dark voice in her head reminded her.

She pushed the thought aside. She knew that the community where her cousin lived was more conservative than the districts in Clover Ridge, but that didn't mean they went as far as the Swartzentruber. They were still in Holmes County, *jah?*

She smiled and handed Kevin the postman the card her delivery man had left in her box yesterday.

"Registered mail, huh? Must be real important. Give me a minute to find it." He slapped the palm of one hand on the counter, then winked. "Be right back."

"Danki." She gave him a quick nod of her head and watched as he disappeared into the back rooms of the building.

She had to look at this move as an adventure. A reluctant, misguided, unwanted adventure. Such was her lot in life. She was unmarried, orphaned, and had very little extended family. Even the community that, under normal circumstances, would have been like a family in her life, had been kept at a distance by her maiden aunt.

When she had first moved to Clover Ridge, injured and grieving the loss of her family, she hadn't minded the seclusion. Now she could see the repercussions, and there were many.

"Here we are." Kevin appeared behind the counter holding an official-looking letter with red, white, and blue stickers and bearing the name and address of the attorney her *Aenti* Katherine had used to finalize all the mortgage details.

Rachel's heart gave a hard thump at the sight of it.

Kevin pushed a small card across the counter toward her. "Sign here by the *X*, and we're all done."

She hated that her hand shook as she penned her name on the line he indicated. She could pretend that moving wasn't a reality as long as she didn't have that paper in her possession. Now, pretending wasn't an option.

"This just came in for you as well." Kevin handed her another letter, this one not as official looking and bearing the return address of her distant cousin in Ohio. Or at least from his eldest daughter who was about to get married and start her own family away from her father's house. That was why Albert Byler needed her help.

You should be thankful that you have a place to go, and family, however distant, that needs you and is willing to take you in. Yet she wasn't. She only felt sadness that she was about to be forced to leave Clover Ridge, as well as a twinge of jealousy that she would remain an old maid, never to have children of her own and the family that she'd desired for as long as she could remember.

She blinked back sudden tears and nodded her thanks to Kevin before hurrying out of the post office and into the bright morning sun. She still had to stop at the general store and pick up a loaf of bread. Of all the accomplishments of most Amish women, bread was not among Rachel's. Baking just took up so much time. Time that could be spent tending her goats, making her cheese. Really, doing anything else.

First she had to see what Albert's oldest daughter, Amanda, had to say.

Rachel stopped at the bench just outside the post office and sat down, tearing into the letter like a starving man tears through a *snitz* pie.

With trembling hands, she held the letter as steady as possible and began to read.

> *Dearest Cousin,*
>
> *I suppose we are cousins even if four times removed. What a joy to learn that you are alive and well in Oklahoma. Everyone lost touch with you after the terrible accident that killed your* mamm *and* dat *and your* bruders *as well. And what a blessing for us that you are coming here to live after all these years. Even though I am saddened at the passing of Katherine, I am so looking forward to meeting you at last.*
>
> *Our farm is not the largest in these parts, but* Vatter *does have a goodly amount of land to till and livestock to care for. It is for this reason that he regrets you will not be allowed to bring your goats here to Ohio. I'm confident that you can find a suitable buyer there in Clover Ridge who will be willing to give them a good home and surely at a fine price as well.*

Rachel felt her heart drop a little more. Her precious goats. And Sugar was just about to give birth. Oh, she knew she could find someone to buy them, but they were her goats. She had bought them at auction, saved her own money for their purchase. Getting rid of them would be like selling the closest things she'd ever had to children.

She pushed the thought away lest her tears grow until she could no longer contain them. The bishop, the elders, most likely even most of the district would think her beyond foolish to give so much credit to critters such as goats, but she loved them with her entire heart.

She blinked hard and continued to read.

> *You are going to love it here in Ohio. We have the largest settlement in America. It's so exciting to be a part of such a big community. (Well, we are on the fringes, but it is still exciting.) Of course some families here are large enough to be a church district within themselves.*
>
> *Our bishop's name is Andrew Stoltzfus. He is very young for a bishop, just twenty-eight years old. Isn't it amazing what God's will can do? All the elders were a bit concerned when he was chosen. I think they felt that he would be a little too liberal with cell phones and other Englisch luxuries. But to their surprise (and delight) Bishop Andrew has turned out to be one of the most conservative bishops we have ever had. He has us wearing the most demur colors—gray, brown, and the darkest plum. At first I thought it would be a trial, but it has turned out to be a greater blessing than I imagined. Wearing subdued colors makes me so appreciate the colors that God has displayed for us instead of trying to reproduce them on my person.*
>
> *Oh, and did I tell you that Andrew is the brother of my intended, Matthew? They are both such gut men. I can hardly wait for you to meet them.*
>
> *I must close this letter for now. Taking care of eleven little ones doesn't leave a lot of time left over for things like letter writing. But you'll find that out for yourself in a few weeks.*

Be safe as you travel and go with our Lord.

Your cousin,

Amanda

Rachel crumpled the letter in one hand and dropped her head back against the wall of the post office. It was all so much to take in.

No goats. No colors. Eleven children.

Her mind swam with the changes that would be expected from her. How would she ever be able to leave her entire life behind and move hundreds of miles away? It was more than an adventure—it was an impossibility.

She closed her eyes against the negative thoughts. Her *aenti* would not approve of such an attitude, but she couldn't help it. The prospect was overwhelming.

Yet what choice did she have?

None.

If she stayed in Clover Ridge, she would have almost no money and no place to live. She could sell her goats, but what good would it do to have money for a place to stay if she sold her means of a livelihood? Clover Ridge might not be as conservative as Ohio, but she felt certain the bishop would frown on her taking up living alone. She was too old to get married and too young to be an old maid.

With a sigh, she smoothed her cousin's letter and folded it to rights, then slipped it back into its envelope. She had a few more days before she had to start collecting her belongings and head for Ohio. A few more days before she had to find a buyer for her precious goats. Maybe in those few days, God would show her His will. With any luck and lots of prayer maybe—just maybe—she would find a way to stay in Oklahoma.

"I'm looking for a housekeeper," Gabriel told Coln Anderson the next day. He'd driven his buggy into town just after Joseph, Simon, and David had left for school. He needed to be in the fields. The back twenty still had to be plowed and planted. Thankfully the wheat was coming along nicely, but he needed to get his corn in the ground soon. Yet this chore took priority. He'd instructed Matthew to start cleaning out the stalls. At fifteen he could handle a plow on his own, but Gabriel hadn't wanted to leave the *bu* alone in the fields. Instead he'd left him in the barn with Samuel, who begged to tag along.

Gabriel felt a twinge of guilt at leaving the child with his oldest brother. He had been through so many changes over the last couple of months. But Gabriel wasn't accustomed to the child dogging his heels. He wasn't sure how a housekeeper could help him with this problem, but at least he'd have warm meals when he came home each evening.

"A housekeeper, eh?" Coln Anderson, owner and operator of Anderson's General, Store wiped his glasses on the tail of his white butcher's apron. He inspected the lenses then gave them one last swipe before settling them back in their place.

He didn't say the words, but Gabriel knew what he was thinking: Hiring a housekeeper instead of finding a wife was about as smart as wearing a metal hat in a lightning storm. But this solution . . . it would work just fine.

"You can hang a notice on the bulletin board." Anderson nodded his head in the direction of the large corkboard the community used to post notices and such, like hogs for sale and lumber needs.

Gabriel held up the stack of white copy paper Joyce at the library had given him. She had smiled politely at him, suggested he draw a map to his house for applicants, and helped with the wording. Then she had showed him how to make copies on the fancy Xerox machine. He was certain the bishop would demand he not use the copies, but hopefully by the time Beachy found out, the matter would be resolved.

He took the pushpins that Coln Anderson offered him and tacked the notices to the bulletin board, one on top of the other, five thick. He'd come back tomorrow or the next day and check it again, add more from the stack in his hands if need be.

"*Danki*, Coln Anderson." He raised his hand in farewell, then walked out the door and straight into someone. Someone small and soft and sweet smelling like fresh-baked cookies. Or honey.

"*Dunnerwetter*," she exclaimed as his papers flew in all different directions. The wind caught a few and sent them tumbling into the street and out of reach. She clamped a hand over her mouth, her big brown eyes even wider at her slip.

"*Ach*, Rachel Yoder. Thunder weather is right. Look at the mess we have now."

"I-I'm sorry," she said, crawling on the planks of the porch leading to the general store as she gathered the papers, pushing them under her knees in order to keep them from flying away again.

Gabriel stooped to help and soon almost all were rescued from the Oklahoma wind. He could only hope that the ones that got away would find themselves in the hands of people willing to help him.

"I—uh, here." She thrust the papers toward him, and for a heartbeat she looked almost frightened.

But what was there to be scared of?

"*Danki*," he said, not realizing until that moment how gruff his voice sounded. Or did it seem so coarse because it followed her softer tones?

He cleared his throat, and she stopped brushing the dirt from the skirt of her dress and turned those bottomless eyes to him once again. "*Jah?*"

He shrugged. "*Danki*," he repeated, though softer this time.

"*Gern gschehne.*" She dipped her chin before brushing past him and into the general store.

Gabriel clutched the flyers in one hand and watched as she disappeared though the glass doors.

⁓⌇ ⌇⁓

She was such a *dabbich*. Rachel dropped her chin to her chest, then cut her gaze back outside through the large glass window at the front of the store. There he stood, looking back toward her like he wasn't sure if he should paddle her or tell the bishop that she was *ab im kopp*. But it seemed she was a little off in the head where he was concerned. Big, frowning Gabriel Fisher brought out the worst in her. Not that she was going to have to let it worry her much longer.

She directed her gaze toward the letters she held in her hands. Or rather, letter. She turned the official-looking envelope over, but her cousin's letter was missing. Perhaps she dropped it outside when she crashed into the solid wall that was Gabriel Fisher. If so, it was long gone by now, tossed about by the wild spring winds of Oklahoma's Green Country.

In her hands she still held the registered letter from her *aenti's* attorney and a piece of paper that wasn't there before their collision—a flyer stating that Gabriel Fisher was looking for a housekeeper.

Rachel gave an uncharitable snort. She'd just bet he was. The man was too stern and ornery to marry. She remembered the hard look in his green eyes. They were the color of the moss that grew down by the creek, lush and deep, but there was a hardness to them that warned anyone within distance to keep to themselves. She shuddered. What made a man so hard and unfeeling? Or maybe the word was guarded. What caused a man of God to be so protective of his emotions that he put up a barrier between himself and the world?

Rachel Yoder, she admonished herself. Who said that something had happened to him? His stern demeanor could be just another part of his makeup as much as his coffee dark hair and broad, broad shoulders.

Her eyes scanned the notice once again, and she looked back to where he had been standing only to find him gone. Good luck and Godspeed to whoever accepted his position.

They were going to need it.

❧ ❧

It was after lunch by the time Gabriel pulled his buggy to a stop in front of the barn. Matthew came out with a wave, Samuel hot on his heels.

"Time to eat?" Samuel asked, his lispy voice hopeful.

"*Jah,*" Gabriel said, handing the reins to his eldest son. "Matthew, take the horses into the barn while I get us something together to eat."

"*Jah, Dat.*" Matthew gave a nod of his head and unhitched the horses.

Gabriel watched him for a moment, saying a little prayer that Matthew would keep his wits about him when he entered his *rumspringa.* For the most part the children in their district strayed little from their Amish upbringing. Very few of them lost their heads and even fewer still left and never returned. Of the ones that did head out on their own, most returned only to leave again and again, breaking their parents' hearts in their desire to live in the outside world but unable to stray too far from their strict upbringing.

He could only pray and hope against all that Mary Elizabeth would find her way back home. Once she returned, he'd do everything in his power to keep her at his side.

"*Dat.*" Samuel tugged at his pant leg, bringing Gabriel back to the here and now. He couldn't dwell on past mistakes and all the sorrow that her leaving left behind; just like when his Rebecca passed, he had to go on. Others depended on him.

"*Jah*, Samuel." He patted the boy's shoulder and steered him toward the house. "Let's see what we can find to fill our bellies this fine day."

Samuel tilted his head back to look up at his father. Most of his face was hidden by the brim of his straw hat, but his smile was evident and warm. It filled Gabriel's heart with hope. In that moment, hope was just what he needed most.

Matthew poked his head in the kitchen. "*Dat?*" He was hesitant and cautious, though Gabriel couldn't blame him. What Amish child could overcome the sounds of their father trying to bake and failing miserably?

"*Jah?*" He glanced up from the mound of dough that he'd thought would eventually turn into biscuits. So far that miracle hadn't happened.

It had been three days since his trip into town, and he hadn't had one inquiry concerning a housekeeper. He'd hoped to go and check on his flyers, but being both the man and the woman of the farm since Mary Elizabeth had left was proving more work than he could have ever imagined. He hadn't realized just how much he depended on the youngster until she was gone.

He spent the mornings plowing and overseeing the children's chores. Then he got them to school and spent the remainder of the day cleaning and cooking. Well, attempting to cook. If it hadn't been for the efforts of the women in his life, his family would have starved. Yet he couldn't put the burden of his family on them any longer. His mother had just gotten her strength back after her cancer treatments. There simply wasn't enough time in her days, what with Katie Rose planning her wedding and Gideon's Annie preparing for her first child. After losing his first wife and child to a tragic accident, Gideon was overprotective and worried constantly about his beloved wife.

Gabriel couldn't blame him. His own Rebecca had died in childbirth just after Samuel was born. She hadn't even held the child in her arms. He couldn't imagine how he would feel if he had a pregnant wife.

"I found this in the buggy. Do you want me to run it over to her?" Matthew held out an envelope. It had been ripped open though the address was Rachel Yoder's.

"You did not read it, *jah*?"

"*Nay*, but I'll take it to her, if you'd like." Matthew's green eyes were lit with eagerness. He loved to drive the buggy every opportunity he could find.

"Not now, *sohn*. Soon the other *kinder* will be home from school. I'll need you here to help oversee their chores."

Matthew looked ready to protest, perhaps even tell him that he could go to Rachel Yoder's and back before school let out. But it seemed he thought better of it and gave a jerky nod of his head. "*Jah, Dat.*"

"Set it down on the sideboard. We'll find a time to get it over to her." When they weren't so busy. When he didn't have to go check on the flyers at the general store. Perhaps another day, after he learned to make biscuits.

He gazed hopelessly at the flour-strewn kitchen and the mound of lumpy dough that seemed beyond inedible. On second thought, he'd send Matthew over to Rachel Yoder's first thing after the morning chores, after the other children headed off for school. It might be a long time before he cracked this biscuit-making secret.

With a shake of his head, he pushed at his rolled-up sleeves and went back to work on the rubbery dough.

The letter stayed on the sideboard all through the day. Every now and again Gabriel caught sight of it and thought of Rachel Yoder.

She was a small thing. Why, she didn't even reach his shoulder. If he had to guess, he'd say Matthew was taller than she by a good few inches. But there was a look in her eyes that said she had survived more than most. A wise light that showed her a fighter with a strong spirit.

He shook the thought away. All this cooking and women's work must have made him a bit soft.

"*Gut nacht.*" He gave Samuel a tiny kiss on his forehead and outened the light. Then he eased the door closed behind him and started down the stairs.

He enjoyed reading the Bible after the *kinder* were all in bed. A few minutes to himself, just he and God. He slipped on his reading glasses and found his place in the soft-bound book: Acts, chapter 3.

> Now Peter and John were going up together to
> the temple complex at the hour of prayer at three in
> the afternoon.

> And a man who was lame from birth was
> carried there and placed every day at the temple
> gate called Beautiful, so he could beg from those
> entering the temple complex.

When he saw Peter and John about to enter the
temple complex, he asked for help.

Peter, along with John, looked at him intently
and said, "Look at us."

So he turned to them, expecting to get
something from them.

But Peter said, "I don't have silver or gold, but
what I have, I give to you: In the name of Jesus
Christ the Nazarene, get up and walk!"

Gabriel's gaze flickered toward the sideboard and the white
envelope lying there. He couldn't help but notice that it had an
Ohio return of address.

He turned his eyes back to his reading.

Then, taking him by the right hand he raised
him up, and at once his feet and ankles became
strong.

So he jumped up and stood, and started to
walk, and he entered the temple complex with
them—walking, leaping, and praising God.

Ohio. His gaze once again flickered to the letter. Wasn't that
where Old Zeke had said Rachel was moving?

What concern of yours is it?

He shook his head at his own wandering thoughts, and
centered his attention once again on the words of his Lord.

All the people saw him walking and praising
God, and they recognized that he was the one who
used to sit and beg at the Beautiful Gate of the
temple complex. So they were filled with awe and
astonishment at what happened to him.

With a sigh, Gabriel stuck his finger between the pages and
stood. He took a hesitant step toward the sideboard wondering why
he even cared. What business of his was it if Rachel moved away to

Ohio? Why did he care that she had a letter and that somehow he had ended up with the opened missive?

He set the Bible down, forgetting to mark its place with the scrap of fabric he's used since he and Rebecca had said their vows. With unsure fingers, he traced the jagged edges where the letter had been opened. Was she wondering where it had gotten off to? Was she looking for it that very minute hoping to recover whatever was contained on the pages?

As if watching from far away, he picked up the envelope and slid the folded pages out. Perhaps he should check and make sure that the letter was safe . . . and not so important that he needed to take it to her first thing on the morrow.

He gave a jerk to his head, one that slightly resembled a nod, and opened the pages.

4

Rachel sat in the yard under the same oak tree and stared back at the house. This had long been her favorite place to sit and think. Perhaps if her aunt hadn't been so ill in those last few months, her favorite place would have been further from the house. Maybe down by the cool creek that ran at the very edge of the property, between her house and the bishop's.

Not that it mattered anymore. Soon she would be in Ohio. The thought sent dread filtering through her very veins.

She took a deep breath and tried to turn her thoughts to the positive. But she couldn't find any. Instead she lowered her head to pray.

Dear Lord, help me see the benefit of what's to come. I know You have a plan for me. Let me be open to Your wishes and all that You have in store for my life. Aemen.

She opened her eyes, her gaze focused on the dark green dress she wore with its pristine white apron. Come wash day she'd put this dress with the others in her box to go to the bishop. She wouldn't be needing a green *frack* in Ohio. According to her cousin, their bishop considered green to be God's color since He bathed the earth in its richness. Who was man to compete with that?

Rachel sighed. She had prayed to be positive, yet her first thoughts were a challenge. The entire move was to be a challenge. No bicycles or untied prayer caps—who tied their prayer *kapps* these days?

Or perhaps the challenge would be in having to change again. It had been so hard on her to come here from Florida. The Amish of Pinecraft were much more liberal, Beachy Amish. She had adjusted then, she told herself. But she had been younger and grieving. And like now, she'd had nowhere to go.

She plucked a blade of grass, twirling it between her fingers before tossing it away and picking another. More time in prayer. That's what her *aenti* would have said she needed.

But it was more than that. When her goats were gone, so was any chance she had of being independent again. Ohio wasn't the place for a woman to support herself. She was well past the marrying age, and most everyone in Clover Ridge thought she was strange. Not that anyone would say anything to her face. Amish were too polite to do that, but that didn't mean they didn't talk about her when her back was turned. Not that she could blame them.

When she had arrived in Oklahoma, she'd had a tough time adjusting to the more conservative ways. So she'd kept to herself, preferring to be alone rather than stand out as different. At first it had been for protection, and after a while, it became simply habit.

Then before she knew it, it was too late to entice a good young man to marry her and raise some babies. In truth that was all she'd ever wanted. At twenty-six, her time for that had long since passed. Even if they didn't think her odd as she tended her goats for milk and cheese, most men her age were already married.

The creak of a buggy sounded from the road. Rachel didn't look up. Someone on their way to town or heading to the bishop's. She plucked another blade of grass, mentally going over the list in her head. She should be inside gathering the items to take to the bishop's and the supplies to take to Ohio. But she couldn't just yet. Maybe she should leave it all and let the bank man sort through it.

She made a face, then turned toward the road as the sound of horses drew nearer. She didn't recognize the buggy as it pulled to a stop in front of the house. But she knew the man who slid open the door and stepped out.

The frowning Gabriel Fisher.

Rachel stood and brushed the blades of grass from her skirt. What could he want?

She pushed the uncharitable thought away. The stress of the move, her aunt's death, and all of the life changes she faced were taking their toll on her. She sent a small prayer for patience and goodwill heavenward and started toward the big man.

"*Guder mariye.*" She nodded toward him, deeply instilled manners keeping her from blurting out all the questions forming in her mind.

He nodded his head in return, the brim on his black hat hiding his eyes from her scrutiny.

It had been four days since she had seen him last. He looked the same. Mostly. But when she thought about him and his son at her aunt's funeral, he seemed changed indeed. The lines around his hard mouth had deepened, seemed more pronounced. The lips themselves pressed into a firm line. Unlike some of the Amish men in the district, he trimmed his beard. The lines were neat and even, and she decided that she liked the look.

See, her prayers were working already.

Rachel stopped a good ten feet from him. It was better that way. The farther she was from him the easier it was to look him in the eye. Any closer and she'd have to crane her neck back to meet his hard green gaze.

Gabriel Fisher shifted from one foot to the other. "I should apologize."

"For what?"

He looked down at the envelope he held in his big hands, then extended it toward her. "I believe this belongs to you."

So that was where it had gotten off to.

She took the letter from him and turned it over. *"Danki."*

Gabriel cleared his throat. "I know it was wrong of me—"

She shook her head. "It was an accident, surely."

"Jah, an accident that I took it home." He took a deep breath and expelled it noisily. "But not an accident a'tall that I read it."

Rachel blinked at him once, then twice more before his words and their full meaning sunk in. "You read my letter?"

He swallowed hard and nodded. "I meant no harm."

She gave him a stiff nod. Of course he didn't. She folded her arms across her middle, a chill stealing over her. She shook off the tingling. There was nothing in the letter to be hidden, nothing to be ashamed of. She was going to live with her kin in Ohio. That was respectable enough. She would take care of the *kinder* . . . and live out her days in gray dresses and black stockings even in the summertime.

Still he stood there.

"Is there something else, Gabriel Fisher?"

He nodded. "It seems to me that we are two people who can help each other."

"What do you mean?"

"Tell me, Rachel Yoder, do you want to go live in Ohio with your cousin?"

"I don't see how my wants factor in as a part of this." She swallowed down the lump in her throat. It wasn't like she had much choice in the matter, now was it?

"That is no answer." His green eyes seemed to cut right through her. Could he see her every thought, know her every wish and prayer?

"*Nay*," she finally said.

"*Nay*, it's no answer or *nay*, you don't want to move to Ohio?"

"I do not want to move." She uttered the words so strained, so quietly that she almost didn't know the voice to be hers. After all, she had never said those words out loud.

Secret revealed, she looked out over the pasture to her goats, frolicking in the warm spring sunshine. They would be the hardest to leave.

"Are you here about the goats?" she asked. That was the most logical reason, even as she held a hope . . .

"I'm here to offer you a job."

Her gaze swung back to his stern expression as a tiny flicker of hope sparked to life inside her. He seemed serious enough. "A job?"

"As my housekeeper."

The flyer she had held in her hands no more than two days ago, flashed through her mind.

Housekeeper.

What good would that do? "That is very kind of you to offer, but I have no place to live." She was proud of herself for saying the words without a tear one in her voice.

"You will naturally stay with me and my family."

Hope flickered again. "*Jah?*"

"We have an empty room upstairs. It would make a fine place for a housekeeper to stay."

It would indeed, but there were still so many other things at stake. Even if she stayed in Clover Ridge . . . "What about my goats?"

He turned partially around and surveyed the prancing kids. "I would welcome them on my farm. There is plenty enough room."

She didn't answer right away, couldn't find her voice among the hope and doubts.

"Listen," he started, propping his hands on his hips and nearly doubling his size. "I have a need. I have five boys at home that need clean clothes and hot meals. It seems to me that you have a need as well."

That was true.

"I think that maybe God brought us together on the steps in front of the general store so that we can help each other."

She dipped her chin, so wanting to accept his offer, but somehow afraid that it was too good to be true. "I keep my goats."

"*Jah.*"

She stuck out her hand.

Gabriel Fisher simply looked at it for a heartbeat before taking it into his own.

His hand was warm and calloused, strong enough to crush the bones of her fingers into dust, yet gentle as he wrapped them around her hand and gave it a small shake. "Deal."

⁂

Gabriel stood next to his brother, Gideon, and his soon-to-be brother-in-law, Zane Carson, as they waited in Beth Troyer's front yard. He always enjoyed church service, though today's was a bit different. It was their communion Sunday. Afterwards they held the foot washing, then everyone had filed out of the house as the ordained men gathered in the kitchen to await their nominations for deacon.

"I can't say that I was surprised that Ezekiel is stepping down," Gideon said with a sad shake of his head.

"He needs to," Zane Carson added. "It's getting harder and harder for him to get around."

Zane would know. He had lived with the deacon for the past two years as he went through the classes and such that had enabled him to join their district.

No one was surprised that Ezekiel Esh was giving up his position as deacon for their district, although most were saddened by his decision. He had held the position for a long time. He deserved a break before his time on earth was through. His wisdom would be missed though. Esh was fair to a fault and much loved in Clover Ridge.

Gabriel nodded in agreement, his own thoughts buzzing with anticipation. Not for the new deacon, but for his new helper. He felt as if a huge weight had been taken off him. Rachel Yoder was going to be his housekeeper. Starting tomorrow. She was reporting in at seven o'clock, just in time to help with breakfast and get the boys off to school. His plan was working. For the first time since Mary Elizabeth left, he felt the tension in his shoulders lessen. Now if he could only get through today without Ezekiel Esh's predictions coming true.

Gabriel glanced back at the house as the first of the congregation tramped back in.

"This is exciting," Zane Carson said, rubbing his hands together.

Gideon laughed. "This from the man who moved here from Chicago. You really have become one of us, *jah*?"

Zane gazed around him. "I love it here."

Gabriel nodded. It was beautiful this time of year. The trees were covered in buds. The grass had turned green. It was truly a blessing to be a part of such a beautiful place.

"So do you know who you're going to nominate?" Gideon asked.

Zane shook his head. "Tell me again how this works."

"We'll each go back into the house and pass by the doorway to the kitchen. When it's your turn, you tell one of the ministers who you think God would want in the position."

"And then they share this information with the bishop?" Zane asked.

Gabriel nodded. "Only men receiving at least two nominations will be included in the lot."

"Maybe even three," Gideon added.

Zane nodded.

Gabriel knew Old Zeke would put in for him to take his place, but that didn't mean much. At least one more person had to recommend Gabriel. Maybe more if some received three or more. Half the people there were his kin in one way or another. They knew the struggles he faced, the hardships he was overcoming daily. Besides, he was a widower. Most of the men chosen were married. Surely that fact alone would work against him.

"Maybe I should nominate you, Gabe." Zane gave a quick nod in his direction.

Gabriel immediately shook his head. "*Nay*. Not me. I'm not the man for this." All his life he'd been taught that to serve God, a man needed humility, but that had nothing to do with his response. He wasn't the man needed for this position. He simply wasn't.

"Why not, *bruder*?" Gideon asked. "You are as upstanding and worthy as the next man."

"As are you."

Gideon was a testament to the healing power of faith. He had lost hope after his wife and son were killed in a tragic accident. But he'd found his faith again with the love of a fancy woman from Dallas. They were expecting their first child soon. Although Gabriel thought Gideon would make a fine church leader, he still needed some time with his wife and his new growing family.

Gideon shrugged. "I suppose."

Gabriel shook his head. "This is not for me."

Gideon elbowed Zane Carson in a friendly sort of way. "That's what they all say."

There were several good men in the district and still others who would benefit from the lessons God would teach if'n they be ordained. Men like Samuel Beachy. The bishop's son had spent many a year with the *Englisch*, after he'd broken Gabriel's sister's heart, before coming home and repenting his ways.

Katie Rose had been all set to live out her life alone as the district's school teacher. That was until a certain fancy *Englisch* reporter came along. What a surprise everyone had when he stayed, and despite the fact that Samuel Beachy returned in humility to Clover Ridge, Katie Rose still pined to marry the *Englisch* man. They would wed soon, his sister all dressed in blue while her fancy reporter-turned-Amish stood by her side.

Gabriel inched along as the members ahead of him in line made their way through the house. Samuel Beachy. Yes, he was the logical choice, and Gabriel was certain that others in the district would feel the same.

They took a step closer. Now they were almost at the doorway. Just a few minutes more, and they would be whispering a name to the ministers. Beth Troyer stood at the door, her keen eyes studying him. Gabriel wondered just how much of the conversation she had overheard.

He lowered his voice so only Zane and Gideon could hear his words. "Seriously, this is not for me."

"And I seriously disagree," Gideon shot back. Then his brother smiled at the lady standing next to them and touched the brim of his hat. "Beth," he said.

She dipped her head in return. Her mouth was pressed together in a thoughtful line. Surely she wasn't contemplating on anything they had said. "To the left and past the kitchen," she told them. "Daniel and John are waiting on you."

Gabriel took his turn, whispering his nomination to the minister and then making his way back into the yard. Samuel Beachy would be deacon and serve alongside his father the bishop, and Rachel Yoder would be Gabriel's housekeeper. She would keep her beloved goats, and he would remain true to Rebecca, his one forever love. Gideon had his Annie, and Katie Rose had Zane Carson.

Gabriel smiled to himself. It seemed Old Zeke was right—God saw a need and He fulfilled it. Funny how interpretation varied from one man to the next. Regardless, Gabriel was satisfied with the way it all turned out.

He didn't know a lot about Rachel Yoder, but he didn't have to. She was a *gut* Amish woman, kin to Katherine Yoder. Course'n she was a bit of an odd duck, Katherine was. But it was no matter. It wasn't like he was marrying Rachel Yoder.

The bishop waved them all back into the house. As custom, the women filed into one side of the room and the men the other. After everyone was settled back in front of the benches, the church elders minus Ezekiel made their way to the front of the room. A table awaited them and the books they carried. In solemn reverence they set the books down and took up a stance in front of the congregation.

"We've heard your choices for our new deacon," Bishop Beachy started, his blue eyes scanning the room. He stepped to the side, and Gabriel could see three copies of the Amish hymnal. Each one had a rubber band wrapped around it. A small piece of paper with a single verse written on it had been hidden inside only one of the copies, the other two had none. Each man nominated would step forward and pick a hymnal. The man who picked the copy with the slip of paper would be ordained as the next deacon of their district.

Poor soul. Gabriel said a quick prayer for the men about to step up. Being a church leader was an honor bestowed by God, but it was also a burden to the man and his family. There was no pay, no compensation for the time a man had to give to his duties. Truly, it was a blessing as well as a curse.

"Samuel Beachy, will you please step forward?" the bishop asked, a note of pride in his voice. Gabriel was sure the bishop would be saying a prayer for humility that very night. "David Troyer." A young man in the front stood. He was newly married, his beard barely enough to cover his face. From across the room his equally young wife gasped. In surprise or dismay, Gabriel was not sure. "And Gabriel Fisher, will you come to the front, please?"

Gabriel's heart gave a hard pound. He wasn't supposed to be in this lot. His nomination was just an old man's fancy. This wasn't really what God intended for him.

Gabriel took a deep breath and stepped out into the narrow divide between the benches. He walked on stiff legs to the front of the room, flanked by the church members—women on the left, men on the right, all eyes on him.

He couldn't help but notice the frown on the faces of both Samuel Beachy and young David Troyer. He sat down on the bench, right next to them, the ringing in his head loud enough to block out the words of John Zook, one of the ministers, as he asked them to pray.

The congregation behind them turned and knelt in silence. Gabriel clasped his hands between his knees and bowed his own head. He needed to pray. This was . . . wrong. He wasn't supposed to be here, and yet he was. It is said that every man has his cross to bear, but this wasn't his burden. He had loved, lost, and was doing his best to raise his children on his own. He had his trials. But to ask God to let this pass from him seemed . . . selfish somehow, though he wasn't sure why. The church needed a better leader than what he could give, or even what young David Troyer could offer. Samuel Beachy was the perfect man for the job.

But when the words formed in his head, it wasn't to ask God to let the mantle of the deaconship pass from him and to fall about the more qualified Samuel. Instead it was a silent plea that God's will be done. That was basically the same prayer. For surely God planned for Samuel Beachy to lead the district. It was the most logical choice.

"*Aemen*," John Zook finished.

The church members rose and sat back down as the bishop stepped forward. "It is time now for you men who have been called to step up and choose a hymnal. Please come forward when the Holy Spirit leads you."

Gabriel wondered what Bishop Beachy would do if he continued sitting after the other men had chosen their book. He'd never know. On wobbly knees he stood and approached the table. There were two books left. David Troyer had already picked his and sat back down.

Gabriel studied each book in turn. They both looked so much the same, each in the same binding, each with a rubber band around it, only one with the verse inside. Or maybe not. Maybe the verse was in the one now held by the young David Troyer.

Something told him to pick the book on the left. He hated the fact that his hand shook as he reached toward it. He picked it up slowly as if in the replay mode that he had seen on the television in town. Book in hand, he returned to his seat. Only one book left and Samuel Beachy palmed it as if he hadn't a concern in the world. More and more that proved to Gabriel that Beachy was the man for deacon's position.

Samuel sat back on the bench next to him.

The bishop stepped toward David Troyer and took the hymnal that he held. He removed the rubber band and thumbed through the pages. Nothing. The bishop gave the young man a quick nod then moved down the line.

Rueben Beachy took Gabriel's book, and he had to fight the urge to snatch it back. Taking it from the church leader would surely be frowned upon and would do no good on top of it all. It would only delay the announcements.

Carefully Beachy rolled the rubber band off the hard cover of the book. Gabriel willed his heart not to beat so fast. He should feel calm and collected. After all, this was not what God had planned for him. He knew it as surely as he knew the color of his eyes and the lay of his land.

The bishop slid the band over the tops of his fingers and gently cracked open the book. He thumbed through the pages, while Gabriel's heart lurched. Then the book fell open in his hands, exposing the scrap of paper placed there just minutes ago by the minister.

The bishop smiled, though Gabriel was sure it was tinged with disappointment. "Gabriel Fisher. The lot has fallen on you."

A numbness filled his limbs as the truth slowly sank in. He, Gabriel Fisher, was to be the next deacon in their district.

5

Rachel pulled her buggy to a stop in front of Gabriel Fisher's house. She sat for a moment staring at the large two-story structure. What had she gotten herself into? How was she going to care for the frowning man and his brood of boys? She had never cared for a child.

She sat up straight, the more confident side of her taking over. *Then again, how hard could it be?* Surely it couldn't be that difficult. Besides, some of the boys were big enough to fend for themselves.

Think of Sadie and the rest of the goats. The living creatures that she had raised. Surely taking care of a human kid couldn't be much different from taking care of a goat kid.

She laughed at her own joke, then snorted and nearly choked as Gabriel Fisher burst out of the house and glared at her from the porch.

She instantly sobered and wiped her hands down her clean black apron. *"Guder mariye."*

He gave a stern nod. "Are you coming inside, Rachel Yoder?"

"I-uh, I . . ." She coughed again, then stepped out of the buggy and onto the farm belonging to the frowning man before her. One thing was certain: Gabriel Fisher was going to take some getting used to. He was big and frowny and seemed to intimidate her just by breathing.

But she had made her choice. This was the only way. Moving to Ohio required too many sacrifices. At least on Gabriel's farm she was in charge of her own life. Well, mostly. At least she was earning her keep, and she still had her livelihood. She wasn't totally dependent on him as she would be on her cousin if she went all the way to Ohio. *Jah*, she had made the choice and she was bound to stick to it.

"*Jah*," she finally managed to squeeze out. "I am coming in."

Gabriel motioned her inside. "Come meet the *kinder*. I'll take care of your horses while you clean up the breakfast dishes."

It was on the tip of her tongue to tell him that he had messed up the dishes and therefore he should be the one to clean them, but washing dishes was one of the chores he expected her to perform. After all, how bad could it be?

Bad. The kitchen looked as if every last bowl and spoon in the house had been used in the making of one meal. She bit back her gasp of dismay and tried not to stare at the mess as Gabriel Fisher stepped forward and introduced her to his children.

He laid his hand on the shoulder of a younger version of himself. "This here is Matthew. He's fifteen and the oldest."

"No, he's not. Mary Elizabeth is the oldest."

Rachel watched as Gabriel Fisher's beautiful green eyes misted over. It seemed he had a heart after all. She wasn't sure if she was more surprised over that discovery or the fact that she thought he had beautiful eyes. Maybe she would have noticed them before now if he didn't go around scowling at everybody all the time.

"That is enough, Simon," he told the second tallest *bu* in the room, who was still taller than she. The youngster had the same eyes as his father but hair the color of faded dandelions. If Rachel had to guess she'd say he was about thirteen.

"*Guder mariye.*" He politely nodded and gave her a smile, but his sweet dimples somehow looked shockingly mischievous. Or was that just her imagination?

"Then there's David. He's eleven. And Joseph. He's eight." Gabriel indicated the next two boys, each one with their father's dark, dark hair, but clear blue eyes they must have inherited from their mother. "And I believe you've met Samuel."

The small redheaded boy smiled, his front teeth missing since the first time that she had seen him, and Rachel felt her heart melt all over again. Sweet, sweet Samuel.

"I'm six," he said with a grin. "How many are you?"

Rachel smiled. "I'm twenty plus six. Do you know how much that is?"

Samuel shook his head.

"We'll work on it together," she said.

"Are you coming to be our mother?"

Rachel blinked at Samuel's blatant question, then gathered her wits enough to shake her head. "*Nay,*" she whispered, though she felt in that moment she would move heaven and earth to give this child anything he needed. "I've come to help your father around the house, cooking and cleaning and such."

Samuel tilted back his head, his red hair shining like a new kettle. "'Cuz Mary Elizabeth is gone." He replaced the *r* in his sister's name with a *w* so it sounded more like "Mawy."

"*Jah.*" Rachel had heard through the talk at the general store that Gabriel's oldest child had gone to join the *Englisch*, but she could tell by the way he shifted behind her, Gabriel Fisher was not comfortable talking about it.

"Are you staying until she gets back?" David asked. Or was it Joseph? They were enough alike to be twins. Only an inch or so separated them in height. Heaven help her when they started moving around.

Rachel gave a quick nod. "Of course."

"*Buwe!* Get your lunches and get on to school. That new teacher will have your hide if you're not there on time."

The boys did as he bade, each grabbing an insulated lunchbox before heading out the door.

All but Samuel. He tugged on her skirt, urging her to kneel down next to him.

"Aren't you going too?" she asked.

He shook his head, his sweet cherub mouth pulled down at the corners.

"Samuel doesn't go to school anymore."

Rachel whirled around, standing up at the same time and almost toppling over. For a moment she'd forgotten Gabriel Fisher was in the room. A miracle she was sure, but she had momentarily blocked him from her mind.

"What do you mean 'anymore'?"

He nodded toward the child. "When his *aenti* was the teacher he went with her every day, but since then . . . well, the new teacher isn't sure that she can give him the attention that he needs."

Nonsense. That was the first word that popped into her head, but Rachel managed to bite it back. It'd do no good to get off on bad footing with Gabriel or the teacher. Really, what concern of it was hers if Samuel went to school or stayed at home? He was quiet and gentle. It wasn't like he would be in her way.

She shrugged. "I guess I should start on . . . the dishes." She glanced around the room which seemed to have soiled kitchenware of one kind or another piled up on every available surface.

"Samuel," Gabriel said in that deep voice of his. "Do you want to go to the field with me or stay here with Rachel?"

The *bu* chewed on his lower lip, looking from one of them

to the other as if weighing the benefits and drawbacks of each decision. Finally he asked, "If I stay here can I have a cookie?"

"Of course," Rachel said on top of Gabriel's "Absolutely not."

She looked to the man who stood, hands propped on hips, as he stared at her like she had just grown a donkey's tail. Or rather he glared at her, green eyes biting in their intensity.

Gut himmel! She hadn't even been there half an hour and already Gabriel looked like he wanted to toss her out with the breakfast scraps.

"I mean," she stammered. "After lunch, maybe." She turned on her heel, but not before she saw the flash of disappointment cross young Samuel's freckled face.

"Come on, Samuel. We have work to do." Gabriel clasped the young boy on the shoulder and steered him from the house.

Rachel shook her head at her own hasty mistakes and twisted on the water handle. Thankfully the water turned warm at the tap, and she breathed a sigh of relief. Not all the districts were allowed to have indoor plumbing and water heated before it reached the pipes. She doubted that this district would be any different from her own, nor did she think Ohio would be so conservative, but she wasn't about to take these things for granted. With the mounds of dirty dishes she now faced, she was glad for the convenience.

She ran some water into the sink, added some dish soap, and got down to work.

In what seemed like half the day later, but in truth was only a couple of hours, she heard the dogs start barking from the front yard. They had visitors. Most likely the truck with her goats. Excitement zinged through her.

For the most part, she had settled into her new room. After washing the dishes, drying them, and putting them away, she had gone back to her buggy to retrieve her things.

She had always been one for simple living, but to see all of her worldly goods packed into one carrying case and a cardboard box seemed sad somehow. She reminded herself that her earthly treasure was in her goats and all the potential they had. So she had hung up her few dresses, her winter coat, and her bonnet and waited for her other "possessions" to arrive.

She ran out onto the porch just as the driver swung down from the truck, a clipboard in his hand.

"Rachel Yoder?" the man asked.

"*Jah.*" She nodded.

"I believe I have your goats."

She clapped her hands in excitement, like she hadn't just seen the creatures a few hours before when she left her *aenti's* house. Well, the bank's house.

"*Gut, gut,*" she said, taking the clipboard and signing her name by the *X*.

Good, except she didn't know where to put them. She and Gabriel hadn't talked about that. She bit her lip and gazed around the outbuildings trying to figure the best place for her goats. She couldn't leave them in the trailer for long. Sadie was bound to lose her spirited temper soon and there was no telling what would happen after that.

Then she spotted the perfect place, just on the other side of the chicken coop. A pen filled with bright green grass for them to eat and just enough room for her seven does and one buck. For a while at least. "There." She pointed out the way as the young driver nodded. He tucked the clipboard under one arm and went to the back of the trailer to unload the first of her sweeties.

Half an hour later, the goats were settled, and the big truck rambled back down the drive.

The only problem with the new goat pen was the fact that there was no water trough inside. Surely Gabriel Fisher had something she could use to make sure her goats had fresh water to drink. With a glance back at her herd, happily munching on the sweet green grass of their new home, Rachel headed toward the barn hoping to find a makeshift trough.

"Is it time for lunch yet?"

Gabriel looked down into Samuel's questioning smile.

He'd kept the child away from the house for far too long, but he had so much that needed to be done. It had been such a burden off him to know that Rachel Yoder was working in his stead, cleaning the kitchen and making them a healthy, filling lunch. Catching up the laundry, sweeping the floors, and in general making his life easier.

He checked the sun and nodded. "*Jah*. Let's head back."

Samuel took up the reins and clicked the horses into motion. He had so many limitations, but driving the wagon back to the house was a chore he had been doing for the last few months. Gabriel was happy to give him something that he could accomplish. The child had realized this year that he was different from the other children, though Gabriel was certain he didn't know to what extent. But with the new teacher not being able to help him or willing to have him in her classroom this year, Samuel had determined that he was not like the other children his age.

Still, Gabriel held hope for his youngest. Hope that soon he would catch up to his peers and be able to attend school like his brothers.

"Look, *Dat*. Goats!"

At his squeal, Gabriel scanned the yard until he found the spot where Samuel pointed.

Sure enough there were goats. In his experimental patch of hybrid red and gold wheat! The beasts were munching on the tender stalks pulling them up by the roots and chewing them to bits like there was no tomorrow. Even worse, someone had dragged a number 10 washtub into the fenced-in area crushing even more of the wheat sprouts.

He snatched the reins from Samuel, not even taking the time to apologize as he spurned the horses into a faster trot. He had to get to the house and as fast as possible before they ate every last bit of his experiment.

But by the time he hollered, "Whoa," he feared he was too late.

With a small grunt he swung down from the wagon and raced toward the goats. "Hiyah," he said, waving his hat at them to shoo them from the tender wheat. They stared balefully at him. Not even one of them stopped chewing long enough to pay him much attention.

He slapped them on the rumps with his hat, but a lot of good it did. They just moved further away from him and resumed their eating on the other side of his wheat patch.

"Rachel!" he bellowed, starting for the house.

The urgency in his tone must have done the trick for she slammed through the screen door, wiping her hands on a dish towel as she came to a halt. *"Was iss letz?"*

"Your goats are eating my wheat! That's what's wrong."

A confused frown puckered her brow as she looked from him to the eating machines. "Wheat?"

He slammed his hands on his hips. "Do something with them!"

Her eyes widened, and she turned on her heel and ran back into the house.

He stared after her in disbelief. "Rachel Yoder!"

But she was gone.

Gabriel dashed past Samuel who stood as if in a trance looking from the porch where Rachel had been standing to him, then to the goats and back to the house again. He had a length of rope in the basket near the front door. He could loop them together and get them out of the test area. Or he could tie the rope into a noose and hang the blasted creatures from the roof of the barn.

He snatched up the rope and said a small prayer to help him keep his temper. He'd worked long and hard on the wheat hybrid and to see it ruined in one morning. . . . He bounded off the porch just as Rachel came barreling out of the house. She held dog leashes in one hand, and it took Gabriel several long seconds to figure out what she intended to do with them.

Then he could only stare as she clipped the leashes to the fancy collars the goats had around their necks, and pretty as you please, she led the goats out of the wheat.

Gabriel sucked in a deep breath as she came near, leading the goats behind as one would a stray horse.

She opened her mouth to speak, but he was one ahead of her. "What were your goats doing in my wheat field?"

"Wheat field?"

"*Jah*. Now answer."

She pressed her lips together. Her brown eyes were as hard as root beer candy. "I have never seen such a small planting. Nor do wheat fields require fencing around them."

"It's my field, and I will do with it as I please."

She lifted her pointy chin in the air, a small muscle in her jaw jumping. "I thought it was a pen."

"You thought wrong."

"Then I must apologize."

She didn't look like she wanted to apologize. She looked more like she wanted to dump a soup pot full of gruel on his head and leave him in the sun to dry.

"I didn't see another place to put them."

"They'll be fine in the main pasture."

A look of horror flashed across her features. "*Nay.* My goats cannot be kept with the other animals. They have to be milked twice a day. Fed premium hay and organic food in order to produce quality milk for the cheese."

She was pulling his leg. But the serious tilt of her jaw stated otherwise.

"Samuel, go on into the house and get you something to eat." He said the words without taking his eyes off his housekeeper.

"*Jah, Dat,*" Samuel said before running to the porch and disappearing inside.

"It seems we have a misunderstanding." Rachel Yoder's words had lost their previous edge. Her breathing had returned to normal, though her cheeks still held a bright pink flush that seemed to make her eyes appear even more bottomless than before. If that were even possible.

"*Jah,* it does."

She looked back over to the patch of wheat now mowed nearly to the ground by her ravenous goats. She bit her lip and looked back at him, apology flooding her features. "I didn't know the grass was special."

"Three years' worth of work," he said. "My own blend of red and gold wheat."

"I'm sorry," she whispered. "I didn't know."

At her quiet tone, Gabriel felt his anger subsiding. They should have talked more about this from the beginning. Too late for that now. "I think we should sit down and set some guidelines for our arrangement."

She nodded.

Who knew hiring a live-in housekeeper would require so much effort? "Will your goats be okay on their leashes for a time?"

"For a little while, *jah*."

"Then let's go inside," he said, with a nod toward the house. "We can discuss our plans over a good meal."

She nodded, then tied the goats to the hitching post. With a jaunty air, she stuck her nose toward the sky, turned around, and marched back into the house.

<hr />

"Where's the food?"

Rachel turned to Gabriel.

He stared at the table now freshly cleared and cleaned.

Surely he hadn't expected her to . . . She stood a little straighter. "I usually have sandwiches for the noon meal. *Jah*?" She nodded toward Samuel who sat at his place at the table swinging his legs and waiting on one of them to feed him. He was such a sweetheart, and Rachel felt a warm rush of affection every time she was near the youngster.

"Sandwiches?" Gabriel repeated the word with such disbelief that she had to bite back the urge to explain to him what a sandwich was.

Instead, she nodded slowly. "Peanut butter with strawberry jelly is one of my favorites."

He just stared and suddenly she got the feeling that he expected her to make the sandwiches. Then again she was the housekeeper.

She shook herself free from her stupor and opened the pantry. But after a quick scan of the shelves, there was no peanut butter. She walked to the cabinets opening each one in turn. Cups and glasses, plates and bowls, pots and pans, but no food, and more important, no peanut butter.

Rachel bit her lip and turned to face her employer.

Gabriel Fisher stood, arms slack at his sides, mouth hanging open as if he could not believe what his eyes were seeing.

Samuel looked from one of them to the other, still patiently waiting for his meal.

"And what do you have for supper?" he asked.

Rachel shrugged. "Usually a bowl of soup."

He adjusted his stance and crossed his arms over his massive chest. "Homemade soup." He announced the words like he'd won a prize.

"Sometimes," she hedged, having the awful feeling that this wasn't the answer he wanted to hear.

"And the other times?"

She dipped her chin unable to keep staring into those intense green eyes. "The kind from the grocer is quite delicious as well."

He shot her a dubious look.

"And quick," she added.

He took a deep breath and she had the strange feeling that he was calming himself. "But you can cook."

"Of course," she scoffed, not admitting that it had been years since she had made more than a pot of stew and a pan of cornbread. But that was cooking, right?

"Tomorrow, I expect you'll plan better."

"Oh. Yes, of course. It's just the dishes and the goats and the—" She stopped at his frown. Maybe she shouldn't bring up the goats right now. She needed this job. She needed this place to stay, and she would do anything necessary to keep it.

Even tell a little white lie.

She added her shortcoming to her mental prayer list and hustled over to the refrigerator. A couple of minutes later she returned to the table, a container of her garlic and chive *chevre* and a loaf of sourdough in her arms. She should have thought of this sooner. Peanut butter and strawberry preserves might be her one of her favorites, but this topped the list by far.

She smiled at Samuel, then shot a cautious glance at his father as she sliced the bread and smeared it generously with the cheese spread. "There," she said with a grand flourish, offering the open-faced sandwich to the boy. He studied it for a moment, then cast a questioning glance back at his father.

Gabriel nodded, that frown still pulling at his mouth. Honestly, did the man never smile?

At his father's "okay," Samuel began to eat. He smiled. "It's *gut*, *Dat*. You should try it."

"Remember your manners," Gabriel said sternly. "We don't talk with our mouths full."

"*Jah, Dat*," Samuel mumbled. Then he swallowed and crammed in another enormous bite.

Perhaps her employer expected her to correct the children as well when they were in her charge, but she was so happy that Samuel liked the meal, everything else flew from her head. After the morning she had, what with the dishes, the goats, and then botching up the noon meal, she was just glad to have one success under her belt.

Perhaps she felt a little bit of pride, but she would add that to her prayer list for this evening, too. At the rate she was going, she would have to start keeping a list on paper. It was no matter. She had a good feeling about this. A better feeling than she'd had in a long time about anything.

And that was a *gut* thing indeed.

6

He really wasn't sure how long he could go on like this. In the three days that Rachel had been at his house, she'd almost set the kitchen on fire twice, she had somehow managed to tear the inseam out of two pairs of his best-fitting pants, and that was besides the fiasco he'd had to endure on her very first day. He just hoped she was handier with a needle and a thread than she was with cookin'.

He'd been surprised to discover that her meals were mostly edible. Sometimes it seemed she forgot about the potatoes she'd started to boil or the chicken she'd put on to fry. Those instances, she'd wander out to check on her precious goats or her cheese that was fermenting on the porch and whatever she had abandoned would be ruined. It was those times that Gabriel wondered if he might not do better with one of those cans of store-bought soup, but he was paying her for a job—to cook and clean for his family. Maybe she just needed time to settle in.

He was making excuses for her, but Samuel had taken such a liking to Rachel that Gabriel felt somewhat obligated to his youngest to keep her around. Though loving and a blessing, Samuel didn't cotton to just anybody—the members of his family, Gideon's Annie, and now, Rachel Yoder. *Jah*, he owed it to his son to make this work. If that weren't enough, he needed her. No one else had answered his ad. Truth be told, neither had she, but Gabriel was standing by the adage that the Good Lord had seen the need in their lives and filled it. This was just part of the process, a time for adjustment. That was all.

He'd built a special pen for her goats to keep them from the other livestock and he'd made sure that they had a trough for water and room to run and play as goats were prone to do. Now if he could just get used to her peculiar ways. Every night he asked the Lord to help him accept her and her strange habits. He guessed that wasn't quite fair to call her strange and said a quick prayer on top of his prayer. She was just so different from the other women in his life—Gideon's Annie aside. Annie Fisher was different for a good reason. She had been raised *Englisch*—wealthy *Englisch*—and had a good enough excuse for her differences. Rachel Yoder . . . well, she was a different matter altogether, though he'd overheard someone once say that she had been raised by the Beachy Amish in Florida. If that were the case, then perhaps he could better understand her ways.

Gabriel took off his hat, wiped his forehead on the sleeve of his shirt, and surveyed his handiwork. He had just finished moving all the hay around in the loft to make room for Rachel's crazy organic stuff that she'd brought to feed her goats. *Jah*, there were adjustments to be made all around. But given some time he was sure they could get to an understanding. He replaced his hat and heard the rattle of a horse and buggy. Stepping out into the blinding spring sunshine, he blinked several times and shaded his eyes to identify his visitor.

"Whoa." Rueben Beachy pulled his buggy to a stop, Daniel

Glick at his side. The two men stepped down from the buggy and waited for Gabriel to make his way over to them.

"Bishop. Minister." Gabriel shook hands with them both.

He had expected them to come earlier in the week. When they didn't show on Monday he knew it was only a matter of time until they did come out to talk.

"Gabriel, we've come to talk to you about a matter most important."

He nodded. His appointment as the deacon to the district. Of the four positions, it was the least complicated. It would be his job to make certain they had any items needed for the service, water for foot washings, and supplies for communion. When the bishop got wind that someone wasn't living within the *Ordnung*, he would dispatch the deacon to talk to the offender first. Also, the deacon always conferred with the parents of the girl before weddings were announced. All-in-all not terribly difficult, but still time consuming and holy just the same.

"I was hoping that this burden might pass from me."

The bishop looked taken aback at his statement, but quickly recovered. "As you know, Gabriel Fisher, the Lord has seen fit to put you in this position within our church."

He nodded. "But I'm not married. I'm a widower, and Mary Elizabeth has left. How can I be a pillar in the district with so many . . . transgressions?"

The minister stared at his feet while the bishop cleared his throat. "That is not why we are here."

Gabriel frowned. "Something else?"

"We should go inside and sit down," the minister said.

"With Rachel Yoder," the bishop added.

"Rachel?"

The bishop nodded. "This concerns her too."

Gabriel nodded and led the way to the house.

"Rachel," he called as he wiped his feet at the front. "The bishop and the minister are here."

She came out of the kitchen, her prayer *kapp* a little lopsided on her head. A few strands of her pale brown hair had escaped their pins and her cheeks were flushed bright pink. What had she been doing?

She stopped short and ran her hands down the sides of her apron. "Bishop . . . minister." She smoothed a hand over her hair, but the crazy curls popped back free of her efforts.

"Rachel." The bishop nodded. "We are here to talk to you and Gabriel about a matter of great importance."

She looked to Gabriel, those big brown eyes questioning.

He gave her a small shrug. The clenching in his gut was due to the serious tone the bishop had used and had nothing to do with the fact that every time he looked at Rachel something in him felt like it was missing.

He sent her a nod which she returned before gesturing toward the kitchen table. "Come. Sit down. I'll make some coffee."

They gathered around the table with Rachel casting glances in his direction every few seconds. Like him, she evidently could feel the tension in the air.

Once the coffee had brewed, she brought it to the table with a plate piled high with chocolate chip cookies. It was no coincidence that chocolate chip was Samuel's favorite kind. Nor was it a surprise that they were slightly burnt around the edges. If he had to guess, she was flushed and disheveled because she had gone to check on goats while the cookies baked. Gabriel wondered how many batches she had burned before getting to the ones she served.

"There has been some talk," the bishop said after everyone had a cup of coffee and a plate of cookies in front of them.

"Talk?" He'd told them he shouldn't have been in the lot for deacon. "I'll step down." He nodded. It was better this way, but the words had barely left his mouth when the bishop shook his head.

"*Nay*. It's not about your position within the church. It's about your relationship with Rachel Yoder."

Rachel gasped.

Gabriel's mouth dropped open, but the bishop and the minister looked as serious as two men of God can look.

"I don't understand. I hired Rachel to help me around the house." As he said the words, the minister and the bishop shared a glance. A feeling of alarm slid down his spine. There wasn't anything in the *Ordnung* against having someone help in your house. There would be a good many fine Amish who were in violation if that were the case. He should have nothing to worry about, but the dread didn't subside.

The bishop cleared his throat. "We had heard something of the sort, but we came out to see if what we are hearing is true."

Gabriel locked gazes with Rachel, then he turned back to the bishop. "And what is it that you've been hearing?"

The bishop adjusted his eyeglasses again and nodded toward the minister.

"That you and Rachel Yoder are living under the same roof," Glick said.

"We are, I suppose." He shrugged. "She needed a place to live, and I needed someone to help with the *kinder*."

Rachel nodded.

The bishop cleared his throat. "There are those among us who believe that your arrangement is not . . . appropriate."

Gabriel opened his mouth to respond, closed it, then opened it once more. "Because I'm the new deacon?"

"That's a part of it," the minister said.

"And the other part?" Rachel asked, her voice small and wounded. Gabriel didn't think he'd ever heard her use that tone before, and it cut straight though his heart.

"That the two of you are not married."

Rachel sucked in a sharp breath.

His gaze jerked up and snagged hers and suddenly he felt like everything was different. It wasn't as if they were really doing anything wrong. There was a need and God filled it. That was all.

Gabriel pulled his gaze from his housekeeper and centered it on the minister. "I hardly think that is fair to Rachel for the gossips to be talking about us like that."

"The gossip has been dealt with, but the source must also be addressed," the bishop added.

Gabriel looked from one of them to the other, carefully avoiding Rachel's chocolate-colored eyes. "There is nothing wrong happening here. Do we need to go in front of the church and testify to that?"

"As I see it, the best thing would be for the two of you to get married."

"What?" Gabriel wasn't sure whose response was louder, his or Rachel's.

"I . . . I . . ." she stammered.

Gabriel couldn't say his thoughts were any more coherent.

"Assuming that the two of you plan to continue to occupy one dwelling, the best future for all involved would be a marriage."

Gabriel could only blink as he tried to get a handle on his swirling thoughts. He couldn't get married again. He didn't want to get married again. He'd had his chance at love, and it had been taken away. True love was rare and surely wouldn't come around more than once in a lifetime.

Besides that, Rachel was young and easy to look at, even if she was a bit independent and scatterbrained. Surely some young Amish buck would find favor in her. Who was he to take that from her?

"Excuse me, if I may," Rachel said, "but are you saying that we have to get married?"

The minister gave an uncomfortable nod. The irony wasn't lost on Gabriel. His job as the deacon would be to talk to anyone in the congregation who had strayed from the ways. Yet here they sat talking with him. "Only if you plan to live here and remain Gabriel's housekeeper."

"But I sleep in a separate room. Upstairs and completely away from Gabriel's."

The minister had enough sense to blush at her candid statement. "It's a matter of how the arrangement looks to the rest of the community."

Gabriel nodded. He understood. He captured Rachel's gaze with his own. "I'm sorry, Rachel. I never meant to put you in this type of situation when I suggested that you work for me."

She gave a quick nod, and to his horror, her big eyes filled with tears. "But . . . but . . ." She heaved a shuddering sigh, and he could tell that she was struggling to keep her composure. Suddenly it broke. She pushed away from the table and fled out the back door.

❧❦

Rachel ran across the yard, around the garden plot and didn't stop until she reached the pen where her goats were kept. She thought she was so smart. She'd thought she had it all figured out. But as quick as that, it all slipped away.

She took a deep, shuddering breath trying to stem the flow of her tears, but to no avail. They just kept coming one after another, sliding down her cheeks as all the changes she faced piled upon her. Changes, always changes.

As if sensing her pain, Sadie, her favorite doe, approached, nudging her soft head through the fence and against Rachel's leg.

She scratched the goat behind her ears, her tears still flowing. How was she going to leave them behind? Her cousin had made it perfectly clear that there was no room for them at his farm, though Rachel suspected he didn't want her attention split between the family and her goats.

She leaned down, breathing in the smell of goat before kissing Sadie on the top of her head.

"Rachel?"

She stiffened at the sound of his voice, using her apron to wipe away her tears before turning to face him.

Gabriel Fisher loomed over her, making her feel smaller and more helpless than ever. Two weeks ago she had everything she wanted, everything she needed, and now—despite her best efforts—she had nothing.

"Gabriel." She nodded toward him unable to say more through the lump in her throat. She just wouldn't think about the changes she faced. She couldn't think about them right now. She didn't want to start crying all over again.

"Don't cry," he said, his voice rough and soft at the same time, gravelly as if he were battling his own emotions. She was certain that he was dealing with the news the minister had delivered to them. He was from one of the most upstanding families in the district, in the whole settlement, even. To have his integrity questioned was a blow in itself.

"I'm not crying," she lied. *Not now,* she silently added, staring at her herd and still scratching Sadie behind her ears. "I guess I should write my cousin and tell him that I've changed my mind." She nearly choked on her last words. She hadn't changed her mind at all, but wagging tongues had done that for her. No wonder it was a sin to gossip. It hurt bad, especially when it wasn't true.

"Have you?" he asked.

She jerked, turning to face him. "Have I what?"

"Changed your mind."

She shrugged. "Does it matter?"

"I think so, *jah*."

Her gaze flew to his face, her eyes snagging his. Something unreadable shined there and in an instant filled her with hope. She pushed it down, tried to contain it. "*Nay*," she finally said. "I have not changed my mind." In fact she had grown fond of his family, sometimes pretending that they were her own. It was silly, she knew. But she also knew that the chances of her having a family that was really hers were slim. What harm could come from a little secret pretending?

"Neither have I."

She studied his face, her hope rising once again. "You want me to stay?"

"*Jah*," he said with a quick nod. "Samuel has grown used to you. He doesn't take to many people the way he has to you."

She laughed. "I'm a terrible housekeeper."

"You are better than none at all." He shrugged. "It is a big chore to take care of so many *buwe*."

"What about the gossip?"

He shifted, appearing uncomfortable as he stared at the ground beneath his feet. "As a newly ordained deacon, I'm expected to maintain a certain standard."

She nodded. He would need to be above reproach. Surely since the minister and the bishop knew the truth they would be okay.

"There is only one way that you'll be able to stay here."

She tilted her head. "What is that?"

"We must get married."

His words fell like a dead duck between them. Was he serious?

She met those hard green eyes and realized that Gabriel Fisher was not the joking sort.

"Married?" she squeaked. Married to this mountain of a man with big hands that matched his constant frown? How could she marry him? "But . . . but . . . but . . ."

He took a step toward her, and she took two back. "Rachel." Exasperation laced his voice. "It doesn't have to be like that. We can have whatever kind of marriage we choose."

"What do you mean?"

"I need a housekeeper, and you need a place to live and keep your goats."

She nodded.

"Our arrangement will remain the same, only we'll be married."

Heat flushed her cheeks, and she was surely as red as the geraniums she had planted in the front of the house. "What if you decide you wish you hadn't married me?" she said. "Or you fall in love? What then?"

He shook his head. "I've had love in my life. I'll not be expecting it again."

She dipped her chin, intently studying the toes of her shoes. "And our sleeping arrangements?" she mumbled.

"Eh?"

She took a deep breath, gathering courage. "Where will you sleep?"

Confusion puckered his brow. "In my bed."

The heat crept down her neck. "Where will I sleep?"

"In your bed."

She was certain she had turned red to the tips of her toes. "Forever?"

"Until it serves us no longer."

What exactly did that mean? She looked away, understanding most of it. For the time being, their marriage would be in name only. She would stay with Gabriel, be his bride and care for his children. She would keep her goats and her independence. What more could a girl want?

True love, a little voice inside her whispered.

But love was the ultimate dream. Gabriel had practically said so himself. It didn't come around more than once—and for some people not at all.

"I accept," she said, sticking out her hand to shake his. Still she couldn't help but wish that he got that same misty look in his eyes when he talked to her the way he always did when he talked about his late wife.

He took her hand into his own, his big palm enveloping hers until it disappeared.

"*Jah*, then," he said. "Let's go talk to the bishop."

⤳⟲ ⟳⤳

"Are you sure they won't mind?" Rachel asked as they neared the turnoff that would take her to his parents' house.

"They will not care if you stay."

"But . . . but . . ."

"Relax," he said, laying one of those large hands on her arm in support. Her flesh tingled where he touched, but she shook off the feeling. It was only natural that she was sensitive right now. She had been through so much in the last couple of weeks: her aunt's death, the move, and now this. A wedding.

The horses turned without hardly any direction from Gabriel. They knew the route so well.

Rachel wiped her hands down her skirt and tried to convince herself that everything was going to turn out fine. She had met Ruth and Abram Fisher several times before, and they seemed to take to her good enough. However, that was before she had agreed to marry their *sohn*. What would they think of her now?

Gabriel pulled the horses to a stop, then unhitched them from the wagon and led them toward the watering trough. They were going to be here a while, explaining and planning. Weddings didn't just happen overnight.

"Gabriel, is that you?"

"*Jah, Mam*," he said. Rachel continued to sit in the buggy until she realized what she was doing. She hopped down.

Ruth Fisher's green gaze centered on her, but Rachel was too anxious to read her expression. Though she did note that Ruth's eyes weren't near as hard as her *sohn's*.

Her feet rooted to the spot until Gabriel came up behind her. One of those big hands wrapped around her arm and pressed her toward the porch.

"I see you have a guest."

Rachel skidded to a stop as Gabriel halted a good two feet from the porch. "We should talk about this inside."

Ruth Fisher nodded. "I'll get us some pie."

Once they all settled around the table, pie in front of them, coffee brewing, Ruth spoke. "So what brings you out today, *sohn*?"

"Rachel and I are gettin' married."

Ruth blinked. "Rachel?"

"Rachel Yoder." He nodded in her direction.

"I know who Rachel is. I'm just a bit shocked. I wasn't prepared for such news." Ruth's voice was calm and even with no trace of how she really felt about the situation.

Rachel looked down at her plate, wishing she didn't have a huge lump in her stomach. Shoo-fly was her favorite.

"As the new deacon, there are church members who feel that it would be better if I were married."

Ruth nodded.

"Rachel and I have a mutual need. She needs a place to live and I need someone to care for the boys. It is a logical solution."

Ruth's keen eyes studied her for a full minute before she turned back to her son. "Many a good marriage has started with less."

Gabriel gave a jerk of his head that she supposed was a nod, then swallowed hard. Was he thinking of his wife? She pushed the thought away. It made no difference; their relationship wasn't based on *that*.

"We will need some help planning."

Ruth's face lit up like the Christmas lights in town during the holidays. She took Rachel's hand in her own and squeezed it. "I'd love to help."

"I want to announce the wedding at the next church service."

Of course he did. As a church leader, he'd need to show the congregation that he had good intentions toward her and his new position.

"We will get married a week from Thursday," he said.

"A week?" Rachel squeaked while Ruth echoed her sentiments. Planning a wedding in seven days was the definition of insanity.

Ruth shook her head. "I'll need at least a month."

"We don't have a month," Gabriel said. "Two weeks. That's the best I can offer."

Rachel wished she could speak past the lump in her throat. Two weeks was not near enough time to get used to the idea of marrying Gabriel Fisher. But the sooner they got married, the sooner they could go back to their normal routine, and that would be best for everyone involved.

Ruth sighed. "Two weeks, then."

"One more thing," Gabriel said. "There are members of the church who believe that it's not appropriate for Rachel to stay with me."

"Gabriel Fisher! Of course it's not. We raised you better than to think it was."

Rachel almost laughed as the stain of red crept up Gabriel's neck, clear up to his hairline. "I was only trying to—"

"Rachel will stay here with us." Ruth squeezed Rachel's hand once again. "That'll give us more time to plan the wedding."

Rachel nodded, glad that Ruth Fisher seemed taken with the idea. Heaven knew she was worried enough about the actual marrying Gabriel Fisher part. She didn't need to have hostile in-laws too.

"Now," Ruth said, standing and adjusting her prayer *kapp*. "Let's get Katie Rose and get a list ready. We haven't any time to waste."

Rachel stood as Gabriel frowned. "What about my noon meal?"

But Ruth was already halfway to the stairs. "I'm sure you'll be able to handle it this one time."

⁓◦ ◦⁓

Two weeks from Thursday . . . Gabriel stared at the ceiling that night after everyone had gone to bed. Two weeks would give the womenfolk time to sew Rachel a new dress and time enough to gather a few friends to witness the event. They already had the bishop's blessing, so that was done. Now he just had to manage the *buwe* on his own until Rachel was his wife.

He flopped over onto his side, staring into the unoccupied half of the bed. "*Becca*," he whispered into the darkness. "I sure hope I'm doing the right thing."

He hadn't walked out of the house that afternoon planning on asking her to marry him. He'd gone to find Rachel to make sure that she wasn't sick. What he'd found was her enormous brown eyes swimming in tears.

His Becca hadn't been much of a crier. She was a strong woman, practical and sure. Rachel's tears had been his undoing. He couldn't stand there while she wiped them away all the while denying their existence and just do nothing. When the plan popped into his head, it slid out of his mouth almost as easily, and there it was, the solution to their problem. The perfect way to stem her sorrow.

A lump formed in his throat as he thought about that moment. He'd never planned on getting married again, much less to a scrap of a girl with chocolate-colored eyes and a love for goats. But there it was. Two weeks away.

In his mind, he knew it was the right answer. But his heart . . . that was another matter altogether. Still the boys needed food on the table, clean clothes to wear, and a father who didn't have to play both parental roles.

For sure and for certain, it would be *gut* to have a woman around the house again.

Samuel's face immediately came to mind. He, more than anyone else, needed the soft touch that Rachel could provide.

Gabriel was worried about the child staying home all day and never attending school. Perhaps he should go in and talk to the teacher and see what he needed to do in order to catch Samuel up to the other *kinder* in his grade. But until then, he would at least have Rachel.

He sighed and closed his eyes. For the time being, he'd made the right decision. He could only hope that his Becca was smiling down from heaven at this new addition to their family.

Ruth thumped the eraser end of her pencil against the notebook and sighed. "Two weeks is not near enough time. I guess we could buy the celery."

Rachel traced the tiny puckers in her apron with her fingers and shifted in her seat. "It doesn't have to be a big wedding. I mean, I don't have any family that would come and well, I don't have a lot of friends." Why did her stomach pang when she said the words? Her lack of social contact had never bothered her before. Just now, when faced with no one at the wedding to stand up for her, it did.

"Well, we'll have to have enough for soup, and *roasht*, and . . ." She made a note on the paper and looked to Katie Rose. "I'm sure your cousins will help. That way we could have the 'going to the table.'"

Rachel shook her head. "We don't have to do all that. Just the family and the bishop. A regular supper."

"You have to have a cake. At the very least," Katie Rose added.

"*Jah*," Ruth agreed. "A cake is not optional."

"It's not that kind of marriage."

Ruth shook her head. "There is only one kind of marriage, and you're about to have it."

Her hands shook at the thought. "But . . ."

"No buts," Ruth said. "We are having ourselves a wedding. Now whether we have six months or two weeks is no matter."

Katie Rose clapped her hands together in excitement. Rachel liked Gabriel's sister. She liked all of his family, from his younger brother, John Paul, to his equally stern-faced father. The Fishers had done nothing if not accepted her into the fold. But this was too much. There would be no one at the wedding for her. All the family she had left lived in Ohio, and though they were welcome to come, Rachel had never met them, not even once. She seriously doubted that they would travel all that way in the middle of the growing season for a distant relative they'd never even seen.

Yet people she hardly knew wanted to make sure that her wedding was something to remember, even if the marriage itself was for convenience sake only. To her dismay, tears welled up in her eyes. She hadn't cried this much since her parents and her brothers were killed.

"Oh, do not cry." Katie Rose jumped to her feet and raced around the table. "We only want to help."

"I know," Rachel sniffed as Ruth handed her a tissue. "It's just . . . everything is happening so fast."

"I'll talk to Gabriel," Ruth said. "Have him give us a couple of months to get everything ready."

"*Nay.*" Rachel dried her tears and stiffened her shoulders. She had promised to marry him and take care of his children, he had promised to let her keep her goats. She had a bargain to uphold, and she would do it. "I'm *allrecht* now. But let's keep this as small as possible. It's not the wedding season and so many will be needed in the fields."

Ruth nodded, though Rachel thought her action seemed reluctant. "Now where are we going to get the celery we need?"

7

The days leading up to the wedding were hectic and filled. Rachel spent the most of her day at Gabriel's house, cleaning and taking care of her goats. Unfortunately, she still hadn't mastered the art of cooking for seven. There just never seemed to be enough food. Most times she cooked the evening meal, then went back to Ruth and Abram's for her own supper. Gone were the days of having leftovers and sandwiches for lunch the next day.

She enjoyed her time at Gabriel's house, even when he came in from the fields tired and sweaty, that perpetual frown marring his otherwise handsome features. She couldn't help but wonder why he frowned so much.

Not that it was any of her business. Even if they were about to get married. It wasn't like they were getting married for real.

She fanned herself even though she was alone in the house with only little Samuel to keep her company. She wasn't comfortable thinking about such things. The goats were milked and the dishes from their noon meal washed and dried, there wasn't a real good reason not to go visiting. It might do Samuel some good too, to see his *grossmammi*, and she could use Ruth's treadle sewing machine to sew a new shirt for Joseph.

Decision made, she gathered her material and Samuel, then hitched up the horses, all the while looking forward to getting out a little. It was a beautiful day—the sun was shining, the birds chirping, the sky the bluest she had ever seen.

John Paul's car was gone from its place behind the phone shanty that sat across the road from Ruth and Abram's house. He was most likely working at the factory that sat between Clover Ridge and Chouteau. Rachel didn't think his father approved of the job, but Abram hadn't said anything directly to her. She supposed every Amish teen experienced *rumspringa* in their own way. Well, she hadn't exactly. She hadn't been interested in sampling the pleasures of the *Englisch* world, more content to stay at home than run around.

She didn't feel like she missed much. Now here she was years later about to be married to a man she hardly knew.

She grabbed her sewing bag from behind the seat and helped Samuel to the ground. "Are you ready to see your *grossmammi*?"

He smiled up at her, glasses glinting in the sunlight, one front tooth missing. "Will she have cookies? The kind without brown edges?"

Rachel laughed as they made their way up the porch steps. "I'm sure she will."

There was no denying it: her own cooking skills hadn't improved much since she had been caring for Gabriel and his sons. It wasn't that she didn't know how, she just got a little impatient while everything baked, fried, or boiled and she would find her mind wandering to other projects—the cheese she had fermenting on the porch, any outstanding orders, a new kid—and she would go to check on these things only to lose track of time and burn whatever it was she was trying to cook. It was an honest mistake and one she was trying desperately to correct.

With a determination to cook supper without a mishap, Rachel knocked on the door. She smiled down at Samuel, his fingers fisted in the skirt of her dress. He was just the most precious child.

She raised her hand and knocked again.

The family buggy was unhitched and sitting to the side of the house. But that didn't mean they were definitely home. Ruth and Abram could have taken off in the wagon. Katie Rose was most likely working on her wedding plans, or at the very least enjoying such a perfect day with her beloved.

Rachel ignored the stab of jealousy and added the transgression to her ever-growing mental prayer list. It was a sin to covet what thy neighbor had, but she was weak. There were so many times when she wished her life had turned out a little more . . . well, normal.

"I guess they're not home." She had been looking forward to spending part of the afternoon with her future mother-in-law. Even having a mother-in-law would make her feel a little more like everyone else.

She turned to lead Samuel back toward the steps when she heard a noise. Had that come from inside the house? She stopped and cocked her head to one side.

Samuel turned questioning green eyes to hers.

"Did you hear that?"

He gave a solemn nod.

She went back to the door and knocked again.

No answer.

What if someone was inside? And hurt? Or what if it was a burglar?

She shook her head at her overactive imagination. Most Amish homes didn't contain items that were considered to be worth stealing. Could be an *Englisch* kid come to play pranks on them.

She took a deep breath for courage and turned the knob.

The house was quiet, the hum of the propane refrigerator and the soft tick of the battery-operated clock, the only sounds.

"Ruth?" she called softly, inching her way into the house. She gently pushed Samuel behind her. "Ruth?"

The sound came again and sounded a lot like a . . . sob.

"Ruth?" Rachel crept down the hall until she reached the bedroom she knew to be Ruth and Abram's.

The door had been left open just a crack. Rachel gently pushed it open unsure as to what she might find, and was utterly dismayed when she found Ruth lying across the bed, silent sobs wracking her body.

"Ruth?"

The older woman jerked, sat up straight, and started wiping her tears on her apron.

Rachel rushed to her side as Samuel hung back at the door. "Ruth, what's wrong?"

"N-nothing. I'm fine." She sniffed once and wiped her tears with the back of one hand.

"That doesn't look like fine."

Ruth pushed herself to her feet. "I'm fine," she insisted.

Rachel crossed her arms. "It is a sin to lie, Ruth Fisher."

Tears immediately started in her mossy green eyes once again.

Rachel turned toward Samuel. "*Liebschdi*, why don't you go to the kitchen and see if you can find some of those cookies."

Samuel nodded. "*Jah*, Wachel."

Once he was out of earshot, she turned back to Ruth. Rachel took her hands in her own and urged Ruth to sit on the edge of the bed. Rachel took up a place next to her.

"Now, tell me what's got you crying like a leaky faucet?"

Ruth hesitated before taking a deep shuddering breath. "I found another lump."

"Oh, Ruth." Rachel felt her insides crumple like an old piece of paper. She hadn't been there when Ruth Fisher went through all of her cancer treatments, but she had heard talk of her illness, seen her around town in her bonnet, near empty from the lack of hair due to the harsh treatments.

Ruth shuddered, and Rachel realized they were forgetting one very important detail. "God's in charge," she said.

"W-what?"

Rachel stiffened her spine and gave the older women a firm nod. "God's in charge here. He didn't bring you all this way for nothing."

"I-I . . . I don't know."

"Well, I do." Rachel folded her hands in her lap and nodded again. "You'll go have the test and—" She stopped as Ruth shook her head.

"I'm not going to the doctor."

"But, Ruth, you must."

She wiped her eyes and sniffed, her shoulders gradually straightening until she seemed to settle into her plan. "*Nay*, I'll not cost the district any more money than I already have."

"But—"

It was Ruth's turn to interrupt. "If the cancer is back, then it was God's will all along. I'll not go against Him again."

"You believe that by fighting the disease the first time that you were going against Him?"

"I don't know." Ruth shrugged. "But I can't go through that again."

Rachel's heart ached at those near-whispered words. "But your family—"

Ruth looked Rachel in the eyes, unwavering. "Won't know anything about it."

Rachel shook her head, the tickle of her *kapp* strings against her throat seemed surreal. "I don't know if that's a *gut* idea."

"*Gut* or not isn't the matter. I don't want them to know."

"Ruth, I—"

She took Rachel's hand in her own. Her fingers were trembling, a little on the cold side despite the increasing heat on the Oklahoma spring day. "Promise me, Rachel. Promise me that you won't say anything." She squeezed her hand, green eyes blazing. "Promise me, Rachel."

"I . . . I promise." Her stomach sank as she said the words.

The day of the wedding arrived so quickly it nearly made Rachel's head spin. But there it was. Two weeks had passed. Her pale blue dress completed, pristine white apron starched and pressed. Her heart pounded. Her hands shook.

She took a deep breath and looked around Ruth and Abram's room, searching for something to ease the anxiety roiling within her.

They had decided to get married at the Fishers. Or rather, Ruth had decided for her. How was Rachel supposed to protest? Aside from the looming threat of cancer, Rachel had no mother to cook her wedding feast, no home of her own to be married in.

"Rachel, *liebschen, was iss letz?*"

She turned to face Katie Rose, her breathing shallow. What's wrong? Everything was wrong. Couldn't she see that? "I—I need to see Gabriel."

"He's in the barn with the other men. You don't want to go out there in your wedding dress."

"*Jah.* I do." She took off for the door, avoiding the front room where some of the women in the community had already begun to gather. She sailed through the backyard, deep gulps of fresh air fueling her flight.

She slowed as she neared the big barn doors. Fine wisps of her hair had worked free of their pins and tickled her face and neck. She brushed one back, then pressed her palms to the flaming skin of her cheeks.

"Rachel?" Gideon Fisher stepped from the dim interior of the barn, his green eyes so like his brother's searching her face.

She took a steadying breath. Gideon's eyes weren't identical to Gabriel's. Her soon-to-be husband's were as hard as rock candy, but the younger Fisher brother had eyes of a soft mossy green filled with hope and understanding.

"Are you feeling *allrecht*, Rachel Yoder?"

"I . . . I need to talk to Gabriel."

Gideon turned and said something to the man closest to him. Rachel hadn't paid much attention before, but saw now that it was John Paul Fisher, the youngest of the family.

John Paul gave a quick nod, his usual smile turned upside down. He disappeared into the crowd of men and returned moments later with Gabriel in tow.

"Rachel, *was iss letz?*"

Why was everybody asking her that? Didn't they know what was wrong? Was she the only one who could see it?

"Can . . . will you walk with me, Gabriel Fisher?"

His brow puckered into a frown, but he gave her a small nod. "*Jah*," he said, casting a quick glance at his brothers before stepping out into the sunlit day.

He had waited until they were a goodly ways from the barn before speaking. "Is there something you want to talk about, Rachel?"

She knew that everyone in the barn was watching. They might not be able to hear, but they sure were looking at this bride desperate to talk to her intended one more time before they wed.

She stopped at the edge of the garden, looking out at the perfect rows of beans and corn. "Are you sure we are doing the right thing?" Her garden wasn't nearly as tidy. Maybe she wasn't cut out to be a wife. Maybe she'd never be. She had heard stories about Gabriel's first wife, how sweet she was. A *wunderbaar* woman who took care of her family and had time to spare for her friends and loved ones. How would she be able to live up to that?

"You don't want to be my *fraa*?"

"That's not what I said." What *did* she want?

"If'n you want to back out, Rachel, now would be the time. I'll not think badly of you."

Then what? Move to Ohio and leave Clover Ridge behind? She wasn't sure she could bear it. In the last sixteen years, this had become her home.

Then there was Samuel and the other boys. They needed her as much as she needed them. And Gabriel's mother and father. They treated her as much like one of the family as if she had been born into it. That was all she had ever wanted, a family like the one she had lost. It was the one prayer that God had never fulfilled. Now that she had one, it'd be mighty hard to just walk away, regardless of the nerves that shook her body from head to toe.

"*Nay*," she whispered. She turned her gaze from the pasture and the new foal frolicking there with last year's addition. Instead she met Gabriel's gaze in all of its intensity. She felt like she was falling, falling, falling into something she couldn't name.

He grabbed her elbow to steady her. She must have swayed. She pressed a hand to her forehead.

"Unlock your knees, or you'll pass out for sure."

Rachel did as he said, wobbling a little as the blood flooded back into her limbs.

"You are positive this is what you want?"

Want? *Nay* . . . but it was what she needed, no doubt. She dipped her chin. "This is what you want too?"

"'Tis." The one syllable clipped the air. He was certain, of that she was sure, but somehow she knew there was more brewing just beneath the surface of their plan. Yet she had no idea what it was. Her only course of action was to pray about it and know that God's hand was at work.

"Will you pray with me?" she asked, feeling suddenly small and insignificant.

"*Jah.*" He took her trembling hands into his own and bowed his head.

She stared at the crown of his black hat for a moment longer before bowing her head as well.

Something in the way he held her fingers in his own brought a calmness to her belly. It was warm and fanned out, filling every part of her as they stood there together, talking to God and just . . . being.

"*Aemen,*" he said, lifting his head and meeting her gaze once again. "Better?"

"*Jah.*" And it was. Somehow she felt so much more calm and in control than she had just moments before.

He reached up and brushed the tendrils of hair out of her face. "Then go let the ladies ready you up and let's get married."

So many of the traditions at a regular Amish wedding had been abandoned. The bride's family was not hosting the ceremony. There would be no "going to the table" in which the eligible young men asked the unmarried women in the community to sit with them during the meal.

Somehow Ruth, despite her worry of the lump that she had found, managed to scour up enough celery for the *roasht* and creamed celery.

As Rachel and Gabriel sat in the *eck*, the special place in the corner reserved for the bride and groom, Rachel was just glad it was over. A couple hours more, then she and Gabriel could go back to his house. Tomorrow everything would return to normal. Well, sort of . . . at least they could start their bizarre life together.

Her smile felt stiff on her lips. Her cheeks hurt from forcing the pleased expression, but she couldn't let her own doubts show. She was all too ready to climb into Gabriel's buggy and wave good-bye.

She breathed a short-lived sigh of relief. They had done it. For all anyone knew, she and Gabriel had somehow managed to fall into a mutual attraction with the other and decided to join their lives into one.

Now all they had to do was keep up the charade for the rest of their lives. Was that even possible? All too soon, the district would suspect the truth. Regardless of how frowned upon gossip was in the community, she knew folks would be talking about why she wasn't going to have a baby. They would look at her at church services, barn raisings, and quilting bees and wonder what was wrong with her. After all, Gabriel had proved his ability to father a child. From there it was only a short jump to the truth. That she and Gabriel Fisher had married out of convenience, and there would be no baby in her future.

The thought made her heart ache, and she cast her eyes to her husband. He faced the front, eyes on the road as he guided the horses home. Night was falling, and the foggy light of dusk made his features impossible to read. Still she wondered what thoughts were going through his mind. Was he thinking about tomorrow's chores? Or the fact that they had just promised themselves to the other until death should part them?

Was he thinking about their bargain and how he would have no more offspring to carry on his name? Probably not. But the thought plagued Rachel.

Just in the last couple of years, her unmarried state had presented her with this deficiency. Not being married was heartbreak enough. But never having children . . . that was more than she thought she could bear.

Rachel cast a glance into the back of the buggy where Joseph and David sat side by side, each looking out the windows at the dusk-coated scenery. Rachel had spent enough time with them to know that they were unusually quiet. She supposed it wasn't every day that your father remarried. *And* to a woman who couldn't bake cookies without burning them.

She kissed the top of Samuel's head as he sat between her and his father and silently vowed to try harder. Gabriel had done her a service. He had taken her into his home and allowed her to care for his children so she wouldn't have to give up her goats and move to Ohio. When that didn't work out as planned, he asked her to marry him. The least she owed him was properly cooked bread and edible meals.

With that very thought pinging around in her head, Rachel closed her eyes and said a small prayer that tomorrow, her first day as Gabriel Fisher's wife would be better than the two weeks she had spent as his housekeeper.

⚮

Gabriel used his fork to peek at the underside of his serving of eggs. At least he *thought* it was eggs. Then he glanced around the table at his sons who were having the same problem with their breakfast.

Once they had gotten home last night, they unloaded from the buggy and went into the house. Matthew and Simon arrived moments later and they all gathered in the living room for a family meeting.

Gabriel explained that they were a family now, and families stuck together. Rachel would be cooking and cleaning for them, and in turn he expected them to respect her and follow her decisions. The boys nodded, their faces solemn. Gabriel knew the younger *buwe* might not understand, but Matthew and Simon were old enough. He expected them to set the example for their siblings.

They all nodded in agreement then tromped off to bed, exhausted by the day's festivities.

Gabriel had gone to bed feeling calm and satisfied. He had helped out a fine woman and took care of his children to boot. He was sure the Lord would smile down on them.

And now this.

Rachel eyed him over the rim of her coffee mug as she took a sip. "Something wrong?"

"*Nay*," he lied, and shot Simon a stern look as he opened his mouth to protest. "What would be wrong?"

She shrugged. "I don't know." She paused, then shook her head. "I'm not the best at making dippy eggs."

You don't say. He cleared his throat, unwilling to add even an ounce of hurt into those bottomless brown eyes. "I like them this way just fine too." He doused the overcooked mess with his mother's pepper sauce and prepared for the worst. With a quick smile in her direction, he forked up a bite and chewed. And chewed. And chewed. He swallowed hard, then pointed at Simon with his fork. "How about you, *sohn*?"

Simon quickly took a bite, gave a grimace which turned quickly to a smile of pretend pleasure. "Mmm-mmm," he said, laying it on a bit thick by rubbing his belly. Or maybe he was preparing it for the next bite.

Gabriel would have to say extra prayers tonight. He'd need to ask God to forgive him for lying to his wife and encouraging, no, *insisting* that his children do the same. But what harm was there really in a lie if it made someone special feel better about themselves and what they had to offer?

He guessed no matter what way it was split up, a lie was a lie. But he couldn't stand the thought of the truth bringing any more tears sliding down Rachel's sweet face.

He choked down the meal and poured the remainder of his coffee down the sink. "I'll be in my *vatter's* south forty if you need me."

She nodded as the three middle boys filed past, grabbing their Igloo coolers filled with who-knew-what and tromped out the door for school. Matthew gave Gabriel a nod and Rachel a fleeting glance as he headed out the door for his day. At fifteen, Matthew was out of school and promised for half of the summer to help Gideon tend to his thriving alpacas so the soon-to-be father could help his *fraa* ready for the new baby.

Gabriel washed his hands and dried them on the dishtowel as Samuel finished eating. At least his youngest wasn't finicky. Course'n young Sam didn't have non-dippy dippy eggs this morning, just an overcooked biscuit filled with scorched bacon.

"You ready, Samuel?"

Big green eyes focused on him as Samuel slowly shook his head. "I wanna stay with Wachel."

Gabriel wasn't surprised. Samuel was more accustomed to staying with his *aenti* and *grossmammi* than with his *dat*. He could find no fault with that. "Is this okay with you, Rachel?"

She nodded, "Of course."

Gabriel smiled at the sprinkling of freckles across her nose. What a strange thing to notice about one's wife the day after the ceremony. But their marriage was nothing else except strange.

"What is it?" She frowned, smoothing her hair and making sure it was all tucked in its pins and properly covered with a snowy white prayer *kapp*.

"Nothing." He shook his head and started for the door, grabbing his straw hat off its peg.

Yes, indeed. Some kind of strange.

***

Milking the goats had to be her favorite time of the day. Her hands knew what to do without any direction from her brain, leaving her plenty of time to think about recipes for *chevre* and ways to improve her cheese. She was secretly proud of her little business operation which seemed to be growing day by day. Course, she had nothing on Annie's pickle business.

Her sister-in-law had started the business after learning of Ruth's cancer. Although Ruth had finished her treatments, Annie had kept the business going in order to add to the community coffers that helped pay for doctor's visits and the like. Annie had said that she wanted everyone who needed medical care to be able to go if they so choose. They still advertised on the Internet, but the bishop—and the district as a whole—had turned a blind eye last year when Jacob Kauffman had fallen off the barn and nearly killed himself. The tumble had broken his back and only the medical care that he'd received, courtesy of Annie's pickles, had saved the boy. After a year of rehabilitation, Jacob could walk again and showed no sign that he'd ever been wheelchair dependent.

Still her cheese brought in enough that she knew she could

contribute to the overall household. Even if she couldn't quite make the meals that Gabriel and his *sohns* were used to.

But she was trying.

Yesterday Katie Rose Fisher had told her that one of Gabriel's favorite meals to eat was black-eyed peas flavored with smoked ham hock. As soon as he had left the house, Rachel had gone onto the back porch and found the bag containing the dried peas hanging just where Katie Rose said it would be.

It had been a while since Rachel had made beans of any sort, but it was—as they say—like riding a bike. She filled a pan with water and started it to boil while she searched through the freezer. A leftover frozen ham bone was just what she needed and she tossed it and the peas into the pot just as it started to boil. She covered it, turned the setting to low and went out to tend to her goats.

So breakfast still needed some tweaking. She had noticed the way Gabriel had chewed his eggs, like they had been made of a sow's ear, but dinner would be fine and dandy. Okay, so she had never cooked black-eyed peas before. How different could they be from regular brown beans? Katie Rose had said as much and everyone in Clover Ridge knew what a *gut* cook she was.

A delicious aroma floated in the air as they let themselves back into the house. The peas seemed to be cooking nicely and she longed to check on their progress. But she resisted the urge to take the lid off the cast iron pot and release all that built-up heat. Instead she took out a loaf of crusty sourdough bread and sliced it.

"You want a cheese sandwich, Samuel?"

He nodded his head so hard his bangs flew in all directions.

Rachel laughed. "Then it shall be," she said with a flourish.

She smeared the thick slices of bread with her favorite herb and garlic *chevre* and turned the oven to "broil." She sliced tomatoes while the bread and cheese toasted and added the leftover bacon to their plates. A few minutes later she and Samuel were enjoying their quick meal.

Rachel smiled to herself. At least she could do something right, and that was make the best goat cheese in three counties. Sure, her bread left a little something to be desired and her eggs were not the best, but her cheese was grade A.

"More, more," Samuel chanted, his mouth still stuffed with the last bite.

Rachel ruffled his hair. "It's not *gut* to talk with your mouth filled with food, *liebschdi*." She glanced at the clock wondering if Gabriel was coming in to eat or if he was staying at his parents' house for the noon meal.

"One more and then we've got some house cleaning to do."

Samuel's face fell into a quick frown. "I do not like cleaning house."

Nor do I, little one. "That's because you've never done the work with me."

"S'pose." His bottom lip protruded even more than usual, and she heard him kick at the chair next to him. "I wanna go to school."

"*Jah*, I know. But if you go to school, who will be here with me to help with the goats?" That seemed to brighten him up just a little bit. At least he quit swinging his feet and instead propped his chin in his hand and thought about her question. "I guess I should stay here then, Wachel."

"Indeed, you should," she agreed with a quick nod.

She made him another cheese toast, placed it in front of him, and watched him eat, a small measure of pride mixed with the warm feeling of love spreading over her.

This *fraa* stuff wasn't so hard. She was definitely improving—and after just one day! When Gabriel came home to his favorite meal . . . why then she would definitely feel that she wasn't the only one who had reaped benefits from their agreement, and that Gabriel Fisher had gotten the bride that he deserved.

8

"Mmm . . . something smells *gut*." Gabriel walked through the front door to the pleasing aroma of . . . "Is that peas I smell?"

"Gabriel!" His wife of one day came flying down the stairs, *kapp* strings trailing behind her like wisps of smoke. A bright pink colored her cheeks and a smudge of dirt ran underneath one brown eye before fading away into her hairline. Her hair itself was once again sticking out from under her *kapp*, little wisps curling around her face in a way that seemed most becoming. Though it shouldn't have.

One, he shouldn't be thinking that way about his wife. And two, she should be more presentable. Even if she were only at home. Who knew who could stop by during the day? The preacher's wife, the preacher, even the bishop himself might decide to come by and see what was going on in this new household.

He frowned.

Her tiny hands immediately flew to her disheveled hair. She smoothed it back into place only to have it pop free again.

His frown deepened.

"I wasn't expecting you."

He raised a brow. "This is my home, *jah?*"

She nodded, her color deepening until it was the color of a ripe fall plum. "I meant to say 'so soon.' I wasn't expecting you home so soon." She slowed her steps and continued down the stairs, easing her way past him.

He grunted, unable to form a reply.

"I was just cleaning the *buwe's* rooms."

"Where are they?"

Her gaze flew to the clock on the mantel just as her hand fluttered at her throat. "I—I don't know. Still walking home from school, I suppose."

"It's fifteen after five. They should have been home two hours ago." All but Matthew, who was undoubtedly still helping Gideon.

She swallowed. "I guess I didn't realize how late it was. Should we go look for them?"

"I have a feeling I know where they are." He brushed past her and stalked to the back door, all too aware that she flitted behind him like a tiny bird. That alone was enough to fuel his trek across the yard and to the tree line at its edge. "Joseph, Simon, Da-vid!"

He didn't have to call twice. In seconds, he heard them crashing through the underbrush. They appeared before him, smiles on their faces as if they had been doing exactly as they had been told.

"*Jah, Dat?*" It was Simon who spoke, standing in the middle of his brothers who suddenly found the ground beneath their bare feet incredibly interesting.

"Where have you been?"

"Fishing," Simon boldly answered.

"Where are *der fisch?*"

Simon's confidence wavered, then stilled on his freckled face. "We, uh, didn't catch any today."

"And your chores?"

Simon's gaze strayed to a spot behind Gabriel that he knew was Rachel.

"Look at me," he commanded.

The *bu* swung his attention back to Gabriel.

"Did you get your chores done before you decided to take your chances on the creek bank?"

"*Nay, Vatter,*" Simon mumbled.

Gabriel crossed his arms and tried to ignore the ball of energy and heat that was standing behind him. He shouldn't be so . . . so *aware* of his wife. "So you're telling me that the chores haven't been completed because you went fishing and caught no *fisch* for your trouble."

"*Jah, Dat.*" The words were directed at his feet.

Likewise, Joseph and David shifted uncomfortably in the dirt, neither willing to look him in the face.

"*Guck* here," he said. The *buwe* reluctantly met his gaze. "Tomorrow you will help Rachel scrub the floors in the *haus*. And Monday you will come straight home from school and finish your chores before you do anything else. Understand?"

"*Jah, Dat,*" the three mumbled in unison.

"Now, get on up to the house and do your chores. I want them all done by supper."

They took off like the devil was on their heels.

Gabriel shook his head.

"I—I'm sorry, Gabriel. I guess I wasn't paying enough attention to the time."

"That trio is a handful, for sure and for certain. You'll have to be careful in the future that they don't find another way to take advantage of you."

"*Jah*. I suppose."

"Come on," he said, reaching for her elbow and then thinking better of the idea. He gestured for her to walk ahead of him. "Let's get back to the house. There's no telling what those three will be into next."

⚜

Failure. Total, utter failure. Well, maybe not *totally*. She had managed to get the floors cleaned upstairs, the beds made up with fresh sheets, and the windows washed in all three bedrooms. Not that anyone would notice. Not now that they were all scrambling around trying to get their chores done before their father took a switch to them.

Rachel stirred the buttermilk into the cornmeal as she fought back tears. She wouldn't cry. She wouldn't cry. *She wouldn't cry*.

The glaring glances shot her way were of no help at all. It was as if they blamed her for their misbehaving. 'Course, if she had been a better mother, she would have been looking for them to come home and not so busy cleaning that she hadn't missed them at all. She could have reminded them of their chores and sent them into the barn straight away.

But she wasn't a good mother. She wasn't a good housekeeper. She wasn't a good cook. All the things that Gabriel had hired her to do and the main reason he had married her. He was probably biding his time until he could throw her out on her ear.

The Amish never divorced, but that didn't mean they had to live together. It didn't happen much, but it did happen that a husband and wife couldn't manage to get along well enough to remain in the same household. And since this was Gabriel's house . . .

She put the cornbread in the warm oven and wiped her hands on a dishtowel as the front door swung open. Matthew led the way with his brothers following behind and their father bringing up the rear. The edges of their shirt cuffs were wet from washing their hands in the spigot outside, their hair shiny and slicked back from the cool water.

She pushed her own hair back under her prayer *kapp* and for the millionth time in her life wished that the strands weren't so unruly. For as soon as she completed the action, the stubborn curls popped free again.

"Mmm . . . that smells gut." Matthew hung his hat on the peg by the door and rubbed his belly. "I'm so *hungerich*."

The other boys removed their hats as well and nodded in agreement.

"*Jah*," Simon said, his mouth turning down at the corners. "We didn't get an after-school snack." His tone implied that it was all Rachel's fault.

She stiffened her backbone and pulled the pickled beets and applesauce from the propane-powered refrigerator. They could have come in any time and gotten a snack, but they had chosen to go down to the creek. That wasn't her fault. But her heart gave a guilty little jump. "Come and sit down. I've made you a good hearty *natchess*."

They looked skeptical and hopeful in the same instance. Rachel made a note on her mental prayer list to ask for humility. But she was proud of herself. She had made dinner, the cornbread was almost done and not black around the edges. For the first time since she had decided to cook for the Fisher brood, she had managed to make a meal that was *gut* and properly cooked. She had a lot to be proud of . . . even if pride was a sin.

"Are those peas I smell?" Gabriel asked.

Rachel peeked in at the cornbread. Just a few minutes more. "*Jah*. Katie Rose said they were your favorite."

He gave a nod, then lifted the lid on the pot. He gave a tiny cough. Then shut it again. "Uh, Rachel?"

She turned just as he was peeking under the lid once more. "*Jah?*"

"Did you check the peas for bugs before you cooked them?"

She frowned. "Bugs?"

"Weevils."

Her gaze flickered to the steaming pot. "Weevils? Was I supposed to?"

"I expect that means no." She thought she saw a smile flicker across Gabriel's face, but when she turned her attention to him fully, his usual frown pulled at the corners of his mouth.

She grabbed the potholder out of his hand and lifted the lid. A delicious aroma wafted up from the cooking peas and ham hock. But they weren't alone in the pot. Dozens of little weevils floated on the top of the water.

"Ugh." She slammed the lid down. "How did those get in there?"

She closed her eyes against the thought of all those floating weevils and the snickering that erupted from the table. But when she opened them again, everything was still the same.

Gabriel cast a stern look toward his boys. "You didn't clean through the peas."

"*Jah*, I washed them," she said.

Gabriel shook his head. "You have to pick out all the ones with little holes in them. They have weevils."

Little holes? She had never done that in her life.

Then again, she and her aunt didn't have peas very often, usually when someone brought some over to them. Rachel had never grown them herself. Truth was, she was as bad at gardening as she was at cleaning. But she made enough cheese to barter and trade and get what she and her aunt needed—fresh corn, sweet potatoes, and okra. That was one reason why she took such *gut* care of her goats. They provided them with much more than milk and cheese.

She glanced at the table where five *hungerich buwe* sat waiting expectantly. She was certain she would never be able to make enough cheese to support them all.

She cut her eyes back to her husband of one day and wondered what he was thinking. It was hard to read his eyes shadowed by the stern ridge of his brow. But it didn't take an *Englisch* education to figure out he was mad. He had worked all day helping his *vatter*, Matthew had been over with his *onkel*, and they were all hungry and waiting. She wasn't sure if she had enough cheese and bread to get her out of this one.

"*Allrecht.*" He gave a firm nod. "Everybody get on your shoes. We're going into town to eat."

~⊘ ⊘~

He should be mad. He'd worked all day and come home to weevil-y peas. He had hungry boys who had worked hard as well. He'd done his part to provide for them, he'd married a woman to care for them, prepare them meals, and wash their clothes.

Except he had trouble picturing her as a woman, and instead thought of her more as a slip of a girl. She looked as if a strong wind could knock her to the ground. Yet there was a strength about her, slats of steel lying just beneath the surface. He'd seen her close her eyes after looking at the mess of peas and floating bugs. She wanted to break down right then and there, but she hadn't. Instead, she had taken a deep breath and moved forward.

He chanced a quick look in her direction. That she cried when faced with the prospect of having to give up her goats said a lot to him. Showed him how much they meant to her. He knew he couldn't be too hard on her.

Slip of a girl. Tiny hands. Solid core.

She was something else.

He turned the buggy into the parking lot at Murray's Pizzeria. Joseph, David, and Samuel all squealed in delight, while Matthew and Simon shared a high slap of hands. High five, he thought they called it. Some *Englisch* gesture they had picked up in town.

He hated it. But only because it just served to remind him of Mary Elizabeth's desertion. He'd gotten a letter from her just yesterday, but he'd put it in the little wooden box under the bed, the special place where he kept all of his keepsakes. He couldn't read it, not yet. He couldn't know how wonderful it was for her in the *Englisch* world. How well she was getting along with whatever family had taken her in. Couldn't stand the thought of his beautiful firstborn among the sinners of the world.

"Pizza?" Rachel asked, as she slid open the door and stepped down from the buggy. She reached out and Samuel jumped into her arms, anxious as ever to devour his favorite treat.

"You like pizza, *jah*?"

She shrugged. "I've never eaten it before."

"Never?" Matthew's eyebrows nearly disappeared under the brim of his straw hat.

Samuel grabbed her arm and tugged her toward the restaurant entrance. "Are you in for a treat!"

Gabriel laughed, surprised at the sound. How long had it been since he had truly laughed? He could not remember. But that was only because a person didn't go around each day tallying their chuckles. He had more to do, more to worry about than how much laughter was in each day.

He adjusted his galluses and followed behind his family into the restaurant.

The patrons of Murray's were mostly locals who didn't give the Amish a second look. Gabriel made his way to the counter to order while Rachel seated the boys around a table.

She was a sight, his Rachel. Once again her hair was flying every-which-a-ways, her prayer *kapp* pinned to the middle of the mess. If there was one thing he could change about her it would be her hair. For the most part she was as neat and tidy as the next Plain woman, but her hair. *Ei, yi, yi.*

He ordered their pizzas and joined Rachel at the booth. The boys knew better than to act out in public, and for the most part they sat together at a separate table and minded their manners.

"I just . . . wanted to thank you for this." Rachel waved a hand around.

"Gern gschehne," he said. "But no thanks are needed. We all have to eat."

She nodded, her chin stiff. She lifted her nose a little higher, and he knew she was warring with her own feelings. "But I wanted your meal to be special."

He rubbed his hands together. "Oh, it will be."

Samuel nodded. "You will love pizza, Wachel."

She smiled at the *bu*, her entire face warming, softening, changing until she hardly looked like the same person. "Let's get you ready, huh?"

Gabriel found himself trapped, staring at her as she shook out a paper napkin and tucked it into the collar of Samuel's shirt. "I wanted to be the one who made it," she said.

"Huh?" He jerked himself out of his thoughts and focused his attention once again.

"I said I wanted to make the meal. I can cook, you know." She crossed her arms on the table in front of her. She had changed back into the other Rachel, the regular one.

"Jah, of course."

Thankfully their server chose that particular moment to bring their pizzas.

"There's pepperoni," he explained pointing to each pizza as he said their kind. "A double cheese and deluxe."

"Cheese is the best," Samuel said with a sage nod.

The other boys shook their heads, calling out their favorites.

"Which one do you like?" She turned those deep brown eyes on him and Gabriel's stomach dropped. Why did he feel like she had asked for more than his pizza preference?

He coughed and then cleared his throat before speaking. "I like the deluxe."

"That's what I want to try then." She smiled, and his stomach fluttered. Maybe pizza wasn't such a *gut* idea. He felt like he was coming down with something.

Or maybe it was the intimacy of the situation. They had come here so many times as a family and now here he was again. Only this time with another wife. He never thought he'd be in this situation again, and the ghosts haunted him. But he somehow felt . . . connected to Rachel. Through more than just their fake marriage.

But it's not a fake, a voice in his head whispered. There was no such thing as a fake marriage among the Amish. They married for life. He had tied himself to the woman across from him, pledged to cherish and protect her in front of friends and family. In private he'd vowed to never demand any more than clean clothes and tasty meals in return.

And yet he felt—

"Are you *allrecht*?" Rachel asked.

"*Jah, jah.* I'm fine."

She pointed to his plate. "Your pizza is getting cold." He picked up the lukewarm slice and took a huge bite. It was just starting over. That was what bothered him. Nothing more, nothing less.

Pizza, Rachel decided, was the most wonderful meal ever invented. Even better, she had talked to the owner about adding a goat cheese pizza to the menu. He'd asked her to bring him some samples and he'd see what he could do. Nothing in stone, but a start, nonetheless.

She smiled into the darkening sky. She loved the long summer days when the sun set late and the sky turned a dozen different colors before finally relinquishing its hold to the stars.

She loved this new family that she had found. She swayed with the movement of the horses, her shoulder brushing against Gabriel's. Samuel sat between them, but she had put her arm around him on the way home, pulling him close so he could rest his sleepy head against her as they rode. Now she wasn't sure that was such a good idea. Her arm touching Gabriel's in the waning light seemed too familiar by far.

He's your husband, a little voice inside her head reminded. Tonight was the first of many more to come where they would find themselves in situations that seemed . . . intimate.

"Sorry," she mumbled, moving a little so that she wouldn't accidentally brush against him again.

He gave a nod of his head, but otherwise said nothing. Between the brim of his hat and the setting sun, she wasn't able to read his expression. Just as well. She didn't need to see his face to know that she confused him. She had seen that look often enough.

Instead she focused her attention on the road and smoothed down Samuel's hair. But she could feel Gabriel's eyes watching her as they continued along.

After what seemed like hours, he turned his gaze back to the road and steered them down the drive that led to his two-story house.

"*Dat?*" Samuel's sleepy voice filled the space between them. "Did you know that Wachel is afraid of gwasshoppus?"

Gabriel chuckled and Rachel had to remind herself that she shouldn't like the sound so much. "Is that a fact?"

She sniffed. "We are all afraid of one thing or another."

"She was milking Sadie today and a gwasshoppu jumped on her. She screamed and screamed. And I laughed and laughed."

"Now, Samuel, it is not nice to laugh at another's pain."

"Sowy, *Dat.*"

"It's not me you should apologize to."

Samuel tilted his head back to gaze up at her. "Sowy, Wachel."

"'Tis nothing, *liebschdi.*" She smoothed down his hair.

Over the top of his head, Gabriel was still smiling. "Grasshoppers?" he asked.

"It's just that they . . . jump," she explained with a shudder.

"I see." He turned toward her again, catching her gaze and seemingly searching her soul.

Rachel breathed a sigh of relief when they pulled to a stop. Until that moment she hadn't realized that she had been holding her breath. She sucked in a gulp of air and hopped to the ground as Gabriel hooked his big hands under Samuel's arms and plucked him from the wagon.

"Oh, my." The world tipped on its axis, and the night sky swam before her eyes. Rachel grabbed the side of the buggy, missing it and shoving her arm through the open window instead. Thankfully that allowed her to catch herself before she went sprawling across the yard or crumpling into a heap on the ground.

"Are you all right?" Big hands wrapped around her arms just above her elbows and pulled her up. Strong, warm hands that felt as if they could support the whole world with room to spare.

"I'm . . . I'm fine."

"Matthew, you and Joseph take the horses in. Simon, take your brothers inside and get them ready for bed."

"I'm all right. Really." She tried to pull away, but her oxygen-deprived limbs wouldn't cooperate.

"*Jah*. That I can see," he said, then barked over his shoulder. "Now."

The boys did as he commanded, and she was left alone with her husband. The thought shouldn't have been uncomfortable, but it was. She had never found herself in that sort of situation and didn't know how to act. She'd get used to it.

He reached up one of those big capable hands and brushed the backs of his fingers over her cheek and the thin scar there.

Maybe in a year or two.

The thought was dizzying, being married to this man for years and years. Yet that was what she had agreed to. *Lord, please help me. I know not what I have done.*

Rachel opened her eyes to find him studying her. She took another deep breath, but this time she felt steady on her feet, even if her stomach felt a bit queasy. "You must think I'm a silly goose."

"*Nay.*" His eyes still fixed on her.

"I guess I'm just tired."

He nodded. "It's a big adjustment taking care of a family when you had none before."

It was her turn to nod. She needed to get out of there, get into the house, away from him and his magnetic stare, but his body blocked her flight path.

The *buwe* were gone into the barn and into the house, leaving her all alone with this man she had pledged her life to. He seemed so close, close enough she could feel his heat, smell the scent that was him, plus the faint aroma of horse and hay mixed with detergent.

The wind whispered softly between them, stirring the escaped strands of her hair. Before she could reach up and brush them back, his fingers were there, tucking them behind her ear and sending tingles cascading where his skin touched hers.

She swallowed hard.

He took a step closer.

Somehow she knew that he was going to kiss her.

Her heart beat hard in her chest at the thought. She didn't know how she knew. It wasn't like she had ever been kissed before. Back in Florida, she had heard the older girls talking when they thought no one was listening, but that's all the information about such things that Rachel had. For once her family had died in the accident, she had come here to Clover Ridge, and her life was forever changed.

As if sensing her thoughts, he traced the scar under her right eye. She could feel the question rumbling in his throat unasked.

She parted her lips to answer, nothing more.

From somewhere in the night a bird called.

Then Matthew. "Everything *allrecht*?"

Rachel jumped back guiltily like a school girl caught by the bishop. "Fine, fine," she said, smoothing her sticky palms down the front of her apron.

Matthew looked from one of them to the other, then gave a quick nod. "*Gut nacht* then." He sauntered toward the house, leaving them alone once more.

She managed to look up and meet his eyes, but none of the earlier intensity remained. If it had been there at all. "I should go check on Samuel," she said. Had she imagined his desire to kiss her? Made it all up in some girlish fantasy?

Perhaps. The thought saddened her.

Gabriel gave a nod nearly identical to his son's gesture and swung an arm toward the house. "After you," he said with a small bow.

Rachel managed to get her trembling legs to steady enough to carry her to the house.

She needed to be more careful. Make sure that she didn't find herself alone with Gabriel like that anymore, husband or no. One thing was certain where Gabriel Fisher was concerned: she couldn't be trusted.

～◎ ◎～

What had he been thinking? Certainly not about the agreement that he'd made with Rachel Yoder concerning their marriage.

Rachel Fisher, he silently corrected.

He'd been caught up in the beauty of the night, the nostalgia of going out for pizza and sitting around the table like they all had before. The pure enjoyment on her face as she had tasted the delicious Italian pie for the first time.

He needed to remember the weevils floating on top of the pot of peas, the dirt that seemed to appear from nowhere and built up in the corners of the house despite her declarations of cleaning, and the fact that every meal he had eaten since he'd laid eyes on her had been burned in one manner or another.

Just as he needed to forget the sparkle in her brown eyes.

With an aggravated growl, Gabriel flopped to his other side and punched at his pillow, as if it were to blame for his nearly kissing his wife.

There was no one to blame but himself. He'd just have to be more careful from now on. True, living with a woman was an intimate thing, even if she slept upstairs in the room that had been Mary Elizabeth's. It was an intimacy that he'd have to deal with. Certainly not by kissing his wife, no matter how sweet she looked in the moonlight. The sun would eventually rise. He'd best keep that in mind.

"Simon? You asleep?"

Simon opened his eyes and turned to face his brother, Joseph. Their beds sat side by side against one wall, a small propane lamp between them.

"Shhh," he said, covering his lips with one finger. "You'll wake David."

They both turned to look at the opposite wall where their younger brother lay, his gently breathing body no more than a lump under the covers.

"Are you sure this is the right thing to do?"

"'Course I am," he said the words even as the doubts plagued him. They had to do *something*. They couldn't just stand by and let their father do this.

"She seems kinda nice, is all."

Nice was one thing, but moving in and acting like their mother was another one entirely. *And* she wasn't even a good mother. She was always burning the food and forgetting things. Why just yesterday she packed him an apple for his lunch. He hated apples and had to trade with Billy Weaver to get a pear. "She's not our mom." Yet they'd have to help her scrub the floors come Saturday. The best day to go down to the creek and play in the cool water and they'd all be in the house . . . working.

"I know," Joseph mumbled into the dark. "But—"

"No buts." Simon raised up on his elbow and peered through the darkness toward his brother. "It's different for you. You don't remember her like I do."

"I wish I did." Joseph's voice turned misty.

"She was the best mom ever." No one remembered her like he and Matthew. Joseph had been nearly five when she passed, but Simon had been almost eight and Matthew going on ten. Only

Mary Elizabeth remembered their mother better. But she was gone now and unable to tell them stories to refresh their dimming memories of the mother who brought them into the world.

"But Rachel—"

"But nothing." Simon lay back in his bed though he really wanted to jump up and . . . well, do *something*. "She doesn't belong here." If their *dat* couldn't see that on his own, then it was up to them to show him.

He thought about Matthew. His older brother said they should give their stepmother a chance, but Simon didn't agree. First *Aenti* Katie had moved back in with *Grossmammi* and *Grossdaadi*, then Mary Elizabeth had moved out, now this. It was all too much. With a woman in the house, Mary Elizabeth would never return and if that happened, nothing would ever be the same again.

"Well," Joseph said finally. "If you're sure."

"I am," Simon replied even as his stomach dropped. "Now go to sleep."

9

It was a brand new day. A day to start over, begin again and focus on her duties. Two days had passed since the family had gone out for pizza, and one thing was certain: The more she kept things simple the more she would be able to keep things on a proper footing with Gabriel, and then she could begin the slow process of forgetting the look in his eyes when he'd almost . . .

"Wachel?"

She felt the familiar tug of Samuel's tiny fist in her skirt. "*Jah?*"

"Can I go down to the creek with the *bruders?*"

Her heart melted at the sight of his sweet upturned face, but she couldn't expect his brothers to watch out for him properly. She would be beside herself if anything happened to him while in her care. "*Nay, liebschdi.* I need you to stay here with me and help with the chores."

His bow of a mouth turned down at the corners as if he were trying to figure out which activity would be more enjoyable. "Chores?" he asked.

"*Jah.*" She gave him a serious nod. "I have too many leftover cookies. I need someone to help me eat them all gone."

He smiled, the gesture lighting up his entire face as well as her heart. "I can do that." He gave a small hop of joy, and Rachel laughed at his antics. If only she could win the other Fisher boys over with such ease. Or even half. Especially the oldest in the *haus*.

Her cheeks filled with heat at the thought. She had agreed to a marriage of strangeness, but she was human. She knew the rules of the *Ordnung*. Amish married for life. This was her one shot at happiness. Was it wrong of her to want some for herself?

Maybe.

She added the thought to her mental prayer list. She shouldn't be selfish or greedy. She had agreed to marry Gabriel so she could stay in Clover Ridge and keep her goats. In turn she had promised to take care of his children and household. Falling in love and bringing other children into the world was no part of their agreement.

"Wachel?" Samuel brought her out of her thoughts.

"*Jah?*"

"Can I eat those cookies now?"

Nothing like a six-year-old to keep a body on task. She got down the cookies and poured him a glass of milk.

"I'm going to clean some upstairs," she said. "You stay here until I come back down, *jah?*"

He nodded, his mouth already full of yesterday's baking.

She smiled and ruffled his hair before starting up the stairs. Her afternoon chore time was dwindling away as she stood and mooned over love and trivial matters. It was time to get to work.

She'd promised the *buwe* that she would clean out from under their beds today. She had suspected that they weren't too happy with her addition to their household, and she had done everything in her power to make them like her. Then she realized that they most likely felt threatened by her presence in what they saw as their mother's house. Rather than tell them outright that she had no intentions of taking their mother's place, she had opted to show them.

What a breakthrough that they had asked her to help with this chore.

Rachel grabbed the broom from the hall closet and started for the room that Simon and Joseph shared with David. It was the largest of the bedrooms with three twin beds and a couple of propane lamps. Each boy had a set of pegs to hang their clothes on and a different color quilt on their beds. Rachel wondered if their mother had made the covering or if they had been gifts from Ruth.

She ran her hand over one of the quilts, a beautiful crazy covering with the brightest fabrics imaginable. The colors had faded a little over time from being washed and hung in the sun to dry, but the vibrancy was still there. Each stitch was tiny and perfect, blending in with the material until the stitches nearly disappeared.

A flash of jealousy shot through her. She had never been the best seamstress. She had practiced and practiced for as long as she could, but as she stitched, she found her mind wandering to other tasks that needed to be completed. Next thing she knew, her stitches were crooked, not at all the same size, and in general, just not up to standard.

She shook her head and made a mental note to pray for inner peace and more pure thoughts. It was terrible to be envious over something as simple as a quilt. Yet she knew deep down that it was more than that. She wanted the boys to accept her into the house, not as their mother, but as perhaps a friend, another adult who cared about them and wanted the best for their everyday lives.

She'd start that process by cleaning their rooms from top to bottom, though she had to admit the more she cleaned, the more it seemed there was to clean. She supposed that was the nature of a house with so many people living in it. But it felt as if she swept a floor one day and it was dirtier than before on the next.

She blew a wayward curl out of her eyes, then tucked the strand under the edge of her prayer *kapp*. She got down on her knees and ran the broom under the bed that David slept in, surprised for sure when she pulled a small cardboard shoe box from underneath, dust bunnies dancing around it.

A treasure box? Or long forgotten trash? She scooted it closer, feeling weight shift inside. Her curiosity piqued, and she lifted the lid. She couldn't stifle her scream when the big bullfrog leapt out of the box and landed squarely on her chest.

She scrambled to her feet, squealing all the while. "Get it off, get it off, get it off!" She brushed her hands down the front of her dress time and time again, though the frog was long gone hopping through the house unchecked.

Gut himmel! That thing was loose in the *haus* free to jump all over everything.

She raced down the stairs, scooping Samuel into her arms and depositing him into the yard before he even had the chance to ask what was wrong.

"*Was iss letz*, Wachel?" he finally said.

She gulped at the air, trying to fill her lungs and tamp back a scream all in the same motion. "I don't. Like. Frogs," she wheezed.

Samuel turned his redhead this way and that, finally giving an understanding nod. "Frogs jump."

Rachel shuddered. "*Jah*," she said. "They do."

"I'll take cawe of it."

Then her brave little man marched into the house, returning a few moments later with the blasted shoe box knocking around in his small hands. "Hewe, Wachel. I got it fow you."

She shook her head, unwilling to even hold the vile creature in a box. "How did that get in the house?"

The words were more of a question to herself, but Samuel answered. "Simon caught it at the creek yesterday."

Oh, he did, did he?

She thought she heard a laugh from somewhere behind them, but when she turned toward the path that led to the creek, she saw nothing. But they were there, she was sure of it. After all, what good was a practical joke if the mastermind was nowhere around when it happened?

She was certain of one thing: She had been set up from start to finish. Simon had wanted her to find the frog. He knew that she was afraid of things that jumped. What better way to scare the prayer *kapp* right off her head than to plant a frog in the house in the one place she was sure to find it? The very place that she had been asked to clean.

"Samuel, I want you to take the . . . ahem, *frog* to the edge of the woods. I'm sure it can find its way back to the water from there."

He gave a small nod. "*Jah*, Wachel."

"Then I want you to return to the house and wash your hands."

He nodded once again.

"And Samuel, you are not to say anything to your *vatter* concerning this matter. Do you understand?"

"Take the frog to the woods, wash my hands, and don't tell *Dat*."

She smiled, though her lips trembled with the movement. "That's right. Now run along, I've got brussels sprouts to cook."

She supposed that it was childish of her, but she was doing it anyway. Brussels sprouts were about the most vile vegetable known to man. Personally she hated them, but had learned to eat them for nutrition's sake. Well, that and the fact that her *aenti*—Rachel shuddered—actually liked the things.

A dinner with brussels sprouts was as good a payback as any for little boys who needed to be taught a lesson.

She should probably tell Gabriel about what happened, but she felt that if she went to their father, then the *buwe* had won. She wasn't about to be run off. She was tougher than that. So she'd take a deep breath and put on her big girl panties, as she had heard some *Englisch* girls say, and fight back in her own way. Sooner or later the boys would give up and all would go back to normal.

Such as it was.

She set the steaming bowl of brussels sprouts on the table and bit back her smile as the boys all groaned.

Gabriel's head snapped up and Rachel carefully avoided his gaze as she took her seat. There was no way she could look into those green eyes and not confess everything right down to her desire for him to kiss her the other night.

She made a big deal out of smoothing her napkin over her lap as he continued to look at each one of them in turn.

"Let's pray," Gabriel said. He braced his elbows on the table and bowed his head.

Everyone bowed their heads.

Rachel dipped her chin, closing her eyes and thanking the Lord for wonderful food and a safe day at the farm. She also asked for forgiveness for her retaliation and for patience when it came to the children. But she reined herself in before she asked God for help with her relationship with Gabriel.

First of all, there was no relationship. Just an agreement.

Second, there seemed to be so many *real* things to pray about—Ruth's health, Katie's wedding, Annie and Gideon's baby—that it seemed self-absorbed to pray for love.

She added her selfish behavior to the list and uttered *aemen* just after Gabriel signaled that prayer time was complete.

"So," Gabriel said as he took a piece of oven fried chicken from the platter and passed it to his left. "Anything interesting happen today?"

Matthew lifted a piece of chicken with his fork to examine the piece just underneath. "*Onkel* wants everyone to get together before the baby comes."

Rachel bit back a gasp. Such matters were surely not appropriate for *natchess* table talk, but it wasn't hers to correct Gabriel's oldest *sohn*. She turned her gaze to her husband, but he was more concerned with picking the too-dark spots of breading off his meat to correct Matthew.

Still, he shook his head. "It's too close to Annie's time for her to be going about feeding everybody."

Or maybe they just viewed her as furniture.

"*Jah*," Matthew agreed. "She's as big as a *haus*."

Definitely furniture.

"I'll be sure to tell her you said as much the next time I see her." Matthew's fork clattered onto his plate. "*Dat*! Please don't."

Gabriel chuckled, and Rachel hated that she liked the sound. He should use it more.

"Then mind what you say about your kin."

"*Jah, Dat*."

For a moment or two the only sound was the clink of forks and spoons against plates.

"I could cook." Even as she said the words, she wished to call them back. She certainly had a thing or two to learn about cooking for a large group. She could barely feed the seven of them without burning most of the offering.

She had to give her husband credit, though, because he didn't even choke on his bite of extra-brown cornbread. "I don't think that will be necessary. I'm certain *Mam* will cook for everyone."

He was sure, but Rachel had her doubts. She hadn't been able to talk to Ruth alone since her confession concerning her health. More than anything, Rachel wanted to talk to her and try once again to convince her to go on to the doctor and have the new lump checked out. Just because it had been cancer once before didn't mean that it was cancer again. It was in the Lord's hands, for sure and for certain.

Rachel took a big bite of the candied sweet potatoes she made as her consolation for having to eat brussels sprouts. Yams were her absolute favorite, the one thing she managed to cook to perfection every time.

Well, it wasn't like they were difficult to make or anything. Or that they required a skilled touch, but she enjoyed them just the same.

"*Buwe*, eat your brussels sprouts."

"Awh, do we have to?" David asked, his tone nearing a whine.

Rachel felt almost sorry for them. Almost. Then all she had to do was think of the—shudder—frog they left for her and all sympathy flew out the window.

Gabriel shot them a stern look, the one that had her running for cover on a regular basis. "*Jah.*"

Joseph gulped, then picked up one and popped it into his mouth. Rachel didn't see him chew even once before he swallowed again and quickly reached for his milk.

"I said eat, not swallow whole." Gabriel pointed his fork at each *bu* in turn. "Rachel went to a lot of trouble to cook this fine meal. You will honor her by cleaning your plates. Every one of you."

She bit back her smile as Simon threw a smoldering look in her direction. He knew she had found the frog. If he was a smart kid—and he was—he knew that tonight's meal had been a culinary retaliation. Now maybe things could go on as normal. Well, at least as normally as possible given their unique situation.

Simon shot Joseph a look, and the two boys gave a silent nod.

Then again, maybe not.

Ruth heard the rattle of horse and buggy and peeked out the front window. Her new daughter-in-law and current youngest grandchild hopped out of the buggy and started toward the house. Rachel had a basket covered in cloth hooked over one arm, her other hand intertwined with Samuel's.

The sight brought a smile to Ruth's face. She had been so worried when Gabriel and Rachel married, concerned for her special grandson who needed more care than most. She hadn't been convinced that Rachel Yoder would be up for the task of caring for a Down syndrome child. Not that Rachel had done anything to cause Ruth's concern, but she knew that playing with someone else's child after church and caring for them on a day-to-day basis were two different matters all together.

She laid down her scissors and smoothed back her hair. Not a strand was out of place, but the motion had become such a habit, ever since her cancer treatments had caused her to lose it all. Once the shorter strands had gotten long enough to pull back and hide beneath her prayer *kapp*, they required constant attention to hold them in place. With each passing month, her hair grew longer and longer, her glory to God reinstated.

And now she had found another lump.

She pushed those thoughts away and instead concentrated on the two smiling faces approaching the house.

Ruth opened the door before they could even knock. "*Guder mariye*, Rachel."

"*Guder mariye*." Rachel smiled in return as Samuel threw himself at her, burying his face in her skirts and muffling his greeting. "I brought you some cheese." As she said the words, Ruth noticed a high pink color staining her cheeks.

She took the basket. "Your cheese?"

Rachel nodded.

"*Danki*. Come in, and we'll have some together."

"I can only stay a little while," Rachel said, leading Samuel into the *haus*. "Gabriel promised to take me into town this afternoon. I have a batch of cheese ready to go to the pizza restaurant. They have offered to try it on one of their pies."

Ruth shook her head with a smile. "It sounds so strange to call them a pie, *jah*?"

Rachel nodded and dropped Samuel's hand to run her fingers over the material lying on the kitchen table. "It's so *schpass*."

"It's for Katie's wedding." The fabric was a beautiful blue with just the barest hint of green to make it interesting. When she'd seen the fabric in the general store, she knew right away that she would have to have some yardage to make Katie's *frack* for her upcoming wedding.

"She will be a most beautiful bride."

Rachel's voice held a hitch at the end. Ruth stopped folding up the pattern pieces and faced her daughter-in-law. "*Was iss letz?*"

But Rachel only shook her head.

"Samuel," Ruth said, turning toward the child. "There's some feed corn on the screened-in porch. Will you take some out and feed the geese?"

"*Jah, Grossmaami.*" He beamed up at her, then raced toward the back door.

She took Rachel's elbow and steered her toward the table. "Now tell me, *dochder,* what has you looking so sad today?"

Rachel shook her head and blinked back her tears. "Have you thought any more about going in to the doctor?"

"*Nay.*" She jumped up and busied herself cutting a loaf of bread and putting on a kettle of water for tea.

So many happy days were ahead of them. She couldn't put a damper on such things as weddings and *boppli* with the ominous threat of cancer.

"I was hoping you'd reconsider."

"Don't tell me you came all the way over here just for that. What else is on your heart today, Rachel?"

"Nothing."

Ruth poured the hot water over the tea bags and placed one of them in front of Rachel.

"Perhaps I can help."

Eyes as big and deep as a sauce pan filled with melted chocolate turned themselves on her, and Ruth found herself wanting very much to help the child.

"I'm not used to having others to talk to."

"Well, now that's what families are for." She laid a reassuring hand on Rachel's.

The young woman opened her mouth as if to speak, then shook her head instead. "I don't think I should talk to you about it. I mean, you are his mother."

"This has to do with my Gabriel?" Her son could be a hard man, but Ruth knew that his calloused exterior was a mere front for the softness of his heart.

"He . . ." Rachel turned her face toward the kitchen window, her fingers twisting a napkin to shreds. "He almost kissed me."

"He almost . . . Do you mean that . . .?" She couldn't finish the statement. It was just too personal.

Rachel cast her glance down to the strips of paper in front of her on the table. "We agreed to have a marriage in name only."

She had said something about that when they were planning the festivities, but Ruth had chosen to ignore her protests. "I'm not sure such a feat is possible." It was a shame, she was nearly sixty years old, and she couldn't talk about the relations between a man and a woman. It wasn't something that the Amish discussed very often, but it seemed that Rachel needed it.

"We . . . we don't sleep in the same bed."

"And you are fine with this arrangement?"

Rachel shrugged.

"You are going to do this for the rest of your life?"

She shrugged again.

"This is what you want?"

"I don't know," Rachel said to her hands. "But it seems that it is for sure what Gabriel wants."

Ruth smiled. "I do not know every thought in my son's head, but I know that he would welcome more children into his family. There is only one way to get those."

Dark pink colored her cheeks. "*Jah*," she mumbled.

"The Bible teaches women to be a servant to her husband. To love him and obey him. But that's not to say that we cannot point their . . . wishes to a different direction."

Rachel's head jerked up, her attention focused on Ruth. "You mean . . . ?"

"I mean that when an opportunity presents itself, that you should take it and see where it might lead." She paused. "Now let's try this cheese."

The wind lightly ruffled her hair as they clopped along to town. Rachel lifted a hand and brushed the wayward curls back into place. Once again they popped free. She sighed.

Ruth had told her to take her opportunities, and she supposed that finally being alone with Gabriel in his buggy was as much of an opportunity as she was going to get.

"Are you *allrecht*?"

She nodded.

"There's a fan under your seat if you are getting too hot."

"I'm fine." But she could feel the heat in her cheeks, and it had nothing to do with the unseasonably warm weather and everything to do with the man beside her.

"Are you worried about what the Murrays will say about your cheese?"

She shook her head and glanced down at the cooler between her feet. She made the best cheese in three counties. The Lord had definitely blessed her with those abilities, but her skills at making a man notice her were sadly lacking.

She bit back a sigh. It had always been that way. Even before she moved to Clover Ridge and dating and singings were only a part of the future, all the other girls had their hearts set on a boy who shared their feelings, but Rachel had been the odd duck out, a little too chubby and more like a kid sister to everyone and girlfriend to none. When she moved to Oklahoma she had slimmed down, but by then it was too late. All the couples had paired off, leaving her as a third wheel at any gathering. So she'd simply drawn into herself and concentrated on getting through her grief over her family and adjusting to the new *Ordnung*. One day a man came out to work on their barn, a Mennonite with thick dark hair and crystal blue eyes.

His appearance alone sparked something deep inside her, but by then it was too late. She was over twenty and an old maid.

She reached up a hand and lightly traced the scar on her cheek.

"How'd you get that?" Gabriel's voice rumbled from beside her.

"What?" She turned toward him, jerking back a little as the sway of the horses brought them closer than before.

"That scar."

She fingered it once again. "In a buggy wreck."

"Car or other buggy?"

"Car."

He grunted, but didn't ask for more details. Yet Rachel felt obligated to share them with him. "My *elders* and *bruders* were killed in the crash. By the will of God, I was spared."

"I'm sorry." His normally gruff voice was gentle and caring. This—*this*—was the Gabriel she wanted to know better, his voice soft spoken, his frown missing from those handsome features. What made a man frown so?

She shrugged. "It was a long time ago."

She had expected for their journey into town to continue, but Gabriel pulled the buggy to the side of the road. Thankfully there was a turnoff that allowed them to get completely out of the path of traffic. He turned in his seat to face her. "Do you want to talk about it?"

"There's not much to talk about."

Those intense green eyes studied her, searched her face, and seemed to dig deeper into her heart than anyone else ever had. "What are you hiding from, Rachel?"

You, she wanted to shout, but to what benefit? How crazy would it sound to tell him that when he turned all kind and concerned, she felt herself falling in love with him? That she wasn't sure which was the real Gabriel—the frowning man or the kind one? Or that she was afraid to ask lest her answer be the one she dreaded.

"Nothing." She had intended the word to come out strong and sure, instead it was a whispered plea.

When had he drawn so close to her? He leaned in near enough that she could see every fleck of gold in those incredible eyes of his, count the whiskers in his dark beard. She was helpless to keep herself from moving toward him, drawn in by this caring streak she had found in her husband.

He hooked his fingers under her chin, gently, bringing them closer together than ever before. Closer than they had been the night they married. Closer and closer still until his lips were almost on hers.

A car horn sounded to let them know they were passing, and Rachel jumped back in her seat. She sucked in a deep breath and smoothed down her dress, her skirt, her hair, anything she could reach. She needed something—anything—to keep from looking at him and knowing that he had almost kissed her.

Wife or no, she couldn't throw herself at him. It was too bold by far. Oh, what must he think of her? Ruth had told her to take her opportunities, but she didn't think his *mudder* meant *that*.

He cleared his throat. "Rachel?" Her name on his lips sounded strange, like a strangled cry of a faraway bird. Despite his frown, he was a good man, and he was doing his best to let her down easy.

She kept her gaze to the front and folded her hands in her lap. "If we do not *mach schnell*, then we will be late."

His gaze stayed on her, steady and searching for what seemed like an eternity but could have only been a couple of minutes. Then he, too, looked toward the road and clicked the horses into motion.

The time for taking opportunities had passed.

Her cheeks were still burning when they pulled up in front of the pizza restaurant thirty minutes later. After their almost kiss, her excitement over possibly gaining the pizza parlor as a client had dampened. She wanted to be excited—she did—but all she could think about was the ride home with Gabriel and what to say to him next.

She slid from the buggy without his help and made her way to the door of the restaurant. It was nearing four o'clock, and the early dining customers were starting to arrive. She had wanted to be there a little earlier, but with them stopping on the side of the road and all . . .

The heat stole into her cheeks once again. Involuntarily she fanned herself as she set the cooler on the counter.

"Rachel! Hi," Mrs. Murray greeted, beaming a super sweet smile filled with perfect teeth and genuine happiness.

She was young, Mrs. Murray, and as they talked, Rachel discovered that she was married to the son of the Mr. Murray who started the business. The couple was hoping to take over soon so the father could retire. Oh, to be so certain of one's future. What Rachel wouldn't give for *that*.

"That's why we want to add a few new items to the menu," Mrs. Murray was saying.

"I see." Rachel nodded, the strings of her *kapp* dancing around her shoulders. She shuddered a little at their tickle but knew deep down that it was the eyes behind her, those green, green eyes that had made her so sensitive. "My cheese has been certified organic. There are a few other growers who have organic produce. For sure and for certain 'twould not be hard to find product to make an all-natural, organic pizza for your customers."

Angela Murray clapped her hands together. "That's a fantastic idea. Let me run it by Ed, and I'll let you know. How do I reach you?"

"There's a phone shanty out in front of my mother-in-law's house. You can leave a message there, and I'll get it."

"All right, hon. Give me the number, and I'll call you as soon as I convince the boys the idea for an organic pizza served with fresh goat's cheese was all theirs."

Rachel laughed though she didn't quite understand what Angela Murray was talking about. But it seemed she should laugh, so she did. Then she printed the number to their phone line on the back of a business card that belonged to the pizzeria. She slipped one into her pocket, then grabbed her empty cooler and turned to go.

"Wait a second, hon." Angela popped her gum as she opened the register and pulled out two twenties. "This is for the cheese you brought tonight."

But Rachel started shaking her head.

Angela froze. "Is this not enough?"

"It's too much."

But Angela pressed the bills into her hand. "A quarter pound in the store is going on ten dollars. Don't sell yourself short, hon."

Rachel's cheeks filled with heat once more as she pushed the money into the pocket on the front of her apron. "*Danki*," she said, flashing a smile at Angela.

"You're welcome. I'll be calling you soon."

Rachel nodded her head then raced to the door, anxious to tell Gabriel about the transaction.

◦◦◦

Gabriel nodded as Rachel chatted on about selling cheese and making profits. Good thing the horses knew the way home by heart, for he was having trouble concentrating on anything except Rachel's pink bow of a mouth and how he had almost kissed her on the way to town.

That was a direct violation of everything they had agreed to, and yet he could think of little else. Not her success with selling the cheese and the potential for her to make money selling to the pizzeria, nor the way she brushed her hair back from her face not bothering to tuck it back under her prayer covering and instead folding it behind her ear.

He smiled as one wayward curl popped free.

Wait, he was not supposed to like that. This was a marriage of convenience for the two of them. He'd do well to remember that.

"What do you think?"

Gabriel took his gaze from the road and fixed it on his wife. "*Jah?*"

"What do you think about buying a couple of more goats?"

He blinked, then turned back to the road. "I suppose."

"I still have some of the money from the sale of the furniture."

There had been very little that she had been able to keep from the house she had shared with her aunt: the china clock her father had given her mother when they had announced their engagement to be married, the dishes that had belonged to her grandmother, and the wooden hutch some distant family member had built long ago. The rest hadn't been needed and had been sold at an estate sale.

"Why not just let nature, ahem . . . take its course?" Even as he said the words he wished he could call them back. It seemed too intimate by far.

"Well . . ." He could almost hear her blush. She pleated her fingers in her skirt, then smoothed it back. "*That* takes a little more time than what I need. If I'm going to take on the pizza restaurant as a customer then I'll need to increase my production by half."

"*Jah.*"

"So I'll need more goats."

He nodded again, finally bringing his wayward thoughts back in. "We could go to the auction in Tulsa. I'm sure they have goats."

"We could?"

His breath hitched in his throat at the sheer excitement sparkling in her eyes. "*Jah.*" He coughed. "If'n that's what you want."

"Oh, it is!" She flung her arms around him, pulling the reins to the right as she pulled him in and soundly kissed his cheek. "*Danki, danki,*" she said before quickly releasing him. She pushed her prayer *kapp* back into place and tucked her hair back under its band. "I mean, that would be *gut.*" She cleared her throat, winding her fingers through her skirt again. Her gaze trained on the road ahead, a dark pink coloring her cheeks.

Thankfully they were nearing the house. He wasn't sure how much longer he could sit calmly beside Rachel and keep the promises that he had made to her. He wanted to pull the buggy over and pull her close, tell her that he would do anything for her. All she had to do was ask, and he would get it for her.

He briefly closed his eyes and sent up a small prayer for strength. This was just an adjustment, that was all. Their relationship was intimate and yet not, and he had no experience dealing with such feelings. There were bound to be a few bumps and missteps along the way.

10

Simon crouched next to Joseph, making himself as small as possible in order to look out the upstairs window and remain unseen. Down in the yard below, his father and Rachel had just pulled into the drive.

"What are they doing?" Joseph whispered.

"I don't know." He scooched to the side to keep his brother's pointy elbow out of his ribs. "Quit crowding."

"Where do you suppose they've been all afternoon?"

Simon shrugged. "Matthew said they were going into town to take some cheese samples to someone."

Joseph smacked his lips. "She sure does make good cheese."

"Cut it out." Simon sent his elbow into his brother's side. He didn't want to talk about Rachel's cheese. He didn't care how good it tasted. They needed to remember all of the things she did wrong. Like not being their mother and burning every pan of cookies she had baked since coming to their farm. Why couldn't she have just stayed wherever it was she had been before?

"You like her cheese too."

"So what if I do?" Simon gritted. "That still don't mean that I want her to be our *mudder*."

"I'm just sayin' is all. We like her cheese and her cookies."

"She burns the cookies." He put a hard, big *bruder* edge in his voice. Couldn't Joseph see that cheese and cookies were not important? That the sacred memories of their mother were?

"Only because we turn up the oven when she's not looking."

"She burns them plenty of times without our help." He looked back down at his father and Rachel. She did have pretty brown eyes . . . He shook the thought away.

"Samuel seems to like her."

"Samuel's dumb." He said the words and hated them. Samuel was precious to them all, but that still wasn't a reason to keep around a woman who should have never been on their farm.

"I'm going to tell *Dat* you said that." Joseph started to get to his feet, but Simon held him back.

"Don't," he said, scrambling around for an excuse as to why. "You know I didn't mean it."

"I guess." Joseph slowly relaxed back next to him as Simon formulated their next prank.

His father grabbed Rachel's elbow the same why his uncle Gideon did for their *aenti* Annie. One thing was for certain: they were going to have to increase their plans to break up this marriage. After seeing the way his father looked at Rachel, it wouldn't be long before the two of them were deep in love.

The rest of the week passed with no more such encounters like the one in the buggy. Maybe because Rachel avoided being alone with Gabriel as if he had some kind of disease. It felt strange to avoid him when he was quickly becoming such an important and special person to her.

She set the pan of biscuits on the table and propped her hands on her hips. She had been extra careful this morning not to burn them and she had finally succeeded. Almost. The bottoms had browned to the color of dirt. But the tops were okay. And the bacon. Well, the bacon got a little done as well, but if she crumbled it up into their gravy, she was certain no one would know the difference.

Strange though. She thought she had turned the stove off before she went out to check on her goats for the morning. Yet somehow the oven and the burner on which the bacon sat were burning when she returned to the house. She was going to have to be more careful. It would never do to burn down the house, and Gabriel surely wouldn't appreciate it if she did.

"Is it time to eat?"

She had been so busy thinking about the meal she hadn't heard Matthew come into the house. He hung his straw hat by the door and studied her. She wished she could figure him out. He was so quiet and grownup, not quite a child but not yet an adult, he always seemed to be working. Even more than most Amish kids. He did his chores, doing the more labor intensive work in the barn with his father. Then he rode over to his *onkel's* house and helped there, most likely doing a fair amount of work to help Gideon so he could be closer to the house as Annie's time neared. Annie was just so small, her belly protruding to unbelievable proportions as the baby grew within her delicate frame.

"I'm about to start the gravy," she said. "Call your brothers so they can get here before it all turns cold. We've got a-ways to go to get to the church service this morning."

This week church was being held clear across the district from them at Betty and Dan Lapp's house. The Fishers had a long piece to travel before they would get there and would need to leave a bit earlier than usual.

"*Jah.*" Matthew gave a swift nod then re-donned his hat to go in search of his brothers.

She sighed as she watched him go. The other *buwe* were not so hard to figure out. She had discovered long ago that they did not approve of their father marrying her. Not that their opinions could carry any weight. The deed was done, and she hoped that eventually they could come to accept her.

That's why she hadn't told Gabriel about their antics. How she had found that frog under the bed or that she suspected they were bringing in extra dirt to coat the floors so it looked like she never did her household duties. Why, this morning she had gone into her room to get dressed only to find that every *frack* she owned had some sort of stain on the front. She had taken the lightest looking one and rinsed the area out in the sink while she prayed it would dry before the service started. Thankfully the dress was a deep green and one of her favorites so even if the stain refused to budge before the next washday it wouldn't be so noticed at church.

Then there were today's biscuits and bacon, she thought as she crumbled the overcooked pork into the gravy. She was fairly certain the boys had something to do with that. Not Matthew and Samuel, though.

She cast a loving look at the youngest Fisher who sat at the table tracing his letters while he waited for her to finish cooking. She felt in her heart of hearts that Matthew and Samuel were among the innocent in the pranks that she faced daily. But the other *buwe* . . .

As if on cue they all marched into the house, hung their hats on their pegs, and went to stand behind their chairs as their father followed them in.

Gabriel looked at her and caught her eye. Her heart skipped a stuttering beat. He wore his everyday frown, but she could see past it now, at least a little ways. For sure he frowned a lot, but Rachel had come to think of it as his thoughtful look. For he often had that same expression when mulling over a problem in need of a solution.

He gave her a quick nod and pulled out his chair to seat himself. The other family members followed suit and they all bowed their heads to pray.

Lord, please give me patience. I have come into this household for the good of everyone involved, but the boys have trouble seeing my role as such. Please, Lord, if it be Your will, allow them to see me for what I want to be to them, a friend as well as a mother, another person in their life to care about them, help them and be there for them in their time of need.

"*Aemen,*" Gabriel said.

Aemen, she silently repeated.

She gave a tremulous smile as her husband reached for the pan of biscuits. He didn't say a word at the too-brown bottoms, just covered them with gravy and a spoonful of molasses.

It was only then that Rachel realized her prayers had only been about the family, and she hadn't thanked God once for the food they were about to eat.

This Sunday marked the third church Sunday since Gabriel had been chosen as the new deacon.

As everyone milled around the yard and visited before the service, Rachel sat with Annie, Katie, and Ruth as they waited for the call to go into the Lapps's house. Her newfound kin talked about babies and weddings, but Rachel only had eyes for her husband.

He stood with Bishop Rueben Beachy and Daniel Glick, one of the ministers. John Zook was nowhere to be seen, and Rachel hoped that everything was okay. It was practically unheard of for a minister—or any of the elders of the district—to not be at a service. That, added to the fact that the Zooks were expecting their thirteenth child, had Rachel wondering if John Zook was at his house wringing his hands and pacing while the midwife attended his *fraa*. But she hadn't heard anybody say.

Well, she hadn't really been listening. She'd been too caught up thinking about Gabriel and the goats and their trip to the auction in Oklahoma City. It would be a late trip, having to travel all the way to the state capital, but the next auction to be held in Tulsa was too far in the future to do them much good. Still, Rachel was excited about the prospect. It would be *gut* to get away for a little while. The boys and their antics were starting to chafe on her patience.

"Rachel?"

She jerked back to the present as Annie Hamilton Fisher laid a hand on her arm. Confusion mixed with care and concern tinted her violet eyes. "The elders have gone in. Are you coming?"

The men in the congregation had already filed in as well. Rachel stood and brushed the grass from the skirt of her dress. "*Jah*, of course." She shot Annie a smile to show her everything was all right and followed the other Fisher women into the house.

After everyone was settled in, with the women on one side of the room and the men on the other, the singing began. For Rachel, this was her least favorite part of the ceremony. The thought immediately made her repentant. It wasn't that she disliked the singing, but the familiar words and smooth drone of the tune allowed her mind to roam.

What would they have for the afternoon meal? How she had forgotten to darn that pair of socks for Gabriel. She had also forgotten to stitch up the hole Joseph had put in the rear of his school pants.

She pulled her thoughts back in. Proof enough she needed to pay more attention to the verses of the solemn hymn. She needed the words of grace and worship. Why, she was fortunate enough to live in a country where she could worship freely, unlike her ancestors who fled religious persecution so many centuries ago.

The first hymn ended. As one, the congregation started to sing *Lob Lied*, the Praise Song, which was always the second hymn sung in the Amish service.

"Oh, Father God, we praise Thee . . ."

Katie's fingers crept into hers and squeezed Rachel's hand tight. Without looking at her, Rachel returned the gesture, thankful to have her sister-in-law at her side. Ruth and Annie were in the back, side by side on padded chairs provided for the elderly and infirm.

Rachel made a new effort to pay better attention, but as they sang the familiar words, thanking God and praying for the ministers to be able to preach the word of God's teachings, her mind continued to drift away.

By the time the song ended, the first sermon began, and word had already spread that the Zooks were indeed at home awaiting their newest addition. Rachel could hardly wait until the service came when she would be able to see the baby. Maybe even hold it close.

Perhaps she should pay the Zooks a visit this week. For sure, she should get with Katie and Ruth. The three of them could make sure Jean Zook had everything she needed, that her floors were swept, and the laundry caught up.

Rachel took hold of her thoughts and dragged them back to the service. Daniel Glick had been chosen to preach. He was a *gut* man, but he was not the most gifted at speaking. His voice tended to hum like the noise of the airplanes that flew over from time to time, and Rachel found herself struggling more and more to pay attention. Instead her focus fell to her husband seated in front of the congregation.

She had to admit that she was secretly proud of Gabriel. Not proud in a sinful way, but in a more gentle way that spoke of the admiration she had for him. He had changed her life. Even with the trials that she had faced at the hands of his *sohns*, she was still very grateful. At least in Clover Ridge as Gabriel's wife she had a more secure standing in her community. The house she shared with him was for them both. They were partners, not just house-keeper and employer.

So he didn't love her. It wasn't like love was necessary for a true and successful marriage. They were making along just fine.

The first sermon ended, and they stood, turning to face their benches, and kneeling for a silent prayer. Rachel prayed for the Zooks, for Annie and Gideon, for the boys to eventually come to accept her into their home, and for Ruth. Her mother-in-law had made no mention of going into Tulsa for further testing, but Rachel prayed that the Lord would move her to do just that. How could they know what to pray for if they didn't know what they were up against?

"*Aemen.*" The stern word, spoken by one of the elders, brought them back to standing, though the women continued to face the back while the men turned to face the deacon for the scripture reading. Her husband.

Gabriel's deep, affecting voice washed across her ears and brought goose bumps to the exposed flesh of her arms. "*Wives, submit to your own husbands as to the Lord, for the husband is the head of the wife as Christ is the head of the church. He is the Savior of the body. Now as the church submits to Christ, so wives are to submit to their husbands in everything.*

Husbands, love your wives just as Christ loved the church and gave Himself for her to make her holy, cleansing her with the washing of water by the word. He did this to present the church to Himself in splendor, without spot or wrinkle or anything like that, but holy and blameless. In the same way, husbands are to love their wives as their own bodies. He who loves his wife loves himself. For no one ever hates his own flesh, but provides and cares for it, just as Christ does for the church, since we are members of His body. For this reason a man will leave his father and mother and be joined to his wife, and the two will become one flesh.

This mystery is profound, but I am talking about Christ and the church. To sum up, each one of you is to love his wife as himself, and the wife is to respect her husband."

Rachel heard the words, spoken clear and true in ringing high German, as were all Amish church readings. But these words pierced her heart like a knife.

Wives, love your husbands.

Husbands, love your wives.

A decree by God.

But she didn't worry about her disobedience, because in that instance she realized that she did love her husband. Or she was starting to. She had learned to see past the wrinkled frown to the thoughtfulness of the man. She had found his so-big hands to be capable, as well as gentle, and his heart to be as large as the sky.

He was a *gut* man. What about him was not to love? He feared God, adored his children, and would die for his family.

She wouldn't tell him. She would not lay that at his feet—that she had fallen in love with him. He would never love her in return. No sense travelling down a road that led to nowhere but heartache. He still loved his Rebecca and always would. She wouldn't make him feel worse about the situation by telling him that she held such feelings for him.

But the emotions within her were warm, radiating from her heart until they made the tips of her fingers tingle.

The bishop recited the benediction from heart, "Finally, dear brethren, rejoice, be perfect, be comforted, and be of one mind; be peaceful, and the God of love and peace shall be with you. Greet each other with the holy kiss. You are greeted by all the saints.

"So I submit myself, with you, to God and His gracious hand, that He be pleased to keep us in the saving faith, to strengthen us in it, to guide and lead us until a blessed end; and all this through Jesus Christ. Amen."

At the sound of the Savior's name, Rachel dipped her knees slightly, a sign of deference and obedience to Christ, as all those did around her. For her, it was strictly from habit, for her thoughts were still filled with her tender discovery concerning her husband. How, oh how had she fallen in love with him and whatever was she to do about it?

11

Gabriel continued to fill her thoughts as she and the other women turned the benches into tables on which to serve the afternoon meal. Her motions were automatic, sure and true, but without thought as her mind was so occupied elsewhere.

Once the men had all been served, the women filled plates for themselves and the smaller children, and they too settled down—men on one side of the yard, women on the other—to fellowship and sup.

Rachel found a spot for herself and Samuel next to Katie Rose. Gabriel's sister was looking as beautiful as ever as the date for her wedding drew near. Several times Rachel saw Katie's green eyes dart to the opposite side of the yard. She knew by the softening look of love in them that Katie was staring at Zane Carson, the fancy *Englisch* reporter who had come to do a story on the Amish but fell in love instead.

Rachel fixed her gaze on the gnarled tree root running alongside her feet and took a bite of her meal. She would not look at the men, she would not look at her husband, for if she did she would gaze all moony-eyed at him and give away her secret for all to see. The thought brought heat to her cheeks.

"Rachel, are you *allrecht*?" Ruth asked. "You're so very flushed."

"I'm fine." She choked on the lie, the bite of cracker she tried to swallow sticking in her throat. She grabbed a drink to wash them both down. How *ever* would she keep her feelings a secret from her husband if she couldn't keep them from Ruth?

Rachel looked up to see three pairs of concerned eyes studying her. Change that: If she couldn't keep her feelings a secret from Ruth, Annie, and Katie Rose.

"Really," she said, sending a wavering smile to back up her statement.

Katie Rose seemed about to say something more when Annie let out a small gasp and pressed a hand to one side of her burgeoning belly.

"Are you okay, *liebschen*?" Ruth tuned her attention to Annie, and Rachel breathed a short-lived sigh of relief.

"Here." She grabbed Rachel's hand and pressed it to her mound of stomach. "The baby's kicking."

Tears sprang to her eyes, stinging with their intensity. Underneath her trembling fingers, the child moved. A miracle. A living miracle was growing, budding, stretching, preparing to come out into the world and amaze them with all the wonder that was life.

Oh, to have that joy as her own.

"Rachel?" Once again Katie's voice was overflowing with concern. "Are you sure you are all right?"

Rachel blinked, sending the tears cascading down her already wet cheeks. She hadn't even realized she had been crying. "Of course." She swiped at the moisture with the back of one hand. She was fine.

"Don't cwy, Wachel." Samuel climbed into her lap and flung his thin arms around her neck. Until that moment he had been sitting quietly next to Katie Rose, playing with the hem of her apron.

She wrapped her arms around him in return and briefly closed her eyes. "I promise I'll stop," she whispered into his shiny red hair.

She didn't have a child of her own or any hope of one in the future, but she had one special little boy who meant the world to her.

For now, that was enough.

Gabriel had gone to the barn to fetch the horses and hitch up the buggy, so Rachel sent Samuel and Matthew to round up the other boys. Church was over and she needed a moment alone to talk to Ruth. When the opportunity presented itself, she pounced on it.

"Ruth." She hooked her arm through her mother-in-law's and led her away from the house. Most everyone was preparing to go home to complete their afternoon chores, but there were still plenty enough listening ears around to cause concern.

Ruth's worried eyes searched her face as if looking for any signs of her earlier tears. Apparently she had given everyone quite a scare with her emotional outburst this afternoon, but she was fully in control now. She had her moment of weakness and self-pity, but God had shown her what was really important. She had Samuel now. He needed her, relied on her to care for him, and he had more than enough love to share with all of them.

"I wanted to talk with you for a moment," Rachel explained. "Walk with me?"

Ruth gave a quick nod, and the two wandered away from the remaining church crowd. The sun was bright, the wind just enough to keep the late spring heat at bay. "Are you sure you're feeling okay, Rachel?"

"*Jah*." She dipped her chin. "I wanted to ask the same of you."

"Me?"

"I was hoping you had changed your mind about going into the city for tests."

She had barely finished her sentence before Ruth shook her head. "*Nay*. I cannot."

Rachel stopped, saying a small prayer for patience and understanding. "I think you should."

"*Nay*."

"Promise me you'll think about it?"

"Have I not already?"

"Then perhaps what I really want is for you to change your mind."

Ruth smiled. "It would seem so."

"It is a hard secret to keep, Ruth." And getting harder by the day, but even more than that, the Fishers had come to mean so much to her. Rachel hated the thought of losing Ruth, of Gabriel and his boys hurting, the rest of the family mourning the loss of one so dear. She shook her head. "We need to know, even if to prepare ourselves for the worst."

Ruth sighed, the sound resigned and staggered.

"Promise me."

Ruth jerked her head upward in what some would call a nod. At least, Rachel took it to be so. "Can't you see how much everyone loves you and needs you?"

"And what difference would it make either way, Rachel?"

But she wasn't about to hear any more excuses. "Shhh. Just make the appointment. If not for yourself and Abram, then for that tiny *boppli* Annie carries."

Rachel pushed a wayward curl off her forehead and punched down the dough once more. This time she would be extra careful when baking the bread, and for the first time since she had married Gabriel, she would not burn it. Or get it too brown. Or scorch it.

The goats had been fed, watered, and milked. Now all she had to do was worry about the bread. And nothing more.

She flipped the dough back into the bowl and covered it with a towel. Then she cast a quick glance at Samuel who sat at the table practicing his alphabet. He had almost mastered all twenty-six letters. He had begged her to teach him to read and she had promised. At the rate he was learning, they might even begin lessons as early as next week.

The back door burst open. Simon, Joseph, and David spilled into the room, tripping over their feet as they rushed inside. "Rachel, Rachel, Rachel, Matthew is here."

She punched down the second batch of dough and gave them a polite nod. So it was the middle of the day, and usually this time of the afternoon he was over with his *onkel* helping Gideon plant and hoe, and tend to his llamas and other livestock. She wasn't concerned. He did live here after all.

Before she could comment about the boys' hyper behavior, the front door crashed in. A red-faced, winded Matthew stood there looking so much like his father he almost took her breath away.

"Rachel. You've got to come. *Mach schnell!*" He hurried across the room and grabbed her floured-covered hands, tugging her toward the door.

She could well imagine the other boys engaging her in a prank, but this was Matthew—calm, assured, even-headed Matthew.

"Was iss letz?"

His wild green eyes swept around the room at the attentive ears and eyes of the younger boys. "It's the *boppli*." He dropped his voice so only she could hear. "It's coming. Too fast I think. Annie . . . she needs help."

Despite the summer heat, Rachel caught a chill as the blood drained from her face and hands. "*Gut himmel*! Have you summoned your *grossmammi*? The midwife?" She couldn't remember if Annie was seeing a fancy *Englisch* doctor or if the midwife had been attending to her needs. One thing was certain: Rachel had never assisted in a birth and didn't have the first notion of what to do.

He shook his head. "*Mammi* isn't home and the midwife . . ." He shrugged, and it was painfully obvious that he knew even less about such matters than she.

Rachel's heart gave a painful thump. "Where's Gideon?"

"He's there with her, but . . ." Matthew didn't have to finish the statement for Rachel to know that Gideon had been rendered near useless with worry for his *lieb*.

She pushed her hair back again, wiped her hands on her apron, and headed for the door. "*Buwe*, stay at the house until your *vatter* gets back." Of all the days for Gabriel to be out dispersing money to the couple who had wrecked their buggy the day before. It was a worthy cause and one of his duties as the deacon, but she *needed* him.

She stopped at the door so suddenly that Matthew, following closely behind, almost crashed into her. She swiveled around. "You have to stay here, Matthew."

A frown puckered his brow, and he looked more like his father than ever.

She glanced at Matthew's brothers. "I can't leave them here by themselves." The other boys she could, but not Samuel. For certain she couldn't take him with her.

Matthew shook his head. "You cannot drive clear out to Gideon's in the buggy by yourself."

It was one thing for her to travel alone to Ruth and Abram's, less than a quarter mile up the road, but driving all the way out to Gideon's without an escort would surely bring repercussions.

She glanced back at Samuel and made her decision. "I have to." She opened the door and hurried out to Matthew's courtin' buggy, still hitched to his team.

She didn't bother to wave as she drove off, though Gabriel's oldest son stood at the door, watching her. She couldn't waste precious time. Not if Annie was in trouble. Or the *boppli* in danger.

The ride across to Gideon's *haus* seemed to take so long. It was a fair piece out, but Rachel's worry made the trip seem twice as far.

She prayed as she flicked the reins, urging the horses to go as fast as she dared. How far along was Annie? Was it time for the baby? A little early, perhaps. But if she remembered correctly, not so early that the tiny life could be in danger.

At least she prayed it wasn't. She also prayed for steady hands, a strong heart, and wisdom to make the decisions that needed to be made.

Oh, where was Ruth?

She would have felt much more confident had their mother-in-law been on the way to the house as well, but it was not so. She would have to see to this alone.

She prayed that Matthew had exaggerated the situation and Annie was merely having those practice contractions she had overheard an *Englisch* woman talking about in the general store. But as she pulled into the drive at Gideon's *haus*, he flew out the door, hoisting her down from the buggy and barely setting her back on her feet before dragging her toward the house.

"I'm so glad you're here. Where's *Mamm*?"

Rachel shook her head. "I do not know." She heard a muffled cry from the bedroom.

Gideon stilled, his face turning white. "You've got to help her, Rachel."

She gave a confident nod. At least she hoped it looked confident and not scared out of her mind. *Dear Lord, please direct me to what needs to be done. It was Your will, Lord, that I am here alone. It is Your will that this child comes today. Show me, Lord, what I need to know to bring this miracle forth. Aemen.*

Gideon stopped in the hallway as Rachel crept into the bedroom. Someone had pinned sheets up over the windows, for privacy she was certain, but the rising summer heat had made the atmosphere unbearable.

Sweet Annie lay propped up on the bed, her dark hair in sweaty clumps around her face. Rachel took note of how short the strands were before remembering that Gideon's Annie was converted *Englisch* and had no doubt cut her hair before joining the church and marrying Gideon.

Her wild violet eyes softened when they saw her. "Rachel."

"It's going to be *allrecht*, Annie. I'm here."

"I told them it was going to be fine, but they wouldn't listen."

"Gideon loves you. He was worried. Matthew too."

She nodded. "It's okay, I know what to do. I mean, I read up on it."

"I can't leave you." Rachel knelt by the bed, taking Annie's clammy hand into her own. She kissed the back and pressed it to her cheek. *Dear Lord, make this right. Let Your will make it right.*

"No, please, don't leave. I just wanted you to know. I guess I had this feeling that something like this would happen, and I wanted to be prepared."

"I suppose that was God preparing you."

Annie smiled, though the motion was tired and a little wan. "I suppose. It's happening a bit faster than I anticipated." As she said the words, a contraction hit her small frame. She leaned forward, panting, her eyes clamped tight. She squeezed Rachel's hand until it went numb.

The pain seemed to go on forever. Rachel counted, though she wasn't sure why, and tried to be patient as she waited out the pain with Annie.

Finally, Annie released her hand and lay back against the pillows, breathing deeply as she tried to relax. "That was the worst one yet."

Rachel shook her fingers to get the blood circulating again. "How long till the next one?"

"A couple of minutes or so. I don't have a watch or a clock . . . I'm not sure. But he's coming today, Rachel. I'm certain of it."

Rachel's heart melted. "You think it is a boy."

Despite the tired lines on her face, Annie smiled. "I hope so. A son for Gideon to teach. He would raise him up to be a fine Amish man."

"But if it is a girl, she would be yours to teach."

Annie bit her lip. "I'm so new at this. I don't know how to teach another what it means to be Amish."

"Nonsense. You're going to be a great mother. Any little girl would be blessed to learn from you."

Annie closed her eyes and laid her head back. "I hope so."

Rachel wanted to run around and get everything ready at once, though she wasn't entirely sure what needed to be readied. *Air.* The first thing they needed was air circulating in the room, and some cool water to wipe Annie's face after the pain stopped. She rose, intending to do just that when another contraction hit.

A strangled cry escaped Annie's lips as she fought through the pain. She grabbed Rachel's hand, crushing her fingers as she battled. The pains were coming quick. The windows could wait. They needed hot water and towels and . . . string.

She had overheard a few women talking about their birth experiences. Between the two of them, she and Annie, they could do this. With the Lord's help, of course.

Annie released her fingers and lay back on the pillows propped against the headboard.

"Annie, I've got to leave you for a few minutes. The baby's coming soon. We need hot water."

She nodded though her eyes were closed. "Gideon. Have Gideon do it."

Rachel nodded. It would give the man something to do besides pace the hallway and worry.

She opened the bedroom door a crack and found him doing just that, his face a knot of concern, perspiration lining his forehead. He kept glancing past her to catch a glimpse of his wife, but Rachel kept him on task gathering the items they would need. He returned soon with a bucket of hot water, cloths, and string.

They could do this. *She* could do this. They had the Lord with them. And the Bible said through Him all things were possible. Even babies.

No more than an hour had gone past, when Annie cried out louder than ever. "I've got to push, Rachel," she said through panting breaths.

Rachel furrowed her brow. She wasn't sure if it was time, but who was she to argue? She helped Annie sit up and get into position: head down, knees bent, then got into position herself.

They could do this.

Rachel said another small prayer and when she opened her eyes, there it was. The *boppli's* head. "He's coming, Annie. Keep pushing." Tears streamed down her cheeks, excitement colored her voice. A baby.

Once the babe's head was free, *she* slipped easily from her mother's body, wriggling and warm, into Rachel's arms. Covered with birth blood and an ashy white substance, she was without a doubt the ugliest thing Rachel had ever seen.

And Rachel loved her on sight.

Her.

"It's a girl," Rachel whispered in awe, her breath catching on a sob.

"A girl?" Annie flopped back on the pillows, her voice dull. "Use the string to tie off the umbilical cord," she instructed.

Just then a knock sounded at the door. "Annie? Rachel?" Ruth peeked her head inside. "The baby?"

"Is fine," Rachel replied, tears wetting her cheeks like happy rain. "It's a girl."

"A girl?" Ruth moved to the side as another woman stepped into the room. Even through her tears, Rachel recognized her immediately as Sue Burkholder, the midwife.

"It can't be a girl," Annie moaned, her eyes closed in sheer exhaustion. "I don't know how to raise a girl."

"Shush, now," Sue admonished. "Let's get this wrapped up here."

Rachel gladly stood back as Sue stepped in, finishing the messiest part of the birth. She lurked in the corner as Ruth cleaned the baby's mouth, washed her tiny body, then wrapped her in a soft blanket.

With a smile on her face and the baby held close to her chest, Ruth stepped from the room to show her son, proclaiming, "It's a girl."

12

Rachel's heart thumped in her chest as she climbed into Bill Foster's van. The Mennonite driver had agreed to drive them into Oklahoma City for the auction. It was a two-hour trip one way, but Bill was a kind man and willing to help them. It didn't hurt none that he had family in Edmond, a brother and three nieces that he didn't get to see as often as he'd like.

She settled down in the backseat.

"Do you not want to sit in the front?" Gabriel asked. "It's better for looking at the landscape."

Rachel shook her head. She had never enjoyed riding in a car. This trip was necessary, and she was looking forward to spending the day with Gabriel, just not the ride.

Gabriel shrugged and scooted into the front seat, shutting the door and pulling the safety belt across himself.

Rachel followed suit as Bill Foster slid into the driver's seat and started the van.

"It's going to be a good day for a drive," Bill Foster said, giving a nod toward the blue Oklahoma sky.

"*Jah*." Gabriel gave a nod of his own as Rachel settled back in her seat and closed her eyes.

"It's a *gut* day for an auction," she heard Gabriel say.

"Or fishing." She could tell by the tone of his voice that Bill Foster was smiling.

"Is that how you are going to spend your day, Bill Foster?"

"My brother and I are taking his daughters fishing. It should be a good time."

"It should at that," Gabriel replied.

Rachel smiled to herself and drifted off to sleep.

⁓◉ ◉⁓

"Rachel?" Someone shook her arm. But she was dreaming a *gut* dream. The fields were so green, stretching out until they touched the flawless blue sky. Beautiful goats roamed across the verdant land munching the tasty grass and giving off the occasional bleat. *Jah*, a *gut* dream in all.

But the shaking persisted. "Rachel?"

She opened her eyes, blinking once as her husband came into focus. She sat up in a hurry, her hands immediately flying to her prayer covering, one straightening the fabric *kapp* while the other smoothed down her hair.

"We're here."

The auction. She strained to see around him as anxious as ever to bid on the new goats to fill the fields of her dreams, but all she could see was the parking lot and rows upon rows of cars.

"Oh," she said, pushing herself out of the minivan as Gabriel stepped back. That's when she saw the rows of horses tied to hitching posts. She pointed toward them, tugging on Gabriel's sleeve much like a child. "Do you see?"

"They must be here to do some kind of exhibition."

"With cowboys?" She couldn't keep her excitement at bay. Cowboys? *Real* cowboys?

"Maybe."

He gave a nod to the man at the ticket counter who handed them a pamphlet outlining the agenda for the day. As they walked through the gates, Gabriel scanned the pamphlet, while Rachel nearly spun in a circle to take in all the sights. She had never been to a county fair, but had heard people talking about them, and certainly this event was close. A throng of people milled around walking and talking to one another. Every now and again someone would lead an animal through the crowd, a proud stepping black horse or a white-faced Hereford calf. The smell of fried treats filled the air.

"The bidding on the goats doesn't start for another two hours," Gabriel said. "Before that there are a couple of pigs I want to see about."

"I smell onion rings." The *wunderbaar* smell trumped any other reply.

Gabriel laughed. "Does that mean you want to see about something to eat first?"

She nodded, with a smile. "I'm sorry. It just smells so *gut*."

"It does at that. Well, come, *Bissli*. Let's see about something to eat, and then we can find someplace to sit and watch the animals."

He held out his arm to her, crooked at the elbow and ready for her to slip hers through.

Rachel hesitated a fraction of a second, then looped her arm in his and smiled up at him. Today with the sweet Oklahoma wind blowing around them and her arm linked with his, it would be so easy to pretend they had a real marriage. And that he loved her in return . . . cherished her even, and would do anything to keep her at his side. That his endearment of "little bit" meant more than a name.

If only for the afternoon.

The thought stilled her smile.

As if sensing the change in her mood, Gabriel peered down at her. "*Was iss letz?*"

Rachel shook her head. "*Nix.*" How could she tell him she wanted more than their original agreement? There were no words. Just like there were none that could take away her love for him, nor his love for his late wife.

"Nothing," she said again, wishing it were the truth.

※◎ ◎✍

Gabriel watched as the auctioneer called out "sold" and pointed to the winning bidder.

He checked the itinerary again, then looked to the big industrial clock hanging on one side of the arena. "The goats are up next."

Rachel nodded, her gaze never leaving the auction block lest she somehow miss something.

"Do you want to go down closer so we can get a *gut* look at them?"

"Can we?" She flashed those bottomless brown eyes at him, and he felt his stomach tighten painfully. Perhaps he should not have eaten that last chili hot dog. It seemed to have set wrong in his belly.

He nodded and stood, taking time to get the blood back into his legs. Still they wobbled a bit as he took her hand into his own and led her down the steps of the bleachers so they could be at the front when the goats were led in.

They had looked at them in their pens, marking certain ones they wanted to bid on. Rachel seemed taken with one doe in particular. She was a pretty thing with chocolate brown fur that looked as if it had been poured over a pure white goat. Rachel's entire face had lit up like the Christmas lights in town when she saw her. Gabriel knew she wanted the playful little creature and had determined to do whatever it took to get it for her.

The auctioneer announced that the bidding was about to begin. Handlers and owners brought the goats in on leads, walking them around the arena so everyone could get another look before the bidding started.

He had to admit that they were beautiful creatures. Silky fur and floppy ears, they had eyes filled with softness and intelligence, brown and bottomless like the woman at his side. Funny, but it seemed these days that whatever thought popped into his head somehow hung around until, once again, Rachel filled his mind.

He blinked hard, pushing those thoughts to the back and forcing himself to concentrate on the auction. That was why they had come to Oklahoma City. He needed to remember that.

Rachel leaned in and spoke closely to his ear. She pointed to the brown and white doe. "That's her."

"*Jah.*" He nodded, readying his marker for the bid. He didn't need to look at Rachel to know that her eyes sparkled and that she was chewing her lower lip in her excitement. If he'd known buying her a goat would bring her this much joy, he would have come here long ago.

He turned back to the front before he gave into the temptation to push some of those wayward curls of light brown hair back under her prayer covering. *That* wasn't part of their agreement. Nor was seeing if those strands were as soft and silky as they looked. Or rubbing his thumb across the curve of her cheekbone . . . the thin line of her scar.

He sighed. What had gotten into him lately?

Maybe it was just the fact that she was living in his house. They were married after all, and there was a certain intimacy that came along with such a pledge. An intimacy they had promised to ignore.

So why wasn't he ignoring it?

"Gabriel!" Rachel tugged on his arm, pushing his elbow into the air. "You almost missed the bid."

His chin jerked up. He'd been too busy thinking about the woman at his side to pay enough attention to the auction. In the process, he'd almost missed his chance to buy her the brown and white goat she loved so much.

He tilted his head in her direction. "*Gut* thing I have you watching out for me."

She smiled as if she liked the idea of them being a team. Or maybe that was merely wishful thinking on his part. Whatever it was, he needed to be more mindful of it in the future. Life would be long and hard if he couldn't hold a thought in his head just because Rachel was sitting too near.

❧ ❧

Despite his lack of concentration, they managed to buy a slew of goats—including the brown and white female that Rachel adored.

"I'm going to call her Sundae."

"Like church?" he asked.

She smiled. "Like ice cream."

Gabriel wasn't sure why the doe had captured his wife's heart, but she acted as if he'd given her a puppy or a kitten and not chattel.

After he arranged for the delivery of the goats and checked on the transport of the hogs he'd purchased, they decided to walk around and check out the other sights, eat more fried foods from the vendors, and drink sweet fountain drinks through straws. They garnered a few looks as they roamed and explored the auction grounds. A few people even openly stared.

Gabriel hated that for Rachel's sake. She seemed so young and innocent, like she had not been out much. He supposed that living with Katherine Yoder was the reason for that. Katherine had always been an odd duck, not so much *ab im kopp* as just . . . different. She rarely visited, or attended many quilting bees or other frolics that the women held between the districts. As a result, Rachel seemed more sheltered than the typical Amish girl.

Woman, he corrected himself. She was twenty-six and married. He could hardly call her a girl. But her small stature made her seem younger, and made him feel more protective.

As if to further prove his point, Rachel's toe caught under one of the big power cables running along the ground, and she started to fall.

He grabbed her elbow. "*Geb acht*, Rachel." Then he hauled her back to her feet before she could tumble headlong across the pavement.

"*Danki*, Gabriel." Her voice was breathless and wispy, her hand braced against his chest to keep her from crashing into him.

His heart thudded. His breath hitched. Slowly he set her away from him, and they continued their stroll.

He glanced at the summer sun, still hanging high in the sky. It had to be about four. "It's about time to meet Bill Foster." By the time they met Bill and started home it would be nearly five, putting them at home in Clover Ridge well after seven.

"*Jah*," she said with a nod. He wondered if her voice really was as wistful as it sounded to his ears or if having her so close was playing tricks on him.

He turned them around, and they headed back to the front gate.

But Bill Foster's van wasn't there. They waited quietly, but still he didn't come. Gabriel talked with a few of the men who had come to the auction while Rachel kept a watchful gaze out for their Mennonite driver.

"Gabriel Fisher? Gabriel Fisher?" He heard his name before he saw who was calling him. An *Englisch* boy of about sixteen was searching through the milling crowd.

"*Jah*." He raised his hand and gave a small wave. "I am Gabriel Fisher."

"I have a phone call for you."

Gabriel nodded, recognizing the teenager as one of the handlers during the auction.

He handed Gabriel a small device, flat and smooth. It took a second for its purpose to register and then he recognized it as one of those newfangled, extra-fancy cell phones.

Gabriel gave a nod, took the phone, and pressed it to his ear. "*Jah?*"

"Gabriel, is that you?"

"*Jah*." He recognized the voice on the other end as belonging to Bill Foster, but there was a lot of noise in the background, talking and buzzing and what sounded like someone making an announcement over a microphone.

"There's been an accident, Gabriel."

His heart sank in his chest. "An accident?" His mind raced with flashes of his boys injured, Mary Elizabeth hurt, his *mamm* . . .

"My niece, Ashley . . . she got a fishhook caught at the corner of her eye. They're taking her into surgery now. She might lose that eye. I can't leave my brother alone. His wife is out of town, and the other girls are here . . ."

"I understand." Gabriel nodded, momentarily forgetting that Bill couldn't see him.

"Tomorrow, we'll know more, and I can take you home then."

"We could get a hotel room for the night." What other option did they have?

"I'll reimburse you for it."

He would not. Gabriel wouldn't allow it. But now wasn't the time to argue about such matters. "We can discuss all that once your kin is out of danger."

On the other side of the line, Bill let out a lengthy heartfelt sigh. "I appreciate that, Gabriel."

"There is not a need to thank me, but *gern gschehne* all the same, Bill Foster. We will say extra prayers for your family tonight."

Gabriel handed the phone back to the boy and thanked him for his trouble.

"What happened?" Rachel asked as the teenager walked away.

"Bill Foster's niece had an accident. He has to stay with her and cannot take us home until tomorrow."

She gave a small nod, then looked around as if searching for an answer to their dilemma. "What do we do?"

He caught her gaze, hoping to still her worries. "We can have someone call a taxi to take us to a hotel." There were no other options. It was too far home for anyone to give them a ride or for anyone else to come and get them. Worst case, they could ride back in the delivery truck with the goats. But either way, they had to spend the night and pray for the best for Bill Foster's niece once the morning came.

Rachel gave him a slow, expressionless nod, as if she agreed with his conclusion, but also had her doubts. If he were being honest, he had a few of his own.

13

"Welcome to the Holiday Inn South. How may I help you tonight?"

Rachel watched as Gabriel took a step closer to the desk and the smiling man in the green jacket who stood behind it. The man's smile never wavered, making it seem forced, like he was covering up his real feelings.

Get a hold of yourself, Rachel Fisher. She twisted her hands together, then dropped her tingling fingers to her sides. There was no reason for the man to be anything but polite, but she still thought that from behind that plastic smile he was mocking them.

She really needed to get out a little more; not a lot, but just enough to keep her from imagining that every *Englischer* was secretly making fun of her.

"I have a double room with a queen-size bed on the second floor," the man in the green jacket said, clicking some keys on his computer and pausing to hear Gabriel's answer.

Her husband let out a little cough, Rachel sure he was choking on their reality. A queen-size bed? *One* bed?

"We were hoping for a room with two beds."

The man looked from Gabriel to her, and then back at his computer screen. "O-kay." Somehow the word sounded anything but fine. "There is an extra charge for a double room, double occupancy," he warned.

"That's *allrecht*. All right." Gabriel coughed again.

The man pushed more buttons and a machine behind him started clicking and humming.

Rachel let go of her concerns as she watched the machine spit out papers. When it finished, she looked at Gabriel in wonder over this modern world she found herself in. But just as quickly, she looked away. For she had noticed a strange light in Gabriel's green eyes, a light that had made her uncomfortable.

She stepped back from the counter and stared at her feet until Gabriel touched her arm. He barely brushed against her before jerking back, as if the fabric of her sleeve had somehow burned him.

"Come on." He nodded toward the elevator, mindful of the clerk's eyes on them as they entered the paneled box.

Gabriel pushed the button marked "6" and took hold of the metal bar running behind them in the cart. "Better hold on," he said.

Rachel didn't have time to reply as the doors slid shut and her world shifted. She laughed a little, her voice strangled and thrilled at the same time. She felt as if she had been lifted off the ground by a giant. It was thrilling and scary and amazing all in the same instance.

"Almost there." Gabriel pointed to the lighted numbers above the door. The four was illuminated. Rachel had only a second to enjoy the return of a normal feeling in her gut before they jerked to a stop, and her stomach shifted once again.

"You okay?" he asked.

She nodded, though she thought she might be sick. And she thought riding in a car was bad!

Gabriel took her arm and led her from the tiny car. Rachel was grateful for his support as he escorted her to their room.

He used a funny little card to open the door. Then he gestured for her to precede him into the room, snapping on the electric light as he shut the door behind them.

"I'm not sure he'd ever seen an Amish person before."

"Hmm?" Rachel looked back at her husband. They had never been alone like this before. As a married couple, it should be no problem, but theirs was no ordinary marriage.

"I said I don't think he's ever seen an Amish couple before." She tried to smile.

Gabriel swiveled a look around. "Do you want to watch the television?"

She turned toward the box directly opposite the bed. "Do you think it's all right to watch it?"

Gabriel raised one dark brow in question. "Are you worried about the clerk, or the bishop?"

"The bishop," she whispered.

He gave her a mischievous grin that transported his face back twenty years. "The bishop need not know."

She would have to pray about the little thrill she got at the thought of doing something not approved by the *Ordnung*. Other than praying and watching TV, what were they going to do all night?

She looked at the bed—thankful there were two—and swallowed hard.

Gabriel cleared his throat. "Would you like to take a shower, or do you want to go find something to eat first?"

"Eat," she said automatically. Anything beat standing in the intimate room with her husband wondering about the next step. At least eating would get them far away from the beds that seemed to mock her very existence.

They made their way back downstairs, this time the elevator was not so much of a surprise to Rachel. Gabriel stopped at the front counter and asked about close places to eat. The clerk said he could call them a cab, they could take a shuttle, or they could walk to the pancake restaurant just across the parking lot.

"Let's walk," Rachel said. The long car trip there and the looming trip back would be enough riding for her for the rest of the year.

They found the restaurant cheery and well-lit, with orange and brown booths lining one wall and tables dotting the way between them and the counter.

The hostess led them to a booth and left menus, but Rachel already knew what she wanted. A cheeseburger. She hadn't had one in years, not since she went with her aunt to Tulsa for a special doctor's appointment. That was just after she had moved to Oklahoma and was still adjusting to the new rules and *Ordnung*.

Yes, she'd have a cheeseburger. With French fried potatoes. And a big Coke.

She pushed the menu to the side, propped her chin in her hand, and stared out the window at the Interstate highway. Big transfer trucks zoomed past, their engines vrooming down the road at a dizzying speed. Rachel was glad to be sitting still. At least for a while.

In truth, she was a tiny bit thankful that they weren't driving back to Clover Ridge tonight. She was sad that Bill Foster's niece had been hurt and had already made a mental note to add her to her prayers tonight. But she was glad not to have to get into the van and race down the roads at speeds God had never intended.

Gabriel looked up from his menu, catching her eye. "You know what you want to eat?"

She nodded.

He closed his menu and soon the waitress began taking their orders.

"And ketchup," Rachel added. "I'd like ketchup with the potatoes, please."

"Sure thing, hon." The waitress stuck her pencil through her ponytail and scooped up the menus. "I'll be right back with your drinks."

"*Danki,*" Gabriel said.

The waitress smiled and hurried away to refill someone's coffee.

"When we get back to the room, I'll call the phone out in front of my *elders' haus. Dat* can get Zane Carson and have him go check on the goats. He and Matthew can do your evening milking."

Rachel nodded. Gideon and Annie had too much on their hands right now with a new babe in the house. "Will Katie Rose stay with the children?"

"*Jah.*"

"Samuel will like that." Even more than the goats, she worried about Gabriel's youngest. He'd had so many changes these last few months that she wasn't sure how he would take another upset. He loved Katie Rose like he would his own mother. Rachel breathed a sigh of relief that he'd be fine for the night.

She looked back to find Gabriel staring at her with that strange light in his eyes. She almost wished he'd go back to frowning. At least she knew what that expression meant.

For a moment they merely looked at each other. Then the waitress reappeared with their drinks, and the connection was broken.

As they waited for their food, Gabriel made small talk. And after it arrived and they prayed, they both fell silent as they ate.

The silence between them was heavy and awkward, but Rachel had no idea how to dispel it. Gabriel was her husband, her life partner, and yet she realized that she could count on one hand the number of times she had been alone with him. Tonight, they would sleep merely feet apart with no one around.

She pushed thoughts of their future reality away, not wanting to think about that right now. She wanted to enjoy this treat, one she hadn't had in so very long. She took another bite of the greasy cheeseburger, reveling in its taste. She had forgotten how good cheeseburgers were. Foods like this were the reason gluttony was a sin.

Enjoying her dinner was one thing, but gluttony was something else entirely, she thought. She added that sin to the list of things she needed to pray about that evening before bed.

Just as she finished her last bite of dinner, Gabriel coughed.

Rachel looked up to find him staring at her, his look guarded. Then he stiffened and rose to his feet.

Rachel turned in her seat, following his gaze to see what had captured his attention.

A young blonde-haired girl stood at the counter, drumming her fingers on the Formica as she impatiently waited.

"Do you know her?"

Gabriel eased back down in his seat and shook his head. "She looks like someone I know. But it's not her."

"Mary Elizabeth?"

He pressed his lips together and gave a short nod.

"Would you . . . would you like to tell me what happened?"

He shrugged, then fished some money from the hidden pocket in his trousers and laid it on the table for their bill. "She left." He slid from the booth and stretched his legs as he stood.

Rachel stepped out in front of him, unsure if she should press the matter or let it be. "I know that."

Leave it alone, the cautious side of her advised. Yet she had a feeling Gabriel needed to talk about the problem to someone. But if she knew her husband at all, he wouldn't turn that information loose without a little prying.

She peered into his face, hooking his gaze with hers. "You can tell me about it, you know."

His face was a mask. "Won't change it."

"It might help you."

He frowned. "*Nay.*"

Stubborn Amish men. That was one thing she had not gotten used to since she had moved from Florida. Her family, at least, had discussed their feelings. Oh, not as much as the chatty *Englisch*, but if they had ever needed to talk to someone close to them, they had the option. Sweeping it all away like it was nothing wouldn't help anyone involved. *Like she'd had to do when she lost them and her home in one fateful minute.*

But the deepening scowl on Gabriel's face said the matter was closed. And maybe it was . . . for now.

They walked in silence back across the parking lot. He held the glass hotel doors open for her, but didn't remind her to hang on when they climbed into the elevator. Rachel managed to keep her dinner in place even though her stomach rose and fell with the motorized cart. The doors swooshed open, and Gabriel led her down the hallway and back to their room for the evening.

"This seems strange," she said, trailing her fingers across the plastic furniture.

Gabriel looked up from untying his boots. "What does?"

"I feel like I should do something. I mean if I were at home, I'd be getting Samuel ready for bed. The older *buwe* would be finishing up their homework. Supper dishes would need to be washed and . . ."

"The house won't fall down without you there to tend it."

"I know that. But I feel . . . lazy."

He set his boots off to one side, then stood and stretched. "I've heard that *Englisch* women like to take hour-long baths."

Rachel's eyes grew wide. "Where did you hear something like that?"

He smiled. "Gideon's Annie."

"Oh." Well, that made sense. Sort of. Being raised *Englisch*, Annie was probably used to talking about such things with all sorts of people, stranger and friend alike. But Rachel was not *Englisch* and even her Beachy upbringing hadn't prepared her for talking about such matters with her in-name-only husband.

"I thought I'd call the phone shanty and see if everything's been taken care of. You could uh . . ." He motioned toward the bathroom, not finishing the sentence as if the intimacy was too much for him as well.

"Uh . . . *jah*. I think I will."

❦

Lounging in the tub for a full hour, Rachel soon learned, was not in her makeup. Despite the closed door and the electric fan that hummed when she turned on the bathroom light, she could still hear Gabriel shuffling around the room. She wasn't able to make out any words, but his deep voice resonated, telling her that he had managed to get in touch with someone about their overnight stay in Oklahoma City.

But after a half an hour, she'd had all the laziness she could stand. She dried off, dressed back in her same clothes and ran her fingers through her hair. She wiped the steam from the mirror and peered at herself in the glass.

The steam had made her fuzzy curls a riotous mess. Should she pull her hair back into its pins? She didn't have a brush or a pony-tail holder to pull her hair off her face like when she was at home. She didn't want to sleep in all those sharp bobby pins, yet she wasn't sure she should face her husband with her hair looking like a crazy rat's nest all over her head.

If only she had a kerchief like she used to wear in Florida. That would solve all her problems. But she didn't have a kerchief or anything to use in its place.

She stuck her tongue out at her reflection. She was being a silly ninny. Just because she had gone and fallen in love with her husband, she was making things harder on herself than they needed to be.

What she needed to remember was that her husband wasn't in love with her.

Her stomach fell at the thought, but it was the truth. He didn't love her. He didn't feel the tension in the air concerning their sleeping situation, what she did or didn't have to wear to sleep in, or what her hair looked like flipping in all different directions.

She took off the apron and hung it in the small closet space next to the bathroom. She rubbed a hand over her stomach, smoothed her fingers through her hair, then took a deep breath before step-ping out of the bathroom and in full view of her husband who sat propped against the pillows on the far bed, galluses hanging off his shoulders, his blue shirt untucked.

She peered at him. "Do you really think the bishop will be okay with us watching the television?"

He sat up as she entered the room. "That is not what I said. I said, the bishop didn't have to know."

She bit her lip. "Oh. I suppose a deacon should keep to the *Ordnung* regardless of the circumstance."

"There's a Bible in the nightstand if you'd rather read. But it's in *Englisch*, so it seems wrong to me somehow."

She walked primly to the closest bed and perched on the corner like she did that sort of thing all the time—sat on a bed, in a hotel room, with her husband. "I just thought it might be fun to—"

Gabriel rose and started pushing buttons on the television. They wouldn't have to worry about what the bishop said, they couldn't figure out how to work the *Englisch* contraption anyway.

"There." Gabriel took a step back as the screen flickered and went from black to a crisp picture of a couple sharing an intense kiss. "Whoa." He blocked her view and pushed another button, all the while not letting her see what was playing out in front of her.

She turned her head. "I'm not sure this is a *gut* idea."

"*Guck datt hie.*" He stood back and allowed her to see.

Rachel read the words written across the screen in large white letters. *Little House on the Prairie*. "Like the books?"

Gabriel shrugged, then padded back to his bed. "We will see in a few minutes."

Rachel scooted back a little farther onto her own bed and pulled one of the pillows in front of her. It was so amazing to her that someone had thought to take the beloved stories by Laura Ingalls Wilder and make them into a moving story. Surely the bishop couldn't protest about that? What was the problem with television anyway?

The image of the half-naked couple kissing on the screen for everyone to see flashed through her mind. Oh, yeah. *That*.

What a shame that a few had ruined the joy for them all.

It was after nine when the shows ended. The sky outside their room was just turning dark.

Gabriel rose from the bed and stretched. "I'm going to take a shower. Do you want me to find something else for you to watch?"

Wide-eyed she shook her head. "I think I'll read the Bible now."

He chuckled. "Feeling the need to repent?"

The look on her face was borderline horror. "Do you think the bishop will be that upset if he finds out?"

Gabriel found himself wanting to cross the room and wrap her up in his arms. He shook the thought away. Perhaps he had teased her too much about the television. "I believe that Rueben Beachy would say that we made the best of the situation. After all, we had to use the electric lights, *jah*?"

She nodded.

"And there were no chores here for us to see to. No family needin' to be fed, or be put to bed."

"I still think I should read." She pulled the book from the nightstand drawer and tucked her feet up under her skirt.

Sitting there, in her blue dress, her light hair spilling around her shoulders, and a book open in her hands made him think of another tale he'd read long ago—*Alice in Wonderland*. He supposed that Rachel might feel a bit like Alice, thrown for a time into a magical world. He felt a little like that himself. What with the dinner at a restaurant and without the *kinder*. Staying the night in a hotel room, electric lights, and fancy television. But tomorrow they would return to the real world. *Their* world. Hopefully by then, this urge he had to hold her close would disappear right along with the *Englisch* magic.

Rachel was not sitting on the bed when he finished his shower. He hadn't needed to take a shower as much as he needed some reason to get out of the same room with his wife. The thought was beyond ridiculous. No man should have to avoid his wife.

But he did.

There was something entirely too intimate about sitting on a bed not two feet from her and being so caught up in her profile that he longed to throw their agreement out the window.

He'd hoped when he poked his head into the room some twenty minutes later that she would have turned out the fancy *Englisch* lights and slipped beneath the covers of her bed. That would have been the perfect ending to a not-so-fortunate day.

Instead he saw her small silhouette standing out of the room on the balcony.

He should make his way to his bed, pull back the covers, and crawl inside. She was twenty-six years old. She didn't need to be told it was time to sleep. She was in no danger outside their room on the tiny rectangle of concrete surrounded by wrought iron rails.

But his feet didn't listen to his brain. Instead they marched out, their steps slowing as they neared where she leaned against the rail.

She sucked in a breath as he came up beside her.

"Sorry," he murmured. "I didn't mean to scare you."

"You didn't." She said the words but didn't bother looking at him. "I guess I should go back in. I hadn't planned on standing out here so long without . . ." She waved a hand toward her uncovered head.

"Now that's something to tell the bishop."

She jerked her chin upward, watching him. "Don't joke about such things."

"Were you out here praying?"

"*Nay.*"

"Then you should be fine."

She shook her head. "I just wanted to see the swimming pool. It is so beautiful."

Gabriel looked down at the patch of bright aqua-colored water. It was beautiful, shining like a jewel into the night.

"I would love to go swimming. I haven't been in years." Her voice turned quiet. "I grew up Beachy Amish. Did you know that?"

"I have heard something of the sort," he said.

"My parents and my *bruders* were killed in a buggy wreck."

He took a step closer to her, rubbing the pad of his thumb across the scar underlining one big, dark eye. "And that's where this came from."

"*Jah.*" She whispered in return.

He should step back, take his hand from her face, but he couldn't move. Wasn't able. Didn't want to. The Oklahoma wind stirred the strands of her long hair, brushing it against the backs of his fingers. Silky, soft hair the color of a doe's hide that framed her big, luminous eyes.

He took another step closer when everything in him told him to step back. But she kept sucking him in, drawing him closer to her, as if he were drowning and she was the only salvation in a churning sea.

He used his thumb to tilt her face to his.

Her gaze snagged his, and he looked at her for a moment. Just looked. She was his wife. His life partner, though they had set out terms of their relationship that most would find unacceptable. He had done that for her. Told her their marriage would be in name only. A piece of paper to stop the gossiping tongues from waggin'. He fully intended to keep his promise.

Just after this one kiss.

Her eyes fluttered closed right before his lips touched hers.

He shut his as well, preferring to enjoy the experience from the feeling alone.

One hand held her chin, kept her steady for his kiss, while the other arm snaked around her and drew her even closer to him.

Gradually, she returned his caress, kissing him back almost hesitantly. Sweetly. Innocently.

She was a strange combination of woman and girl, and he found that he wanted to know more about her. How old her brothers had been when they died, how it felt moving into a new, more conservative district.

And how she had managed to be twenty-six and kiss him as if she was as innocent as . . .

He wrenched himself away from her. "Forgive me." His voice rasped, as if the devil himself had him by the throat. Perhaps he did.

What had he been thinking, kissing her like he did? Of course she was innocent, and he had married her, but he had promised not to touch her.

"It's . . . it's okay."

"I'll . . ." He didn't know what he was going to say. Only that he needed to get away from her. And quick. "I'm going to get a cup of coffee." He rushed back through the room and was halfway out the door before he realized he'd forgotten his shoes.

Her eyes were on him as he marched back in and grabbed them up, not stopping to put them on before closing the door behind him.

He'd go get a cup of coffee at the pancake house, get himself back together. Maybe a couple of cups and he would remember that theirs wasn't a traditional marriage.

He sighed and raked a hand through his hair. But it would take more than coffee for him to forget the smooth texture of her skin under the pads of his fingers, and the sweet taste of her lips beneath his.

14

Bill Foster called first thing the following morning. The surgery had been a success. His niece would not lose the eye, but any damage to her sight was still unknown. The girl's mother had returned home, and Rachel breathed a sigh of relief. Their prayers had been answered.

Before ten, they were on their way back to Clover Ridge.

This time Rachel couldn't sleep on the trip, still wide awake from her adventure. She and Gabriel had come to the city to buy goats and ended up spending the night in a fancy hotel. Quite an adventure for an Amish girl.

And his kiss.

She shivered from the memory. If kissing was always that wonderful, she couldn't understand why people didn't kiss all the time. Or maybe they did. Maybe couples in more traditional relationships kissed all the time. There was no way for her to know, though, unless she asked someone.

The thought brought a blush to her cheeks. She couldn't do that. She couldn't ask Katie Rose or Ruth. No, that would be too embarrassing by far.

But maybe this was what Ruth had been talking about when she told Rachel she should take opportunities as they presented themselves to her. She stared out the window, confused. She just didn't know what to do next.

Well, she knew there was more than kissing when it came to romantic love, but she had no idea of the next step in the process—or even if Gabriel wanted more from their relationship.

Perhaps that was the reason he had stayed out half the night. She had looked at the shiny red lights on the alarm clock between their beds when he slipped back into their room some time later. By then, it was nearly two o'clock in the morning.

That accounted for the dark circles and bags under his eyes and the return of his surly manner.

Still, kissing was an enjoyable endeavor, and she hoped against hope that she might get the chance to kiss Gabriel once again.

She gazed out the window at the landscape whizzing by. If she kept her eyes ahead, she could make out things before they zoomed past: huge signs, cars and trucks of all kinds, the occasional stray animal. They even got to see a transfer truck hauling an enormous blade thing that Bill Foster said would eventually make its way onto a wind turbine.

But no sight was as welcome as the big white and green sign that welcomed them back to Clover Ridge. 'Cept for maybe the mailbox and driveway belonging to Gabriel.

When they pulled up in front of the white two-story house, Katie Rose and Samuel immediately peered out the windows and came to stand on the porch to greet them.

"*Guder mariye*," Rachel said, waving as she got out of the car, while Gabriel stayed behind to settle the price of the trip with Bill Foster.

"*Goedemiddag*," Katie Rose corrected with a dimpled smile.

Rachel took a quick glance at the sky. "So it is afternoon," she said, holding her arms out for Samuel. "And a *gut* one at that."

Samuel raced toward her, and Rachel scooped him up in her arms. Oh, she had missed him so. If the way he squeezed her was any indication, he had missed her as well.

Rachel gave Samuel one more squeeze, then set his feet back on the ground. "*Danki*, Katie Rose. For staying with the boys."

Katie dipped her chin in a quick nod. "Did you have a good trip then?"

"*Jah*, we got the goats, and Bill Foster's niece is healing just fine. All in all, a *gut* trip."

Katie watched Rachel with those jade green eyes of hers, saying nothing. Rachel suspected that her question had meant something more.

Or maybe she was just imagining things.

Katie Rose nodded again. "Something about you seems different." She turned her head this way and that as if studying Rachel from every angle. "I do not know what it could be, but *jah*, different."

An involuntary blush stole its way into her cheeks. "There is nothing different about me, Katie Rose Fisher, except that I am a day older."

Katie smiled. "If you say so."

"I do at that." Even as she said the words she knew them to be a lie. At the very least, they were not the truth. Something was different, but she was as stumped as Katie Rose as to what it could be.

～∽ ∾～

"*Dat. Dat*! Slow down!" Simon squinted up into the hay loft where his father was pitching down bales of hay.

"*Ach*." His father propped his arm in the handle of the pitchfork and wiped his brow. "That's enough?"

Simon looked around at the two dozen bales of hay scattered across the barn floor. "For now," he replied dryly.

Something was wrong, but Simon couldn't figure out what it was. Ever since the auction his *dat* had been acting strange. And Rachel . . . well, Rachel always acted a little odd, but she was acting weirder than usual.

Something happened on that trip to Oklahoma City, but for certain he didn't know what it could be. Maybe they had argued about the goats . . .

His father settled his hat back on his head and climbed down from the loft. "Go and see if there's any lemonade left, Simon. I could sure use a drink."

"*Jah*. Okay."

His *dat* never stopped work in the afternoon to go to the kitchen for a drink, Simon thought as he tromped toward the house. And if he did, he always went himself. Was he avoiding the kitchen?

He shrugged. Why did he care? He'd be able to get a drink for himself and see if he could get any cookies before all the not-burned ones were gone. It might be his imagination, but it seemed to him that Rachel was even worse these days about forgetting what was in the oven or on the stove until it was too done to eat.

His *vatter* didn't say a word, just ate the food without comment, not saying anything until their evening Bible reading. Then Simon and his brothers took turns getting ready for bed.

It could be that things seemed different because school was out, and Simon was at home more, watching this interaction for himself. He shook his head just as Matthew came in the front door, and let it slam behind him. Maybe Matthew knew what was going on.

"*Goedemiddag, bruder,*" Simon greeted as Matthew hung his hat on the peg.

Matthew squinted until his eyes adjusted to the dim light of the house. "*Jah, goedemiddag.*" He walked into the kitchen and grabbed a glass of the cool lemonade for himself, then drank it down in two big gulps before pouring himself a second serving.

Simon turned away, digging through the cookie jar for any edible cookies. He would have rather had some pie. His *grossmammi* made the best pies, but she hadn't made one for them in a week or so. Rachel, it seemed, couldn't roll out a crust if'n her life depended on it.

"So, *bruder,* anything of interest happening here?"

Simon looked back at his brother and considered his not-so-innocent question.

Matthew propped his hip on the counter and continued to sip his lemonade as he waited for Simon to answer.

"*Nay,*" Simon turned back to his chore, not able to find even one cookie without black edges.

"That's not how David tells it."

Simon stilled, keeping his eyes on the cookie jar. "What do you mean?"

"What are you hoping to prove by making her leave?"

Simon resisted the urge to slam the lid of the cookie jar back in place to rid himself of the burning anger. But the cookie jar had belonged to his mother and needed to be treated with the carefulness that it deserved. He held his temper in check knowing that he would have to add the episode to his prayers that night. "I do not know what you are talking about."

"Don't add lying to your other sins, Simon," his brother said. "Look at me. I'm talking about all the pranks you've been playing on Rachel."

Simon looked at his brother over one shoulder. "David was in on it too." Only after the words had left his mouth did he realize they had proven his guilt.

"Promise me that you will stop trying to make her leave."

Simon mumbled something he hoped Matthew would accept as an answer.

Matthew stood up straight and set his glass on the counter. "She loves him."

Simon shook his head. "How do you know?"

"I can tell by the look in her eyes when she catches sight of him. She hides it though, when she thinks someone is watching."

Simon let that sink in. He didn't know if it were true or not. He was only thirteen. What did he know about love except that his *vatter* once loved his *mudder* very much.

Matthew continued to eye him. "He loves her too, you know."

Simon shook his head. "That's a lie!" He hadn't meant to yell.

"It is not. He loves her, but he doesn't know it yet."

"How do you know?" Simon scoffed. "You're just fifteen."

"I remember," he said, his voice quiet. "I remember how he looked at *Mamm* when she was still alive. He looks at Rachel like that."

Simon shook his head, not wanting the words to be true.

"Either way," Matthew continued. "Leave her alone. She hasn't done anything to you."

"She burns the cookies."

"Really, Simon? Is that your objection to this marriage?"

Simon shrugged.

"Tell me this: What did you hope to gain?"

Simon dropped his head and stared at the scrubbed planks beneath his feet. They were clean now, because neither Simon nor David had the opportunity to drag in dirt from the garden. Shame filled him. "I didn't want her to take *Mamm's* place."

Matthew sighed, and even to Simon's ears, it sounded sad. "*Mamm* doesn't have a place here anymore," Matthew said, and to

Simon's dismay, tears filled his brother's eyes. "Her place now is with Jesus."

Simon wiped his nose on the back of his sleeve. "But—"

"There are no buts. *Dat* is married to Rachel now. If she leaves it's not like he can get married again. He'll be lonely and miserable with no way out. Is that what you want for him?"

"*Nay.* But we thought . . ."

"Of yourselves. From now on, think about *Dat* and what he needs. Like it or not, Rachel is married to him. He loves her, and she's here to stay."

<hr />

He was avoiding her, that much was certain. Rachel supposed it was for the best that he kept his distance, but him putting that space between them hurt all the more now that she knew how it felt to be held by him.

She bit back a sigh and started hoeing down the next row of the table garden. She was quite proud, in a humble sort of way, of how her garden was coming along. She'd tended the garden at her aunt's house, but it was nothing compared to this. She straightened for a moment and looked across the patch of land. So the rows weren't as even as she would have wished them to be. There were still all these beautiful green plants raising their heads toward the sun and a multitude of tiny flowers that would soon turn into fruit. It would be *gut* to see the many vegetables mature and feed her newfound family.

Rachel smiled and went back to work, stopping minutes later as she heard an engine rev from the road. Not an unfamiliar sound to have cars and trucks zoom by, but this one stopped.

Her goats!

"Samuel," she said, calling out to the *bu* as he sat in the shade of the large oak tree. He had wandered out of the house after

completing his alphabet tracings and now played with finger pup-
pets while he waited for her to finish.

"*Jah?*"

"The goats are here."

He looked around in all directions. "The new goats?'

"*Jah.*" She propped the hoe against the tree and reached down
a hand to help him up. "Are you ready to go see?"

He stood, brushing off the seat of his pants.

Rachel smiled with love for the child. What a blessing he was.

Hand in hand, they walked around the side of the house
expecting to see the large livestock truck delivering the new goats
she and Gabriel had bought at auction.

Instead, a slim teenage girl walked slowly toward them. She
was dressed in the way typical of *Englisch* youth—faded jeans and a
loose T-shirt, flip-flop sandals slapping against the dirt drive. Her
steps were heavy and weighted with what tragedy Rachel did not
know. But it seemed this wayward traveler needed something.

The girl stopped halfway to the house and held her arms open.
"Samuel?"

"Mawy!" He turned loose of Rachel's hand and ran toward the
girl, not stopping until he collided with her.

She dropped her backpack in the dirt and swept him into her
arms, holding him tight. "You've grown so much."

Rachel stood, rooted to the spot, not sure what to make of this
new development, but somehow knowing . . .

The girl continued to hold Samuel close, raining kisses on
his sweet freckled face. Then she picked up her bag, still juggling
Samuel on her hip as she tottered toward the house.

"Wachel! Wachel! Look, it's my *shveshtah.*"

Mary Elizabeth Fisher had come home.

15

I'm sorry your father's not home. He should be back soon, though."

Mary Elizabeth nodded as Rachel ran out of words. She wished that she had something more to say, a better welcome to offer the girl. She looked dead tired, her eyes listless, as if she had seen things better left unseen.

Rachel shook away the thought. She was being dramatic. Most Amish children who left during *rumspringa* returned. Though some left again. It was hard out in the *Englisch* world. Everyone knew that. But Rachel wished she had something more to offer the girl besides half-burned pie and lemonade. At least the latter wasn't burned.

What she really wished for was a way to contact Gabriel to let him know that Mary Elizabeth had returned. Surely he would be happy to see her whole and healthy despite the sad, sad look in her eyes.

"He's the deacon now, you know."

"No," Mary Elizabeth replied without remorse in her voice, without any feeling at all, as a matter of fact. After dealing with Gabriel's *sohns* and all their pranks and tricks, Rachel found it hard to believe that his *dochder* was so . . . unenthusiastic. Or maybe she took after her father, more on the quiet side than the *buwe.*

"Well, he is." Rachel eased down in the chair opposite Mary Elizabeth and tried to think of something more to say. When was Gabriel coming home?

After all of the excited "Welcome homes" and "We missed yous," Rachel had made the boys—including Samuel—go outside and finish up their chores.

Gabriel would be home soon, she would serve dinner, and that would be that. The day would go on like nothing momentous had happened—when that was far from the truth.

"He's out talking with Beth Troyer. Seems she started hanging her undergarments out on the line and her *Englisch* neighbor doesn't cotton to that."

A ghost of a smile flickered across the young girl's lips. "She's been trying to get that neighbor's attention for nigh on five years now. I don't know why. He's *Englisch* and she's Amish, but she's sweet on him—it is a sin to gossip." Mary Elizabeth shook her head as if confused by her own behavior, as if ashamed at what the outside world had done to her.

"I just thought you should know where your father is."

Mary Elizabeth nodded.

"Once the boys get back in, I'll feed them their supper, and they can go to bed early. Though I doubt anyone will sleep much tonight."

She nodded again.

"Would you like some more pie?"

Mary Elizabeth glanced at the pie on the sideboard and shook her head.

"I'm sorry. I know the crust is awfully brown, but . . ." She had no excuse. She just got sidetracked when it came to baking . . . and frying . . . and cooking in general.

"I'm not a *gut* cook," Mary Elizabeth muttered. "Even on an *Englisch* stove, I burn everything." Her shoulders seemed to droop as if holding herself so stiff had become a burden unworthy of the effort.

"I suppose it's strange coming home and finding your *vatter* married."

She shrugged.

"I was supposed to just help but—" Why was she telling Gabriel's daughter all of this? It was his responsibility to explain these matters to Mary Elizabeth, not hers.

She glanced toward the ceramic clock on the fireplace mantel. Surely he would be home soon. How long did it take to tell Beth Troyer to watch where she hung her unmentionables?

Just then the front door slammed open. Rachel's heart jumped into her throat. But it was only the boys back in from their chores. "All of you, get back outside and wash your hands. Your father will be home any minute." *She hoped.*

The boys, so happy to see their sister, hugged her once again before trudging out to do as Rachel told them. She wasn't sure why they had picked tonight not to argue with her over their responsibilities, but she was grateful nonetheless.

"I'll just . . ." Rachel rose to her feet and went to the stove, stirring the big pot of soup for something to do with her hands. The weather was almost too warm for soup, she thought. Then she switched to wishing Gabriel could hear her thoughts and hurry home.

She just hoped he hadn't picked tonight to avoid her altogether.

Joseph elbowed Simon at the wash stand. "I told you she would come home."

"Quit pushing." Simon winced but continued about his business. Their prayers had been answered. Sort of. Mary Elizabeth had returned, and that was *gut*. Now maybe their *dat* would send Rachel away. Then life could go back to the way it was. The thought should have made him jump for joy, but it didn't. All thanks to Matthew, it made his stomach hurt instead.

How could his father love Rachel? What about their *mamm*? How could he love two women?

Matthew's words came back to Simon as he waved his hands about to dry them. *Mamm doesn't have a place here anymore. Her place now is with Jesus.*

Tears stung at the back of his eyes, but he blinked them away before they could fall. What if Mary Elizabeth took off again because *Dat* had married Rachel, and she no longer felt welcome?

"We gotta do something, Joseph," Simon said.

Matthew, David, and Samuel had all left to go back into the house, leaving Simon and Joseph with a moment alone.

"What do you mean?"

"I mean, something," Simon repeated. He pushed back Matthew's words. Thankfully he hadn't promised to stop trying to make Rachel leave. "Something to get our family back to the way it was."

"You want Rachel to leave."

He nodded.

"I think I like her," Joseph confessed.

"You're just saying that because you're happy Mary Elizabeth is back. But who knows how long she'll really be here. What if *Dat* makes her leave because he doesn't need her to take care of us since he married Rachel?"

Joseph chewed on his bottom lip in what Simon considered his thoughtful look.

"Matthew starts *rumspringa* next year, and Samuel will go to school in the fall."

Joseph shook his head. "Teacher won't take him 'cuz he don't know his letters."

"Rachel's been teaching them to him. You can count on it, he's going to school. With all of us in school and Matthew running around, why would he need two womenfolk in the *haus*?"

"*Dat* won't make Mary Elizabeth leave." Joseph's words sounded tiny and hollow.

"Are you willing to take the chance on that?"

Simon was just about to go back into the house when the creak and rattle of a buggy reached his ears.

"*Dat's* home," Joseph cried, jumping up and down with excitement.

Simon stilled his steps and turned to wait on his *vatter*.

Gabriel pulled the buggy to a stop and swung down, giving Simon and Joseph a questioning look. "*Wie geht, buwe?*"

"*Gut! Gut!*" Joseph hopped into the air as if Christmas had come early. "Mary Elizabeth's home, *Dat*! Ain't that great?"

Gabriel's hands stilled on the harnesses. "What did you say?"

"Mary Elizabeth's come back," Simon answered this time, but with less enthusiasm than his *bruder*.

His heart gave a painful thud. His baby girl had returned? "Mary Elizabeth?" He turned to his son. "Simon, take care of the horses."

The boy complied without complaint, taking the reins and leading the beasts toward the barn, but to Gabriel everything moved as if in slow motion. His Mary Elizabeth had come back. Gabriel tried his best to dampen his excitement, to slow his steps as he neared the house, but his emotions were all there, tamped down but alive and beating with every thump of his heart.

He wrenched open the door and rushed inside the house. There she was, sitting at the table like she'd only been gone for the afternoon instead of nearly two months.

"*Dat*."

She stood, and he stumbled trying to get to her. He wrapped her into his embrace and held her tight. His baby girl had come home.

Reluctantly, Gabriel released his daughter, soaking in her very presence. The world hadn't gotten to her. She might be dressed like an *Englischer*, but she had returned, a little pale, but home.

She lowered herself into a chair, and he pulled up a seat next to her.

As he studied Mary Elizabeth, he began noticing the tiny differences that he hadn't seen before. Her normally sparkling blue eyes seemed dull and sad. She was thin, many pounds lighter than when she had left. He supposed the *Englisch* world was not all that she had imagined or she never would have returned, but it was the changes in her that worried him the most.

"It's so *gut* to see you again," he said, containing the tremble that threatened his voice. "I was so worried about you."

She wiped away her tears. "I'm so very *froh* to be home."

If'n she was so happy, why was she crying?

Rachel caught his eye and stood. "I sent the boys upstairs," she said, standing and taking the lid off the bubbling pot of chicken soup. "We should eat now, before it gets too late."

"*Jah*," he agreed. The dinner smelled *gut*, like it hadn't been scorched. The blessings just kept coming. He took Mary Elizabeth in again. There was still so much to talk about, so many things that he wanted to ask his *dochder*. Then again, she was home and those many questions could be answered tomorrow.

Mary Elizabeth stood. "I'm so very tired," she said, with a shake of her head. "I think I'll just go on up to my room and lie down."

He didn't want to, but he couldn't help but be caught in those bottomless brown eyes belonging to his wife. She had been sleeping in Mary Elizabeth's room. Now that his daughter was back, they were one bed short.

With Mary Elizabeth asleep upstairs, Rachel was strangely quiet throughout the meal. Or maybe it was that the boys were exceptionally chatty. They all talked at once, making plans to take Mary Elizabeth down to the creek and over to see Annie's baby. Samuel wanted to take her out and introduce her to Rachel's dairy goats and the new litter of kittens that were born the week before.

Gabriel used the opportunity to relax, or rather try to. His meeting with Beth Troyer had been a chore at best. That woman walked the line between *Englisch* and Amish like none he had ever seen. But that was a problem for the bishop to see to. Gabriel had told her to quit hanging her private laundry for all the world to see and left it at that.

He now wished that he had hurried home instead of stopping by Gideon's to check on Annie and the new *boppli*. Michelle, they had named her. Michelle Elizabeth after Annie's mother and his daughter—the one currently upstairs sleeping in the bed he'd promised his wife.

After supper, they sat down for the Bible reading, but Gabriel had trouble paying attention. He so wished Mary Elizabeth had stayed downstairs and heard the Good Lord's word, but he could see the exhaustion on her pale face. She would have plenty of time to soak up the verses she needed, and until then, he had five sons that needed their daily dose of the truth.

Still he cut it short, and watched with his heart thumping as Rachel shooed them all upstairs and into bed a full half hour before their normal bedtime.

Which left him exactly thirty minutes to decide what to do with his wife.

"I'll sleep on the couch," she said quietly. Rachel made her way from the kitchen to the living room, wiping her hands on a dishtowel as she approached. The action didn't hide the tremor in her fingers. Nor could it mask the familiar light in her eyes.

He shouldn't have kissed her that night at the hotel. He should have tempered his response to her, fought the forces that seemed to be pulling them together. He hadn't expected love from this relationship. This marriage was about needs—his need to provide for his family and hers to remain in Clover Ridge. He had been honest with her from the start, but perhaps he should have hinted that it could be about more. Because now, as she stood there, tendrils of hair escaping her bun, a small smear of flour on one shoulder and a smudge of cherry pie across one cheek, he found himself sucked in by her chaos.

He stood to fight the pull and moved as far from her as possible. "I think I'll turn in now." He walked stiff legged past her and to his bedroom in the back of the house. It had been a long day and was proving to be an even longer night.

❧ ❧

Gabriel opened his eyes in the darkness, hardly aware that he had been asleep. He had dozed off and on for the past few hours, dreaming of Mary Elizabeth when he was asleep and thinking about her when he was awake. A body could hardly call that resting.

He threw back the covers and stood. Lying there awake wasn't accomplishing anything. Maybe a drink of water would help, or a glass of milk, a piece of pie . . .

Quietly he crept into the kitchen and filled a glass with water from the tap. He didn't really need anything to eat. He wasn't hungry. He wasn't even thirsty—he was anxious. Anxious to know what had caused that terrible sad look in his daughter's eyes. Yet he didn't want to know, was afraid that he couldn't handle what life experience with the *Englisch* had caused such melancholy.

He stared out the window over the kitchen sink, watching the night. Not much moved in the yard, just the wind blowing the trees and an occasional bird braving the dark.

The couch springs squeaked behind him and he stilled, listening for signs that he had disturbed Rachel. There was no sense in both of them being awake, but her footsteps padded quiet and sure across the bare floor.

He felt her before he knew she was there, and he jumped when she touched him, that small hand on his back sending fire right through him.

"It's going to be *allrecht*," she whispered.

But it wasn't. Nothing would ever be the same again.

He turned without thinking and swept her into his arms, holding her close, burying his face in her neck. He breathed in her familiar scent, tried to lose himself in her warmth. How long he stood there holding her, just holding her, he did not know. She kept his tears at bay, the realities yet unfaced, the truth and tragedy and every clawing demon he fought far from him.

"I can't . . . I don't want to let you go." If he turned her loose, he'd break to pieces.

"Then don't." Her words were quiet, but like a shot to his heart in the darkness. He lifted her from her feet, and with arms still wrapped tightly around her, he carried her to his room.

16

Simon looked from his sister, to his father, to Rachel, and then back to Mary Elizabeth again. Everyone was acting *kshpassich*. Rachel acted like everything was full of sunshine to the point that she was tripping over her words and her smile had gone stale. His *vatter* seemed grumpy, well grumpier than usual, and Mary Elizabeth was quiet and withdrawn. What was the matter with everybody?

His brothers seemed either not to notice or not to care.

"And then Rachel came over and delivered the baby," Matthew finished his story with a grin and sat back in his chair.

Rachel turned from the pot she was stirring on the stove to give them all another of her too-big smiles. "I didn't do anything more than hold Annie's hand. She was so brave."

"A *boppli*," Mary Elizabeth said in wonderment. "I'd like to pay Annie a visit today. Maybe stay for a while if she needs some help."

"I'll take you after while." Her father said the words but looked at no one in particular.

"I'm heading that way this afternoon," Rachel chirped. "You can ride with me if'n you like."

Mary Elizabeth nodded, head down, eyes hidden. "That would be *gut*."

Simon bit back a groan. Rachel was already chasing Mary Elizabeth away, and she hadn't even been back for one day!

"Mawy, you need to see the goats." Samuel beamed. He was happy because now he had everything—Katie Rose next door, Mary Elizabeth back, and Rachel who tended his every need.

Simon frowned. Samuel was far too young to understand what was going on.

"How about we do that right after breakfast?"

Samuel beamed again.

The whole family was falling apart. Simon had to do something about it.

And soon.

Rachel escaped the kitchen as soon as she could. Thankfully her goats arrived in the big livestock truck giving her the perfect excuse to leave the room, and the tension, behind.

Gabriel hadn't said two words to her. The magic of the night was over. She could see the look of remorse in his eyes, though she was more than thankful that he didn't say the words out loud. Hadn't told her what a mistake he had made last night. It was one thing to know it, another all together to hear it from his lips.

She'd had big hopes after the night they'd shared. He might not love her, but at least their marriage was now on a proper footing. Then the light of day had intruded.

What did you expect? she chastised. It was beyond fanciful to believe that one night as his wife in every sense of the word would change his feelings for her. She knew where his heart lay the moment that door closed behind them. But she had hoped against hope that that the morning would come and things would be different . . . loving . . . everything a marriage should be.

A fool, that's what she was, she thought as she watched the goats frolic in the warm sunshine. More than a fool.

As if it were not enough to have Gabriel avoiding her to the point where he couldn't even look directly at her, she'd had to face his daughter as well. There was no way around it—Mary Elizabeth had to have noticed Rachel's things in her room. Her *fracks*, prayer *kapps*, her *grossmammi's* quilt on the bed. There was no hiding the fact that she had been sleeping there.

But not last night.

"They're so *schpass*," Mary Elizabeth said, smiling at the playful beasts.

Rachel couldn't help but return her grin. The goats were pretty creatures, so useful and *gut*.

"Do you think Annie needs help with Baby Michelle?"

Rachel shrugged. "You don't have to stay there if'n you don't want to. This is your home."

But Mary Elizabeth was already shaking her head before Rachel could finish her statement. She heaved a great sigh. "Nothing's the same."

"It never is."

Mary Elizabeth tossed the end of her ponytail over her shoulder and stared out at the pasture. She was still dressed in the green T-shirt and blue jeans from the day before, but had covered her head with a kerchief akin to the Beachy Amish. She sighed again, this one shaky and rough as if she was on the verge of tears.

A million horrible deeds at the hands of the *Englisch* flashed through Rachel's mind. She pushed back the thoughts. There was no sense in jumping to conclusions. Best to keep calm. Right now

Mary Elizabeth needed her. "Do you want to talk about it?" What better way to ignore her own problems than by concentrating on someone else's?

Mary Elizabeth shook her head. "There's not much to talk about."

"Something happened while you were gone."

"Nothing bad. Just . . . it wasn't like I thought it would be." She wiped a tear from her cheek. "I thought it would be so special. I would go and finish school. But *Englisch* school is different."

Rachel nodded, though she had no idea how the schools compared.

"The other kids made fun of me." Her voice hitched on a sob.

She wrapped an arm around Mary Elizabeth's shoulders and gave her a quick hug. "You're home now."

A sad laugh escaped the young girl. "But it's not the same. I can't be who I was before. All I wanted was to study to take care of animals, and I can't do that. I don't know who I am anymore."

Rachel had felt the same way when she moved from Florida, and again when she married Gabriel. She had felt exactly like that when she'd awakened in his bed this morning. "You're the same person you were when you left."

Mary Elizabeth smiled through her tears. "If only that were true."

And if only Rachel could believe it for herself.

※ ◎

She had cried.

Gabriel stuck the pitchfork into the hay with more force than necessary. He had taken her into his bed, and she had cried.

He hadn't been loving enough. He'd let his feelings rule his head. He had suppressed all his grief and anger and a hundred other emotions for so long, and they had broken free, bubbled to the surface, and he had made a mistake.

He spread the hay around, wondering why he was doing Simon's chores. *Because he needed to get away from the house, needed to keep busy, needed to forget her tears on his shoulder.*

He had avoided Rachel all morning. Not the most mature of actions, but he found himself in a difficult spot. He just needed time was all. Time to figure out what to say to her, which words to use to convey how sorry he was that he'd broken their agreement. How much he regretted that moment of weakness. How unfair he'd been.

But he didn't know where to start.

With a sigh, he braced his elbow on the handle of the pitchfork and surveyed his work. Done. He'd completed every task he could, and he had no more excuses to avoid her. He shouldn't have made those promises if he wasn't going to keep them. "Ah. Becca. What have I done?"

The very last thing he wanted to do was compare the two of them, but it was so hard not to. Rebecca had been such a big part of his life. Now Rachel was. He'd made so many mistakes, but he couldn't let this happen again.

Alone there in the barn, Gabriel dropped his head and prayed for direction and forgiveness. But the one he needed to beg forgiveness from was outside those big wooden doors.

If he thought it unfair to her last night, his actions this morning were more than unjust. He should apologize, even if he could find no reason for his lapse. No reason more than he was weak, overwhelmed, so tired of fighting his every thought. He owed her that much.

He hung the pitchfork on the wall and blinked as he made his way out into the bright sunlight. There was his bride, hitching up the carriage to take Mary Elizabeth over to see Baby Michelle.

"*Oi*, Rachel."

She stopped, momentarily shading her eyes as he neared. Then she went back to her task. He supposed he deserved her indifference. That was exactly what he'd given her this day.

"Can I have a word, please?"

She nodded, then turned to Mary Elizabeth. "If'n you get the buggy loaded, we'll leave after I talk with your father."

Mary Elizabeth looked from one of them to the other, then gave a small nod. Her shoes slapped against the heels of her feet as she went back into the house to get the food and gifts they were taking to Gideon and Annie.

Rachel turned her attention to him. "*Jah?*" She looked the same, hair defying the confines of her bun and prayer covering, but her mouth was pinched tight and her eyes cool.

"I was hoping that you could do me a favor today."

"*Jah.*"

He wasn't certain if it was an agreement or a question. Still he plunged forward. "Mary Elizabeth . . . she . . . I think she sorely misses her mother."

Rachel nodded. "Any young girl would."

He remembered that Rachel had lost her mother at a young age as well. "Would you talk to her today? About what happened while she was gone?"

"You mean us?" Her voice cracked on the last word.

Gabriel shook his head. "No, I mean what she was doing. She's not the same girl that left."

"She and I have already talked. I can tell you more when I get back."

He hid his surprise that Mary Elizabeth would confide in Rachel before she even talked to him. "That would be *gut*."

She turned to leave and go to the buggy, but he caught her arm.

She looked down at his fingers then back into his eyes. "Yes?"

She seemed so calm and composed, not at all the emotional woman he'd held the night before.

"I'm . . . I'm sorry about last night. I overstepped my bounds. It won't happen again."

She swallowed hard and gave a firm nod. Then she tugged her arm from his grasp and swung herself into the driver's seat.

As if she'd been waiting just inside the door, Mary Elizabeth came back out of the house, a basket of goodies swinging from one arm. She gave him a stern nod and climbed into the buggy next to Rachel. Neither one of them so much as cast him a glance before Rachel clicked the reins. The buggy headed toward the road, leaving Gabriel to wonder when everything had fallen to pieces.

～◎ ◎～

Rachel wasn't sure she could love a child more than Baby Michelle. The *boppli* was perfect in every way—silky cap of black hair, eyes bluer than the sky. She was her mother all over again, and just as sweet.

"Oh, Annie." Mary Elizabeth cuddled the baby close, tears glistening in her eyes. "She is so beautiful."

Annie beamed. It seemed motherhood agreed with her. Who could have imagined that a woman of such wealth and leisure would have turned out to be such a great Plain mother?

Rachel blinked as tears of her own stung her eyes. A *boppli*. What a blessing. She had never really given children a whole lot of thought growing up. Getting married and having a family was almost guaranteed.

Yet it wasn't. She had never wondered about the course of her life. Until now.

She tried to push away the image of Gabriel's face this morning, but it resurfaced like a bobber thrown into deep water. She had failed. Now here she was, wholly inadequate and incredibly in love. Her heart had been set up for failure from the start. What had she been thinking to marry a man who was still in love with his deceased wife? There was no way she could compete with those kinds of feelings.

Trust in the Lord, her aunt would have said. Rachel wanted to trust that everything was going to turn out just fine. But what if she had forced her hand and not trusted in what God wanted for her. What if she had gone against His wishes and stayed in Oklahoma instead of moving to Ohio? What if—

"What do you think, Rachel?"

"*Jah?*" She looked from Annie to Mary Elizabeth and back again. "What do I think about what?"

"What do you think about Lizzie coming to stay here for a while?"

"Just to help with the baby," Mary Elizabeth added quickly. "Unless you need to me stay . . ." Her statement should have included "please don't" for it hung in the air unsaid like a lingering wisp of smoke.

Rachel stiffened her spine. She had to trust the Lord, despite her doubts. "I . . ." She shook her head. "You don't have to do that on account of me."

"I'm not. I just . . . I mean, we don't have very much room, and Annie could use the help." She gave her an expectant look. "Right, Annie?"

Rachel felt those exotic lavender eyes scan her face. "There's something different about you today."

"Pshaw," Rachel said a little too loudly. Baby Michelle jumped, then snuggled back into her blanket, her pink cherub mouth working in her sleep.

Annie looked from one to the other. "What's going on here?"

Rachel shook her head. "Nothing."

Mary Elizabeth nodded in agreement. "Nothing at all."

"Uh-huh." Annie continued to study them, no doubt looking for a crack in the façade. "I could use some help. But I don't want to take you away from your father. You know, he blames me for you leaving."

Mary Elizabeth shook her head. "I'm sorry, Annie."

"He had to blame someone, why not me?"

"I could stay and help," Rachel offered. "Maybe should have offered before now."

"No, it's not that," Mary Elizabeth protested. "I didn't mean to take your bed last night."

"It's *allrecht*," Rachel said, but she could feel Annie's inquisitive gaze on her.

"If she slept in your bed, where did you sleep?"

"If you must know, I slept on the couch." Heat rose into her cheeks as she said the words. They were true. Mostly.

"I see." But her words sounded even more suspicious. "It's up to you, Lizzie. You can stay if you want. I'll deal with your father if he has a problem. It'll be good to have help and to be able to catch up." She turned to Rachel. "And you need to stay home. Samuel doesn't need so many upheavals."

But Rachel had the feeling that Samuel had nothing to do with the sparkling look in Annie's eyes.

～☙ ❧～

Simon grabbed the grasshopper and carefully placed him in the shoe box with the others. It'd do no *gut* if he accidentally tore the insect's legs and it couldn't jump. He spied another and chased after it, aware that someone had turned their buggy down the dirt lane that led to their *haus*.

He shaded his eyes and looked toward the road. Rachel was home . . . and without Mary Elizabeth.

Simon wanted to sit down in the grass and cry. His sister had barely made it back before Rachel had convinced her to leave again. His only hope was that his *dat* would be so upset that Mary Elizabeth had been carted off to his *onkel's* house that he would go and get her himself. Simon wasn't supposed to know, but he'd heard his *dat* talking to his *grossdaadi* about his *Englisch aenti*. His *dat* wouldn't want Mary Elizabeth anywhere near Annie. He thought she was a bad influence.

Simon wasn't sure exactly what that meant, but if it was bad, he was certain that Rachel was worse.

He remembered his father's strange reactions that morning. How no one hardly spoke at the breakfast table, and none of the adults seemed to look at each other. Something strange was going on and he couldn't trust anybody to do like they should. Everyone was acting *kshpassich*. He'd have to take care of this himself.

He plucked up another grasshopper and deposited it in the shoebox.

Poor Mary Elizabeth. She was sad this morning. No doubt because Rachel had come to take her place. Matthew didn't seem to care. He just kept saying that it was their father's business, and Simon should stay out of it.

But he couldn't. He couldn't stand by and let Rachel chase off his sister and his mother's memory.

He scooped up another grasshopper for his growing collection. A few more in the box, and he would make his move.

17

Ruth stood and looked around the table. "I have an announcement to make."

Rachel's heart skipped a beat. Everyone else seemed to feel the same for a quick hush fell over the family. It had been two days since her night with Gabriel. Two days of walking around on eggshells and pretending her heart wasn't breaking in two. Now this . . .

"I know we gathered here to celebrate Mary Elizabeth's return. But, well, since everyone's together I need to talk to you." All eyes on her, she took a deep breath. "I found another lump."

Katie Rose gasped, slapping a hand over her mouth as Zane Carson pulled her close, his natural reaction showing that instead of being born into the Amish, he had converted.

Annie stilled from bouncing the fussy Baby Michelle who, as if sensing the importance of the moment, quieted as well.

Abram half rose from his chair as he reached across the table toward his wife. "Perhaps the *kinder* should go outside."

Ruth closed her eyes and shook her head. "I wasn't going to say anything. I wasn't going to do anything, but Rachel—" Those green eyes met hers and filled with tears. "Annie, I'm sorry I wasn't there to help bring Baby Michelle into the world. I'd gone into Tulsa for a doctor's appointment. He ran some tests. I got the results back today."

"And?" Gideon asked the question that was on everybody's lips.

"It is benign." Ruth exhaled as if she had been holding her breath the entire time.

In fact, everyone breathed a heavy sigh of relief and thanks. At the far end of the table, Noni, Abram's beloved mother, bowed her head and prayed.

"That's *gut*. That's *gut*." Abram made his way around the table to take his wife's hands into his own. "Why were you not going to tell us?"

"I prayed about it day and night, but I knew I couldn't go through that kind of treatment again. Rachel convinced me that we needed to know regardless of the outcome."

Abram's gaze swung to her. "Thank you, Rachel Fisher. You have done us a great service."

She shook her head, unable to speak through her tears. She had done nothing but pester Ruth into going to the doctor. Now she was so incredibly thankful that she had.

"Come, we'll have a special Bible reading then pie, *jah*?"

Ruth laughed through her tears. "*Jah*, that would be *gut*."

As if one unit, the family rose from the table and gathered around the rocking chair in the living room. Abram started to read.

Und der Friede Gottes regiere in euren Herzen, zu
welchem ihr auch berufen seid in einem Leibe; und seid
dankbar! Lasset das Wort Christi unter euch reichlich
wohnen in aller Weisheit; lehret und vermahnet euch

selbst mit Psalmen und Lobgesängen und geistlichen
lieblichen Liedern und singt dem HERRN in eurem
Herzen. Und alles, was ihr tut mit Worten oder mit
Werken, das tut alles in dem Namen des HERRN Jesu,
und danket Gott und dem Vater durch ihn.

Colossians chapter 3. One of her favorite passages.

> And let the peace of the Messiah, to which you
> were also called in one body control your hearts. Be
> thankful. Let the message about the Messiah dwell
> richly among you, teaching you and admonishing
> one another in all wisdom, and singing psalms,
> hymns and spiritual songs, with gratitude in your
> hearts to God. And whatever you do, in word or
> deed, do everything in the name of the Lord Jesus,
> giving thanks to God the Father through Him.

As Rachel looked around the room at the faces there, this family who had taken her in, her husband who had pledged himself to her without love or bitterness, she was thankful. So thankful that she could be a part of something so grand.

Aemen.

Rachel slipped into the kitchen and behind Ruth as she sliced the pie. "I'm so glad you went to the doctor."

Her mother-in-law turned and gave her a hug. "So am I." She patted Rachel's hand and went back to slicing. "How are things with you and Gabriel?"

She would have given about anything she owned to stop the blush creeping into her cheeks. The heat alone was enough to singe the edges of the pie Ruth cut. "I think the *buwe* are getting used to me." She kept her head down, her eyes on the task of getting down plates.

"That's not what I'm talking about."

Rachel sighed. "I know."

Ruth raised one expressive brow.

"He still loves Rebecca."

Ruth nodded. "He may at that, but my Gabriel is a smart man."

Rachel sighed. "It has been my experience that brains don't often become involved in matters of the heart."

Ruth shot her a cryptic smile. "You might be surprised."

Rachel wished she had some of Ruth's positive opinion. Gabriel loved Rebecca. He had all but called their night together a mistake. She was glad he hadn't. For sure and for certain that would have broken her heart clean in two.

Ruth led the way out of the kitchen, carrying the sliced-up dessert on a large tray. "Time for pie."

Samuel scrambled down from Mary Elizabeth's lap and ran to the table. "Come on. Time for pie."

His sister laughed as he motioned for her to follow him. Other than their visit to see Baby Michelle, it was the first smile Rachel had seen from her.

Before this week, Rachel had never spent much time with Mary Elizabeth. They had lived in separate districts, though she had the occasion to run across the young girl from time to time. Clover Ridge wasn't Lancaster. There were only about six hundred in their settlement. The times she had been around Mary Elizabeth Fisher, she had seen a bright girl, charming and sweet, full of energy and smiles. This Mary Elizabeth was vastly different: withdrawn, somber, not at all the *maedel* she remembered.

Mary Elizabeth acted as if she didn't belong. Rachel had hoped her spending time at her *onkel's* house with Annie and the baby would bring a sparkle back into her smile, but so far her plan was failing.

Maybe a new dress was in order. Mary Elizabeth had lost weight while she'd been out with the *Englisch*, and her *fracks* all hung loose on her frame. At least she had taken to wearing a dress again along with a prayer *kapp* and apron. But how could she feel that she was truly the girl who had left if the clothes she wore back then were too big for her now?

Rachel knew just the fabric too. She had been planning on making new shirts for Matthew and Gabriel. But that could wait. She had found a better use for the fabric. Tomorrow after morning chores, she'd send for Mary Elizabeth and perhaps then she could put a smile back on her face.

❧ ☙

"Rachel?"

At the sound of Mary Elizabeth's voice, Rachel called down the stairs, "Up here." She had been so excited to start the dress she hadn't waited on Mary Elizabeth to show. Instead she'd thrown a batch of cookies in the oven to bake and ran up the stairs to work on the dress. She was proud of her plan to use one of Mary Elizabeth's old dresses as a pattern. She had carefully laid the fabric and pattern on the bed and started to cut it out. A couple more snips and she'd be ready to start sewing it together and fitting it.

"What are you doing?" Mary Elizabeth asked.

Rachel spun around, her smile stretching her face. "I'm making you a dress."

"Me?"

"*Jah. Kumm guck.*" She held up a piece she had already cut out. "I used one of your old dresses for a pattern." As she said the words, another piece of fabric fell to the floor. This one wasn't the blue of the fabric or the green of the dress pattern, but the vibrant red and orange of the quilt underneath.

It took several beats for Rachel to realize what had happened. "Oh, no." She started picking up the pieces of pattern and fabric, searching the quilt underneath for damage. "Oh no, oh no, oh no."

"*Was iss letz?*"

Rachel sank down on the bed holding the pieces of fabric in her hands. Tears welled in her eyes, but she blinked them back. Why was she so *dabbich*? Why couldn't she do anything right?

"Rachel?"

Tears wouldn't bring back her grandmother's quilt. She sighed. "I cut the quilt top when I was cutting out your dress. She held up the scraps for Mary Elizabeth to see.

Mary Elizabeth blinked once, then started laughing.

"I don't see what's so funny," Rachel scolded as her own laughter bubbled up inside her.

"You're a worse Amish woman than I am." Mary Elizabeth wiped the tears of mirth from her face.

Rachel sobered, pretending that she was offended by the words. "I wouldn't know."

"Trust me. Just ask Annie about me teaching her how to make chicken pot pie."

Rachel grimaced. "That bad?"

Mary Elizabeth nodded. "What's that smell?"

"The cookies!" Rachel jumped from the bed and raced down the stairs. Smoke had already filled the kitchen.

Mary Elizabeth threw open the windows and the back door as Rachel pulled the crispy black discs from the oven. They were still smoking when she tossed them out into the grass.

What else could go wrong today?

Joseph appeared around the side of the house, Samuel on his

heels. "Look what we found." In one hand he held a wriggling baby snake.

Rachel recoiled. "Joseph Fisher, get rid of that snake this instant."

"It's not poisonous. I don't think."

"You shouldn't get close enough to them to find out. Now go." She withheld her shiver of revulsion until he had released the snake at the edge of the woods.

Raising boys was certainly a challenge. At least snakes couldn't jump.

She carried the blackened cookie sheet back to the house and laid it on the sink. It would take a *gut* scrubbing to get all the burn marks off of it. But that could wait until after dinner. Right now all she wanted to do was get back upstairs to work on Mary Elizabeth's dress.

"Rachel, Rachel. *Guck, guck!*"

"*Ei, yi, yi!* What now?"

Simon raced in the front door, an old shoe box in his hands. "This came for you."

"For me?"

"*Jah*, open it."

"Who brought it?" she asked, shifting the box into one hand so she could pry the lid off with the other.

Simon danced around impatiently. "Just open it."

"*Jah. Jah.*" She wedged the lid free and screamed.

Hundreds of grasshoppers leapt in the air.

Nay, thousands, it seemed.

Rachel dropped the box in the living room floor, screaming like a banshee while she frantically brushed the horrible insects from her dress. Her face. Her hair. She ran out the front door, still screaming as she closed it behind her tight.

Breathing heavy, she managed to get all of the bugs off her and not have a heart attack at the same time. But there was no way she was going back into that house again. No way a'tall.

Two hours later, she was still on the front porch when Gabriel arrived home.

❧❧ ❧❧

Gabriel could see something was wrong the minute he pulled his buggy to a stop in front of the house. His wife was sitting on the front porch looking more *strubbly* than usual.

"Rachel." He gave her a nod of greeting, instinctively knowing something was wrong. It was written there in the rigid set of her shoulders, the brittle line of her lips.

"Gabriel." She dipped her chin in return. "How was your morning?"

"*Gut, gut.*" He saw it for what it was: a polite introduction into whatever was bothering her.

"We've had quite a time here." She looked off toward the pasture, her expression as far away as the grazing cows. "I burned the cookies."

He scratched his head just under the line of his hat band, then settled it back in place. What way did that make today's cookies different than yesterday's? "It's okay."

She nodded. "I can't go in the house. We are infested with grasshoppers."

So that's what this was all about. She had seen a grasshopper in the house and was now afraid. "If'n you saw a grasshopper, I'm sure it's gone by now."

She shook her head, then closed her eyes and shuddered. "*Ach,* there was more than one."

"How do know this, Rachel Fisher?" He hid his smile. He was growing accustomed to her name on his lips.

"Because Simon gave me a shoebox full of them. I opened it . . . and now they are everywhere in the house." Despite her aversion to all things that jumped, she managed to say the words with barely a tremble in her voice.

"The *buwe* did this."

"They've been . . . testing me ever since I moved in."

"What do you mean by that?"

She shrugged. "Little things. Stains on the laundry, dirt in the house, a box with a frog in it. Just little things."

He'd been so bent on adjusting to Rachel that he hadn't noticed all that was transpiring in his house. "I'll go talk to them."

She stood and placed one hand on his arm. "*Nay*. Don't."

"They should not be treating you this way."

"Do you think they will like me any more if they are punished for this?"

He stopped, propped his hands on his hips, and exhaled. "*Nay*, but you are my wife now. They should treat you with courtesy and respect."

She looked up at him, searching his face with those big eyes. "How do you expect them to treat me as such when you don't?"

Her words cut like a hot knife through butter, quick and searing. "I never meant to show you disrespect."

"I know. It's just the situation we find ourselves in."

He gave a quick nod.

"I was aware when I walked into this marriage, that you still harbored feelings for your wife."

"Rachel, I—"

She raised a hand to stop the flow of his words. "Please. Let me finish."

He exhaled, trying to dispel the pent-up emotions bubbling inside him.

"Your sons do not know, and they are afraid of losing their mother."

"They've already lost her."

Rachel's lips trembled and a sad little smile appeared. "*Nay*, they have not. You have kept her alive and well in your own way."

"I—"

"I am not criticizing." She shook her head. "Nor am I willing to ignore the truth."

"What would you have me to do?"

She got that faraway look again, and he had to resist the urge to see what was so intriguing on the horizon. "You'll find a time to tell them how you feel about their mother and also about this marriage. When it comes, just promise me that you will take it. For their sakes."

She had been chased out of her house by the one thing she feared the most. What could he do but agree? "*Jah*, then. I will."

"What did you do?"

Simon cringed as Matthew cornered him in the barn.

"*Nix, nix.*" Yet he felt a stirring in his heart at the lie. "I gave her a shoebox full of grasshoppers."

"That is why she left to spend the night with *grossmammi* and *grossdaadi*?"

"I guess, *jah*."

Matthew visibly relaxed, and Simon breathed a sigh of relief. His brother was not above twisting his ear if he felt it would keep him in line. "Why would you do that when you know she is afraid of things that hop?"

Simon stared at his feet. "It was just a joke."

"Joke or not, she is gone for the night. Now it is up to you to make sure she comes back tomorrow."

He jerked his head up to stare at his brother in disbelief. "But—"

"*Nay*. Tomorrow. She comes back, or I will tell *Dat* about all the jokes you have played on her."

The next evening, Gabriel looked around the table at his wife and his children. All were there, except Mary Elizabeth, but she had at least returned home, back with the Plain people where she belonged.

His dinner was cooked fine without a burnt taste or the smell of scorched in the air. The *haus* was clean, and his wife even looked a little more presentable this eve.

He and Matthew had rounded up all the grasshoppers and had Simon take them far into the pasture before releasing them. Simon had apologized to Rachel, and the world had settled down.

For the first time since marrying Rachel, his world seemed to be going along right smooth. Annie's baby was fine and healthy, his *mudder* still cancer free, and soon Zane Carson would marry Katie Rose.

Life was *gut*.

Maybe this was one of those moments that Rachel was talking about. A perfect moment that could not be shaken by a little truth.

But he couldn't risk the peace that had descended on them. He'd talk to the *buwe* later. Right now he wanted to say a prayer of thanks and savor the moment.

18

Rachel wiped the sweat from her brow with the back of her hand and set back to milking Sundae. The brown and white doe that Gabriel had bought her at the auction had quickly turned into her favorite. Funny disposition, eager to play, and so gentle Samuel could ride her around the pasture.

"Can I wide now? Can I?" He tapped Rachel on the shoulder for the umpteenth time in so many seconds.

"Not, yet, *liebschdi*. Let me finish getting her milk. Would you like to help?"

He shook his head. "I wanna wide."

Rachel swiped at her forehead once again. She must be coming down with something. She'd felt terrible all day. All week. Ever since church last Sunday when Beth Troyer had offered her a piece of mince pie. One look at the sweet treat, and she hadn't been the same since. It was strange, indeed. She'd always had a fondness for mince pie.

She stopped, pressing a hand against her churning stomach. Maybe some buttermilk would settle it down. That would have to wait a minute. She wanted to get finished with Sundae before she stopped. She had just been so tired lately. No doubt it was the heat and whatever bug was ailing her. It had been unseasonably warm with the temperature reaching nearly one hundred degrees even though it was just June. If July was much worse, she didn't know how she'd be able to stand it.

"Rachel?" Simon called around the side of the house. "We're going down to the creek."

She cast a glance back over her shoulder. Simon, Joseph, and David stood at the side of the house, fishing poles over their shoulders. "Are your chores done?"

"*Jah*." David nodded, and the rest followed suit.

"Fine, then. But don't stay gone too long."

"I wanna go." Samuel jumped up and down, excited at the prospect of spending the afternoon with his older siblings.

Rachel moved the bucket out from under Sundae so she wouldn't kick it over. She released the goat back into the pasture. "You don't want to go for a ride?"

Samuel looked from his brothers to the goats and back again. "I wanna go fish."

If Samuel went with his brothers, she could lay down on the couch and catch up on her rest. With any luck she'd feel better by supper. And definitely back to herself by tomorrow.

The thought was selfish.

She shook her head. As tempting as it was, it was not a *gut* idea. "*Nay*, Samuel. You don't know how to swim."

"I don't wanna swim. I wanna catch some *fisch*."

Her resolve slipped a notch, and she yanked it back in place. "You would be in a world of hurt if'n you fell in."

"Awh," Simon interjected. "Me and Joseph can swim. Besides, we haven't had any rain in weeks. The creek is so low it barely covers our feet."

"It couldn't be that low or the fish would all be dead." She looked back to Samuel's eager face.

"Pwease, Wachel. Pwease." He danced in place so anxious to follow after his *bruders*.

She looked to Simon who nodded importantly. "We'll look after him."

"Who's going to look after you?" She asked the question, but she was just so tired. Too tired to argue with four determined *buwe*. An afternoon's rest in the cool house was almost more than she could stand.

"We'll look out for each other."

Against her better judgment, Rachel nodded. Samuel was getting older now. He needed a few more freedoms, and his brothers wouldn't let anything happen to him. "Fine," she said with a sigh. "Just stay out of the creek."

Samuel danced a little jig and threw his arms around her neck. "*Danki*, Wachel. *Danki*."

"Mind your brothers."

"I will. *Ich liebe dich*."

Tears of exhaustion filled her eyes. "I love you too."

It was his scream that woke her an hour and a half later.

She jackknifed into a sitting position, hardly aware that she had been asleep. She must have been more tired than she realized.

Then the scream sounded again.

"Samuel?" She jumped to her feet, her heart plummeting as he continued to cry. But they say a mother can tell the difference in her child's cries and this one meant he was hurt. Bad.

"Samuel!" She tore out of the house, not stopping until she reached the edge of the yard. If he was screaming and crying he wasn't drowning. He was still taking air, and that was a *gut* thing. Or so she told herself.

She crashed through the woods nearly colliding with Joseph as he ran to get her. Tears streamed down his face, leaving little tracks in the dirt on his sunburned cheeks.

"Rachel, Rachel," he sobbed. "It's Samuel. *Mach schnell.* Please hurry!"

Dread filled her and propelled her faster and faster through the woods. Branches pulled at her dress and snagged in her prayer *kapp* and hair, but she continued to run, following Joseph as he stumbled along. "What happened?"

He shook his head, so winded from his sprint that he couldn't form the words to tell her.

A giant fist squeezed her heart. "Please, God, let him be okay. Please let him be okay."

Finally the trees thinned, Samuel's cries grew louder in her ears and suddenly she found herself on the mossy bank of a small creek.

Simon and David crouched near a fallen log on the other side, Samuel on the ground between them.

They muttered nonsensical words in *Deutsch*, tears on their cheeks as they patted their *bruder*, trying to console him.

"Samuel!" They turned at her voice, gratitude and relief shining in their eyes.

Rachel splashed through the creek and to the other side, not bothering to take off her shoes as she crashed through the cold water. "What happened? *Was iss letz?*" she asked, dropping down beside them.

Samuel twisted on the ground, crying and cradling one hand in the other. Blood stained his shirt, smeared his face.

"*Shlange.*"

The word sent panic searing through her. *Snake.*

She had a hundred questions on the tip of her tongue, but all she could think about was getting Samuel to a *doktah*.

She gathered him in her arms, his body hot to the touch. "Wachel," he managed to sob through the tears. It was next to impossible to determine how much of his reaction was from panic or pain, but Rachel feared the worst.

She'd no more lifted him off the ground when he turned his head and vomited.

"It's going to be *allrecht*," she crooned as she started out of the woods. But she was unfamiliar with the path. "Simon, you need to lead us out of here and quickly. Do you understand?"

Tearful and frightened, Simon nodded. "This way."

She followed Simon through the woods, praying with every step even as she struggled under the weight of Samuel's prone body. He was conscious and moaning, crying her name as she raced toward the house.

Lord, please let him be okay. Please don't let anything happen to him. Please, please, please . . .

It seemed like an eternity before they finally broke through the thicket and back into the yard. Thankfully, the laundry wagon was still next to the line. She gently laid Samuel inside.

Eyes closed, he blindly grabbed for her. "Wachel, don't leave. Don't leave me."

Tears filled her eyes at his request. He wouldn't be in this state had it not been for her. If she hadn't've let him go down to the creek with his brothers.

"I'm not going to leave you." She choked on the words, biting back tears that would serve no purpose. She had to remain calm for both of their sakes. "We're just going for a little ride, *jah*?"

"*Jah*, okay."

She brushed his sweaty hair back off his forehead, hating that he already seemed feverish. There was no time to waste. "I need you to be quiet and still. Can you do that?"

"*Jah*." His voice was thready and weak. He was about to lose consciousness.

Maybe that was for the best. The poison wouldn't spread as quickly if she could keep him still.

"Here we go." She wiped the tears from her face and grabbed up the handle.

She couldn't walk fast enough. She had only one destination in mind and that was Ruth and Abram's. She could get there on foot much quicker than if she took the time to hitch up the buggy. John Paul had a car. He could take them into town, to the doctor.

She just couldn't run fast enough.

Her breathing was ragged by the time she reached Ruth and Abram's *haus*. But she couldn't take the time to catch her breath. She needed to get Samuel tended to and quick.

She ran up the stairs, her breathing raspy as she knocked on the front door. But no one came. She knocked again, louder, more raps. Someone had to be home. They just had to be. She knocked again, nearly doubled over in her attempts to catch her breath.

The door swung open, and Ruth was there. "Rachel, *was iss letz*?"

"It's Samuel," a voice behind her supplied. *Simon*. Simon had followed her all the way to his grandparents' *haus*, and she hadn't realized he was with her. Her attention had been completely wrapped up in the unconscious boy bleeding in the laundry wagon. "He got snake bit."

Ruth flew into action. "Simon, go find John Paul. He's down by the barn somewhere. Tell him to come. *Mach schnell*."

Simon nodded and raced off.

"Rachel, let's get him in the car. That way you can leave as soon as John Paul gets back to the house."

Rachel nodded and pulled the wagon back across the road.

Behind the phone shanty, where Abram didn't have to look at

it, sat John Paul's faded blue car. By *Englisch* standards it wasn't a nice car, but it would sure go faster than a buggy pulled by a horse.

"Easy." Ruth helped Rachel load Samuel into the back of the vehicle. His head lolled to one side, his breathing swallow and wheezy.

Rachel slid into the back seat next to him, cradling his head in her lap. She kept his neck straight, his airway open even as she ran her fingers through his bright red hair. He was such a sweet and precious child.

Please don't let him die. Lord, I know Your will is above all else, but please don't let him die.

She didn't even have a chance to say *aemen* before John Paul slid into the front seat. "*Ach*, Rachel. Hold on. We'll get him into the doctor."

She nodded as he cranked the car, and for the first time since this nightmare started she let her tears flow.

"Hold on, *shveshtah*. He's going to be okay."

She looked up and met John Paul's steady gaze in the mirror. Normally full of mischief and delight, his expression was solemn and sad. His lack of confidence did nothing to bolster hers.

"We have the car," he said, as if knowing she needed more reassurance. "We'll take him into Pryor. They have a bigger hospital."

She nodded. Chouteau was a better idea than Clover Ridge and Pryor a better one than Chouteau. The few miles distance would be nothing when compared to the speed of the car. They would make it. For his sake they had to.

She hated riding, but it was excruciating sitting there with Samuel, knowing that his death would be on her hands. She should have never let him go down to the creek with his brothers.

His skin felt clammy to the touch, but thankfully he hadn't thrown up since they had loaded him into the wagon. That had to be *gut, jah*? As much as she tried to console herself, she knew that it was all her fault.

"I'm sorry, Samuel." She closed her eyes against the image of his pale face, his shiny hair such a contrast to the pasty skin. Even his freckles seemed to stand out more.

Don't let this be the last time I see his face, she prayed. *I'll do anything. Just please don't let him die.*

When they pulled into the Emergency Room entrance, a team with a stretcher was waiting for them. Most likely Ruth had called from the phone shanty to let them know that Samuel would be there soon. Rachel almost hated letting them take him from her as they loaded Samuel onto the gurney. They wheeled him inside, doctors and nurses hovering around him.

She exhaled, near bereft as they disappeared behind swooshing glass doors.

An arm came around her. "Come on, Rachel. They need some information from us."

John Paul turned her around and led her back to the front desk. She could feel the eyes of the other patients and families on her as she sat down in front of the admissions desk and started filling in the appropriate paperwork.

Name, date of birth, next of kin . . . the list went on and on, driving her near mad with its monotony. Where was Samuel? What were they doing with him?

She returned the clipboard to the woman behind the desk. "How soon till we can see him?"

"I'm sure the doctor will be out to talk to you as soon as possible."

Rachel nodded. That wasn't really an answer, but it was the best she could expect for now.

She returned to her seat by John Paul. He had his elbows braced on his knees, hands clasped together and head bent. Praying.

Closing her eyes, she leaned her head back against the wall and started her own prayers once again.

"Mrs. Fisher?"

Rachel jumped, startled by the voice and the name she had never gotten used to being called.

"*Jah?*"

"I'm Dr. Williams." He was a kindly looking man—dark skin, eyes, and hair. Dressed in green cotton pants and matching shirt, he smelled like toothpaste and antiseptic. He took the seat next to her. His lips pressed together, worry puckering his brow. "We're preparing the helicopter to take Samuel into Tulsa."

A loud buzz started in Rachel's ears. She shook her head to dismiss the sound, but it only grew louder.

"Mrs. Fisher, are you okay?"

"Rachel?"

The words floated to her in a tunnel.

The kind doctor pressed a hand against her back and shoved her head down. "Breathe," he commanded.

Rachel complied. *In, out, in, out,* but she was still seeing gray around the edges of her vision as he started talking again.

"We have him stabilized for the trip. Do you know what kind of snake bit him?"

She shook her head. "*Nay.*"

The good doctor's lips pressed together. "We're treating it like a rattlesnake bite. Whatever it was, he seems to be unusually sensitive."

"Is that why you're sending him to Tulsa?" John Paul asked.

He nodded. "Do you have a way to follow?"

"I can't go with him?" Rachel cried.

John Paul patted her hand. "You hate riding in a car. How are you going to get into a helicopter?"

This was different. "I want to go with him. I *have* to go with him." Rachel grabbed the doctor's arm. "Please, he doesn't speak a lot of *Englisch*. I don't want him to be scared."

The doctor shook his head. "I'm sorry. That's just not possible."

Tears blurred her vision once again. "I don't want him to be scared."

The doctor patted her hand. "He'll be sedated for the flight. He won't even know he's in a helicopter."

She didn't have time to think about what the bishop would say about Samuel flying in a helicopter; it was the only way to save him. It had to be done.

If only she hadn't let him go to the creek. If only . . .

19

This had to be what Gideon felt like when his son, Jamie, was missing. Hollow, numb, yet a white hot pain cut him to the quick.

His Samuel.

Gabriel leaned his head back and closed his eyes. He'd prayed until he couldn't pray any more.

"Another fifteen minutes and we'll be there," Bill Foster said.

Gabriel nodded. When he'd returned home from yet another visit with Beth Troyer, this one concerning her cats getting in her *Englisch* neighbor's garden, he'd found his mother sitting on his porch, silent tears on her cheeks.

His other boys sat around her solemn, quiet and still, and he had immediately known tragedy had struck.

Simon was as composed as a thirteen-year-old could be, recounting the tale.

They had all gone to the creek to fish and play in the cool water. Samuel had been walking along the bank poking a stick into the various holes in the ground. No one had been paying him too much mind until he screamed.

The best they could figure, he had found a snake, a rattler, and decided to pick it up. But the snake had other plans for the day, striking quickly before slithering off into the woods.

Rachel had come to the rescue, carrying Samuel back to the house and onto Ruth and Abram's.

Now Gabriel was on his way to Tulsa to catch up with his wife and son.

"Let's go around back," Bill Foster said, turning the van at the traffic light in front of the big pink building, Saint Francis Hospital. "It'll be quicker than trying to navigate through all that construction."

He gave a quick nod and took a deep breath to calm his nerves.

Samuel was so innocent and sweet, such a joy to his family despite the tragic circumstances surrounding his birth and the handicaps he had to overcome each and every day. Samuel was a blessing for sure and for certain, and Gabriel couldn't imagine life without him.

Bill stopped near the entrance of the Emergency Room. "Go on in. I'll park and catch up with you."

"Thank you, Bill Foster." Gabriel slid from the cab of the van and shut the door behind him. He tried not to look at the helicopter as he made his way across the paved entry. Or think about how serious Samuel's injuries had to be in order for them to warrant a ride in such a machine.

He faltered a step as he walked through the automatic glass doors and past the guard. To the left a woman sat behind a desk. "I'm looking for my son."

She gave a quick nod. "We were wondering when you'd get here, Mr. Fisher. They've taken Samuel to the Children's Hospital."

"Where is that?" He tried to remain calm when he wanted nothing more than to yell and scream until he found his *bu*.

"It's next door. Just go out the way you came in and turn back to the left. Follow the sidewalk on around. You can't miss it."

He gave her a nod. *"Danki."*

How much longer until he found Samuel? He met Bill Foster coming in as he was going back out. "He's at the Children's Hospital."

Bill nodded and they set off around the building.

The bright colors in the Children's Hospital seemed to mock him as he made his way across the room to the check-in desk. His footsteps on the polished floor echoed and made him want to scream at their hollow sound. He wanted to see his boy, make sure he was okay. Only then could he take a breath and relax.

The nurse behind the counter sent them upstairs. Samuel, it seemed, was in surgery. Gabriel could only imagine how terrifying the experience was for him. Alone with strangers.

He saw Rachel the instant he got off the elevator. She sat alone in one of the fabric chairs provided by the hospital. Her head was bowed, her body bent nearly in half as she rocked back and forth.

"Rachel?"

She turned toward him, confusion then relief shining on her features. "Gabriel. I'm so glad you're here."

She was covered in blood, a chunk of her apron torn clean off, her sleeve ripped. She had scratches on her face, no doubt from her sprint through the woods. She looked tired and her big brown eyes swam with tears. She launched herself at him, throwing her arms around him, trembling as she held him close.

As if realizing what she had done, she released him just as quickly and straightened her prayer *kapp*. "They took him to surgery about an hour ago."

He nodded, built-up energy coursing through him. He'd raced to get here to wait once more. He lowered himself into the chair next to his wife.

Bill Foster jingled the change in his pocket. "I'll go find us some coffee."

"*Danki*, Bill Foster."

A few minutes of eternity later, a doctor wearing a cap on his head and those green shirt and pants they seemed to prefer came toward them. The soles of his athletic shoes squeaked against the waxed tiles. "Mr. and Mrs. Fisher."

"*Jah.*" Gabriel nodded in time with Rachel.

"Samuel is in recovery now, but he's got a long road ahead of him. As far as the actual bite is concerned, the poison has been contained, but he has had a bad reaction to it. We're keeping him sedated due to the pain caused by such venom."

Gabriel took a big breath in through his nose and pressed his lips together, just how blessed they were to still have Samuel with them ringing in his ears.

"Typically it's a couple of weeks before such patients are well enough to be released from the hospital," the doctor continued. "Until then, he'll have constant monitoring. We'll do everything in our power to keep him comfortable."

From the corner of his eye, Gabriel saw Rachel wipe away her tears with the back of her hand. He couldn't turn and look at her, knowing that if he did, he'd fall completely apart himself. Instead, he kept his eyes trained on the doctor and hung on his every word.

"He has sustained a great deal of damage to the digits of his right hand. We are particularly concerned about his pinkie and ring fingers."

"What do you mean damage?" Rachel's voice sounded tiny and wounded, as if the injury were on her own hand.

"Snake venom is tricky stuff. Basically, venom of this sort

attaches itself to the blood and changes it, effectively cutting off the supply to the affected area. So in a sense, his fingers have been denied the blood they need to remain healthy. Only time will tell if we got the antivenom to him in time to protect his digits, particularly the two I mentioned."

"When can we see him?" Rachel's question reflected Gabriel's own thoughts. He needed to see his *sohn*, needed to know that he was alive and lying in a hospital bed as he had just been told.

"We're moving him to ICU as we speak, so once he's settled in we'll allow short visits."

"What does ICU mean?" Somehow Gabriel managed to find his voice enough to ask the question, though even as he spoke he had trouble recognizing the words as his own.

"Intensive Care Unit. Samuel is going to need extra careful monitoring until the worst of this has passed."

⚬

The next time Rachel allowed herself tears was one week later when they had to amputate two of Samuel's fingers. She had refused to leave him, sleeping on the couch in the waiting room when visiting hours were up for the day. Bill Foster had brought her extra clothes and taken her bloodstained ones away. Gabriel had stayed as long as he could, coming back every other day to check on the progress.

Rachel knew he loved his son, but she was there and he had five other *kinder* to see about as well as a farm that needed tending. It wasn't his responsibility to see after Samuel—it was hers. *She* had done this to him. If she hadn't let Samuel go down to the creek, if she hadn't been so tired, so selfish in wanting a rest. If . . . if . . . if . . .

Now he was fighting for his life, handicapped beyond even his mental challenges, and it was all her fault.

She looked Samuel over for the countless time that day. He was asleep, still drugged by the doctors to keep him still and quiet while the second dose of antivenom did its work. In a couple more days, they would stop the drugs, re-bandage his hand, and send them home.

Unworthy.

That one word played over and over in her mind. She was unworthy of this child who had loved her so unconditionally. Unworthy of the family God had given her. Unworthy of the blessing He had so generously provided.

Completely unworthy.

Rachel climbed into the back seat of Bill Foster's van and buckled herself in. Samuel had been settled in the front, his seat leaned all the way back so he could rest during the long trip back to Clover Ridge.

In the back, Gabriel climbed in beside her, not even looking her way. Their shoulders touched, as Rachel sat in the middle of the long seat, giving Samuel ample room to recline. His rest was more important than her discomfort. How she hated being so close to Gabriel, yet unable to communicate with him.

It had been a long two weeks, but finally they were going home. Gabriel had hardly said two words to her in those fourteen long days, had hardly spared her a glance.

Not that she could blame him.

Mary Elizabeth was right: She was a terrible Amish woman. She couldn't cook or clean properly. She burned everything from eggs to cookies, her house seemed constantly untidy, and now this. She was woefully lacking in the care of the *kinder*.

But to have Gabriel reflect that attitude toward her was almost more than she could bear.

He had done so much for her: taking her in, giving her a home, marrying her when there was no other choice that would allow her to stay in Clover Ridge. And how had she repaid him? By endangering his son's life.

Then there was this burning love she held in her heart. How stupid to go and fall in love with her husband. They had an agreement, and she had broken it.

She laid her head back against the seat and pretended that she couldn't feel his every breath, didn't love him so much it hurt. The worst part of all was not that he didn't love her in return, but that he held her in such contempt.

Ach, he was a good Amish man. He would never go so far as to say as much, to show her how he felt, but the anger came off him in waves, burning her with its intensity.

How could she live with him now? She couldn't stand the thought of him being mad at her, hating her with his every breath. That he was unable to even look at her spoke volumes about his true feelings, even if he was too godly of a man to say as much.

He had to know that she'd rather die than have anything happen to Samuel. Yet she had let them down, had made a decision that had nearly cost him his life. She couldn't be trusted with *kinder*. Even those who she loved more than life itself.

It was only a matter of time before Gabriel would send her away. Only a matter of time till looking at his son, maimed as a result of her poor choices, was more than he could bear.

Mind made up, she knew what she had to do.

Gabriel settled the still sleeping Samuel into his bed. He propped up his injured arm on an extra pillow to protect it, then pulled the covers up over his son, tucking him in tight, as if that could protect him from further ill.

Then Gabriel sat on the edge of his son's bed and wept.

How close they had come to losing him. How very, very close. Had it not been for Rachel's quick action and thinking—getting him to John Paul and then onto the doctor in time, breaking the *Ordnung* and letting them take him in the helicopter . . .

His heart broke that Samuel's hand was forever altered, forever less than God had made it, but he knew also in his heart of hearts that it could have been so much worse. He owed Rachel so much, owed her more than he could ever repay. Yet he hadn't been able to say those words to her. Hadn't been able to thank her for saving his son's life. The emotions were too raw, too real just yet to share with another. So he'd shoved them down inside until a time when he could deal with them.

Still they burned his insides like flames, clawing at him to get out. He was a man, protector and provider. He couldn't allow emotions to rule above all else. It was not a man's way. It was not the Amish way.

He wiped the tears from his face, planted a kiss on his sleeping son's forehead, then let himself out of the room. He took extra care avoiding Rachel that evening, knowing if faced with her he'd have to bare his soul, and that was something he wasn't prepared to do. Not yet.

Maybe not ever.

20

It took Rachel three days to get everything into place. Three days of holding back her tears, of hiding the pain in her heart. It was a beautiful day, this third day of Samuel's home recovery. The sun shone brightly, birds chirped, growing crops swayed in the warm breeze. She put Samuel down for his afternoon nap, his rest deep and untroubled, aided by the pain pills the doctor had prescribed.

She brushed his hair back from his face, resisting the urge to dot each freckle, trace the shape of his eyes, the line of his nose. Anything and everything to etch his sweet face into her memory. She could only hope that one day he would forgive her. She could only hope that one day she could forgive herself.

"Good-bye, *liebschdi.*" She placed one last kiss on his sleeping cheek, then made her way to her room.

Her suitcase lay on the bed, packed and waiting. It was almost time. The Mennonite driver would soon be waiting for her at the end of the road to take her to the bus station. She hadn't hired Bill Foster, certain that he would try to stop her and that would never do. It was going to be hard enough to walk away from this family that had come to mean so much to her.

That's all she had wanted. Since the accident that had taken her *elders* and *bruders*, a family had become her dream. An unfulfilled one until recently. She had thought in marrying Gabriel she would have the family she had always wanted.

But some things just weren't meant to be.

She should have prayed more, listened with her brain instead of her heart. Just because she wanted something, didn't mean it was part of God's plan for her. This just proved it. Now it was time to do what she should have done from the start.

She would soon be on her way to Ohio.

She pressed a hand to her queasy stomach, the stress of gathering her things together, of doing what she knew she must was getting the better of her. She swallowed back what little breakfast she had eaten.

With a heavy sigh, she picked up the suitcase and turned toward the door.

"What are you doing?"

"Mary Elizabeth!" Rachel dropped her suitcase with a thud and pressed her hand to her heart. "You scared me. What are you doing here?"

"I came to check on you and Samuel."

Rachel nodded and reached for her suitcase handle.

"You didn't answer my question." Mary Elizabeth's voice was firm but full of inquiry.

Rachel pressed her lips together. She thought she had been so clever. She had waited until everyone was gone. Samuel would rest for a solid hour. By then Gabriel would be back, Matthew would come in for *middawk*, and she would be gone.

"Rachel?"

"I'm leaving." On unsteady legs she pushed forward, thinking she would brush past Mary Elizabeth and keep walking until she hit the door. She only made it to the hallway leading to the stairs.

"Why?"

She stopped, unable to take the rest of the steps that would allow her escape. "I can't do it anymore," she said without turning around. "I can't look at Samuel knowing that he would be whole if not for me."

Rachel felt a hand on her arm, the caring of another's touch seeping through the fabric of her dress to warm her. Tears filled her eyes.

"You can't leave. We need you too much."

Rachel managed the courage to turn and face her stepdaughter. She would have liked to have gotten to know her better, to do some quilting and canning together as she did to help her own mother once upon a time. She would have liked to help Mary Elizabeth settle back into the community, to heal from all the disappointments of the *Englisch* world.

"No one here needs me. Matthew is practically a man, and the other boys have been trying to get rid of me from the start." She turned back toward the door.

"What about *Dat*?"

What about Gabriel? He needed a housekeeper, someone to cook and clean, do the laundry, and get the *buwe* to school on time. But that was it.

She had been a fool to take him up on his marriage proposal, a hopeless romantic fool. She could see that so clearly now. She had been too naïve to recognize that it was a disaster waiting to happen. She had forced it, made a relationship where there was none, had fallen in love with a man who said he'd never love again. A hopeless romantic fool.

"He doesn't need me." She started down the stairs, Mary Elizabeth dogging her heels.

"Then why did he marry you?"

Together they burst through the front door nearly side by side. "He needed a housekeeper," Rachel said over her shoulder.

"I don't believe that for a minute."

Rachel kept moving, her words flying into the wind. "It's true. He married me because he needed someone to take care of the house and the *kinder*. The church elders thought it improper for us to be unmarried and under the same roof." Once she got to the drive she started walking faster. She didn't know the driver well and he might not wait for her. He might just as soon leave thinking that she had changed her mind. She had to leave now, while she had the courage to go through with it.

"He could have built you a room on the back. A *dawdihaus*. But he married you."

Rachel didn't want to think about that. How she could have moved in with Ruth and Abram, rented a place in town, or maybe went on to stay with an unmarried widow like Beth Troyer. Instead she had jumped at the proposal, seeing it as pulling her into a family, a replacement for the one she had lost.

She breathed a sigh of relief as she stepped into the county road. There, up ahead, was a blue sedan. Her driver had parked the car on the small shoulder at the end of the cornfield.

"Rachel," Mary Elizabeth's voice filled with concern. "Are you really going through with this?"

She bit back her tears. "I don't have any other choice."

"You could stay."

She shook her head. She couldn't remain in a hopeless marriage. There was too much pain surrounding her. She couldn't look at Samuel's sweet face every day knowing that she had directly caused his disfigurement. She couldn't live with Gabriel knowing that he could never love her. It was too much to ask a person. Entirely too much.

She peered through the passenger side window to the young man she had hired to take her to the bus station.

"Rachel Fisher?" he asked.

She bit back the pain. "*Jah.*" She opened the back door to the car and placed her suitcase inside. She closed it with a thud.

"Rachel, don't do this."

"She going too?" the Mennonite asked, with a nod toward Mary Elizabeth.

"*Nay.*" Rachel grasped the handle on the passenger's side door and slid inside.

The Mennonite started the engine.

"Rachel, please." Mary Elizabeth clutched her arm through the rolled down window.

She hated the tears that slid from her eyes to roll down her cheeks. She looked into Mary Elizabeth's face. "Take care of Samuel for me."

The Mennonite put the car in gear.

"Rachel!"

She turned toward the front and stiffened her backbone against the pounding of her heart. "Let's go."

He paused for only a second before pulling the sedan onto the road, leaving Mary Elizabeth running behind and calling her name.

"It's okay if you have changed your mind." Perhaps the Mennonite could feel the regret pounding through her veins.

She shook her head. "It's too late for that." Way too late.

Rachel looked back only once to see Mary Elizabeth still standing and watching her drive away. Then they turned the corner, and she was gone.

Gabriel was surprised to see Mary Elizabeth sitting on the porch
when he returned from town. Even more surprised to see the shiny
tracks on her cheeks left by tears.

He pulled the buggy to a stop and hopped down as she stood
and wiped her hands down the front of her apron. *"Dochder, was iss
letz?"*

She had been so melancholy since returning home, so sad after
trying to live her dream of being a doctor to animals, yet unable
to hold her own in the tough *Englisch* schools. But this, *this* seemed
more than that.

"It's Rachel," she sniffed. She held out a wrinkled envelope, his
name penned on the front, the letters slightly smudged.

"What?"

She shook the letter at him. He took it, not yet comprehending
what she was trying to say. "Rachel," Mary Elizabeth started again.
"She's gone."

Gone. The word knocked around in his head, pinging off his
whirling thoughts. "Gone where?"

Mary Elizabeth shrugged. "Ohio, maybe. *Dat,* you have to go
get her." Fresh tears spilled down her cheeks.

"Go get her . . ." the words sounded foreign. He stopped, not
quite able to comprehend what had happened. Then he walked past
his daughter and into the house. Everything was clean and neat,
nothing out of place. He checked in the kitchen. Nothing cooked
on the stove. His wife was nowhere to be seen. Maybe they would
have sandwiches for their noonday meal. Or one of those cans of
store-bought soup.

He peered out the window that overlooked the backyard. He
could see the goats frolicking in their pasture. Rachel wouldn't
leave without her goats.

From upstairs he heard Samuel stir. "Wachel?"

Gabriel left the kitchen and headed for the stairs. But Rachel wasn't in any of the rooms. Just a sleepy Samuel rubbing his eyes with his un-bandaged left hand.

"Hi, *Dat*." His boy smiled, that sweet snaggle-toothed grin that melted hearts. "Where's Wachel?"

Gabriel could deny it no longer. He sat on the edge of Samuel's bed and tore open the envelope. His eyes devoured the words.

"*Dat*?"

"She's gone." His voice broke, cracked like thin ice in early spring.

"When will she be back?"

Gabriel bit back his tears, folding the letter to rights and placing it back in its envelope. "I don't know, son."

Samuel yawned. "I'm hungry."

Gabriel nodded.

Rachel was gone.

Life went on.

He ruffled Samuel's hair and tried to smile. "*Kumm* then, I'll fix you something to eat."

He somehow made it through their noon meal with his *buwe* looking at him as if they expected him to jump up and run after her. Pride kept him glued to his chair, though, slowly eating as if nothing was wrong in the world.

Haste had gotten him into this mess. A rash promise to marry a girl he hardly knew. He had acted without thinking when he had taken her into his bed.

No, this time he would measure his steps, think through a plan. But that didn't mean he was going after her. Why should he follow her if Ohio was what she really wanted? From the words of her letter it seemed they both harbored regrets.

Marrying you was a mistake. I can see that now. I'm sorry for the pain that I have caused. So very sorry that I bent the Lord's will to fit my own.

He'd let her go for now. Give it a week or two . . . maybe three. Then he'd decide.

Gabriel knocked once on the door and let himself in his parents' house. "*Mamm*?"

"Gabriel? Is that you?" His mother poked her head out of the doorway that led to the kitchen. "Come on back."

Reluctantly, he did as she asked. Some things had to be faced head-on.

She had gone back to kneading the dough, but his sister was nowhere to be seen. "Where's Katie Rose?"

"She and Zane Carson headed over to the deacon's house to check on him."

Gabriel nodded, not bothering to point out that he was the deacon. Some habits were too hard to break, and calling Ezekiel Esh the deacon was one of those.

He cleared his throat. "Rachel left." Some things were better said quickly, lest he lose the courage to utter them at all.

His mother stopped kneading the big ball of dough. "Left?"

He nodded, unable to repeat it. It was hard enough to get out the first time. "She went to Ohio."

"What did you do?"

"Do?"

"To make her leave?"

His brow furrowed at her question. "Why does it have to be something I did?"

His *mamm* wiped her hands on a dishtowel and clasped his face in her palms. "Gabriel, you are my firstborn, and I love you dearly, but you are not the easiest person to live with."

Her touch nearly sent tears streaming down his face. The last two weeks had been filled with so much trauma and emotion, he felt lucky to be standing on his own two feet. And now Rachel. He pulled his *mamm's* hands from his cheeks. "I came home for lunch, and she was gone."

She nodded as if to say, *There you have it.*

Until that moment, he hadn't realized how telling that statement was. He pulled out one of the chairs surrounding the table and sat down, his legs wobbling and unable to hold him up any longer.

"Perhaps if you wanted to keep your wife, you should have treated her as such."

"Like I wanted to keep her?"

"Like a wife."

What was it about the Fisher women that made them so mouthy? He'd tried to make Rachel his wife, in every sense of the word, but . . . "That's not what we agreed upon."

"I guess that's neither here nor there."

He grunted and gave a nod knowing it wasn't an answer, but it was the best he had to offer right then.

"You are going after her."

"I thought I would give her some time."

His mother shot him a shrewd look. "Pride is a dangerous thing."

Best if he ignored that. "I'll need some help with Samuel."

"I can help." John Paul picked that moment to walk into the room. He wore his shirt from his job in a nearby factory. He'd taken the job to help pay the medical expenses for his *mudder's* cancer treatment, and then stayed on despite his father's objections.

Gabriel shook his head, touched by the gesture. "What about your job?"

"I don't work all the time, *bruder.*"

"He has a point." Ruth nodded.

"Him or me?" John Paul asked.

"Him. What would you do about your job?"

John Paul shrugged. "I suppose I could ask for some time off."

Their *mamm* turned to Gabriel. "Or you could bring him here. One of us is around the *haus* most all of the time. Samuel will have someone to care for him every hour of the day."

Gabriel hated the thought of being away from Samuel when he needed his father the most, but what choice did he have? Matthew was watching him now, but he was needed at Gideon's. His family would care for Samuel—that was the Amish way. But it wouldn't be necessary if Rachel hadn't left.

A tiny spark of anger burned in his chest. It wasn't much, but it was a start. He needed to be angry with her for leaving. He needed to feel hurt and resentment. Otherwise, he'd have to deal with the other feelings, of being abandoned, sadness, and like someone had bored a hole straight through his heart.

The first Sunday service after Rachel left was the hardest for Gabriel. Word had spread like wildfire, most likely through Beth Troyer and Hester Stoltzfus. Whatever the cause, everyone in the district—in the entire settlement—knew that Rachel Fisher had left her husband.

He supposed that was the reason why Bishop Rueben Beachy

preached on the sins of gossip that sunny Sunday morning, and it was the reason why he felt like everyone was watching him.

He had been chosen by lot, deemed by God to serve his church, but to face the district newly anointed and wifeless was almost more than he could stand. Surely they had made a mistake in choosing him. There was no other answer that added to the sum. He should have never become deacon of the district. For if it were God's will that Samuel was to be bitten by the snake, then surely it was God's will that Rachel left. How could God expect him to hold others to the *Ordnung* if he couldn't even keep a wife? *Nay*, someone had made a mistake, and it needed to be corrected and soon.

Gabriel filled his plate with Sunday afternoon fare and went in search of Rueben Beachy. He found him just about to sit down on the bench next to Ezekiel Esh.

"Bishop? A word, please?"

The light in the bishop's eyes said he'd been waiting on this summons. He nodded toward the plate in Gabriel's hands. "Finish your *middawk* and we'll walk."

Reluctantly, Gabriel complied, easing himself down onto a patch of grass and casually eating as if he hadn't a care in the world. As if he hadn't lost not one, but two wives. As if his mother wasn't able to attend the church service because she was taking care of his youngest *sohn*.

In due time, the bishop finished eating and gave Gabriel a nod. He pushed himself to his feet, and they headed off alone. Gabriel could feel the eyes of the congregation on him as he and Bishop Beachy walked. He suspected they were thinking the same thing as he, how unworthy he'd become of the title of deacon.

"I know what you want to talk to me about and the answer is *nay*."

"You will not even allow me to voice it?"

Rueben Beachy gave a stern nod. "You may, if that's what you care to do."

Gabriel nodded in return. "I'd like to have my say."

"It will not change matters any a'tall. The elders of the church are chosen for life. Whatever God's plan is for you, you have to work with it, adapt to it. It is how our people have survived all these hundreds of years. We adapt ourselves within our own spirit and let the world move ahead in the direction it's going. Let me ask you this, Gabriel Fisher. Did you do anything to make Rachel want to leave?"

It was a question he'd been asking himself time and again since he'd found her note. "*Nay*," he said, though doubts still plagued him.

He could say that she didn't want to be there. If she did, then she would have stayed. Yet she had given up on them when times got tough. If that were the reason, then he was better off without her. All of them were better off without her, even Samuel who asked about his Wachel with nearly every breath.

How did a body explain to him that he had to fight to live, fight to relearn all of his tasks with his hands, writing and such, yet Rachel had given up? How did he explain that indeed.

"If you can look at yourself in the mirror, could stand before God and say with truth in your heart that you played no part in the choice that Rachel made, then there is nothing more to talk about."

Gabriel let those words wash over him, let them sink in. Could he say that Rachel's leaving was her decision and nothing more? Thoughts pinged through his mind: the day at the auction, the evening in the hotel, the kiss they shared, the night she spent in his arms. Had any of those moments steered her course?

He couldn't be certain.

"You're very quiet, Gabriel Fisher."

"I—" He cleared his throat and tried again. "I'm thinking."

"I'll not ask you what about, but I will point out that the time it took to mull over the answer could be the answer in itself."

Monday came and Tuesday too, and still Gabriel was no closer to an answer than he had been on his walk with Rueben Beachy. He looked out over the field of corn, the neat green rows splitting the red-brown earth. New crops, a new beginning, and yet he was haunted by the past.

Past mistakes.

He took off his hat and slapped it against his leg before placing it on his head once again.

So many mistakes.

Simon, Joseph, and David were waiting on him when he made his way back up to the house. They sat in a cluster on the front porch, all huddled together as if the closeness of their bodies was a comfort in itself.

As he neared, Simon stood and wiped his hands down the sides of his pants. "*Dat*? Can we talk with you?"

Gabriel nodded. "Let's go into the house and get some lemonade, *jah*? We can talk inside over a cool drink."

For a moment he thought the *buwe* might protest, then Simon nodded and led the way into the house. Gabriel couldn't help but notice how quiet the boys were as they poured the four glasses full of the lemonade. They were more solemn than he had ever seen them.

Something was up.

Once everyone was settled around the table, Simon spoke up once again. "We're sorry," he blurted out, tears filling his eyes.

"Sorry for what, *sohn*?"

"Samuel getting bit by the snake."

Gabriel shook his head. "That is not your fault."

Joseph nodded with David mimicking his every move. "*Jah*, it is too."

"Rachel wasn't going to let Samuel go down to the creek with us, but we begged and begged until she let him go," Simon said.

"If we had listened to her the first time, then Samuel would have never been there to get snake bit," Joseph finished.

"You don't know that for certain." But the boys had their minds made up.

"We have prayed and asked for God's forgiveness. But we need yours too, *Dat*."

A big hand squeezed his heart. "Of course, I forgive you." There was nothing to forgive them for, but it seemed they needed to hear those words. It was one thing Gabriel could do for them.

"There's more," Simon said the words while studying his fingernails. "We made Rachel leave."

Gabriel's mouth went dry. "What do you mean?"

Tears splashed onto Simon's fingers.

"Look at me, *sohn*, and tell me what you are talking about."

Simon raised watery green eyes and met his father's gaze. "We made Rachel leave. Oh, *Dat*, we're so sorry, Matthew told us not to and—"

"*Halt*. What does Matthew have to do with this?"

Simon hiccupped. "Matthew told us to leave well enough alone, but we didn't listen."

Gabriel pinched the bridge of his nose. A pang of white light throbbed behind his eyelids. "What exactly did you do?"

"We made it hard for her."

"Simon put a frog in a box under the bed," Joseph accused.

"You turned the oven back up so the cookies would burn."

"Well, you—"

"*Halt*!" Gabriel hollered once again. "This is not the time to be accusing each other." He looked from Simon to Joseph, then on to David. "What part did you play in all of this?"

"None, really."

"You didn't let her goats loose or put a lizard in her bed?"

"*Nay, Dat.*"

"Then why are you here?"

"I didn't stop them. I figure that's as bad as doing it myself."

Gabriel ruffled David's dark hair. "That is a fine sentiment, *bu.* I'd tell you that next time you should speak up, but there had better be no next time."

The boys nodded in unison.

"You may go."

Chairs scraped as they got up from the table and prepared to take their leave.

"And boys . . ."

They turned toward him, relief and remorse still painting their faces. "Don't think there won't be repercussions for this. We'll discuss a punishment after supper."

Their shoulders sagged, but all knew better than to whine or protest. They tramped from the house, shutting the door quietly behind them as they left.

Gabriel stared down into the glass of lemonade in front of him. It seemed a lot had been going on in his house that he hadn't been aware of. Rachel hadn't let on the extent of their pranks, instead calling them "little things." It seemed it wasn't so little after all. Not if they felt they were responsible for her leaving.

But were they really to blame? *Jah,* she was terrified of anything that jumped, but that didn't mean that she would turn tail and run if things got a little difficult.

Nay, there had to be more to it than that.

21

One month faded into the next. He had thought time and again about going after Rachel, but managed to make an excuse not to whenever the idea crept into his thoughts. She had written letters telling them how much she was enjoying getting to know her family in Ohio. Asking about Samuel and Baby Michelle. She never mentioned if she missed them, she never once wrote and asked about her goats. It looked to Gabriel as if she had moved on. Perhaps it was time for him to do the same.

His family slipped into a new sort of routine. Gabriel missed having Samuel at the house, but he understood. They all had to do what was right for Samuel and staying with his *grossdaadi* and *grossmammi* was the best thing for now. Still Gabriel looked forward to the time when he could bring his son home.

Simon had taken to caring for the goats, milking them twice a day and selling the milk to Plain folk and *Englischers* alike. Gabriel never knew that Simon cared about such things, but it was *gut* to see his *sohn* grow up and take initiative. Simon put all the money he earned into the fund to help pay for Samuel's hospital bill and ensuing physical therapy costs.

"*Dat*?" Simon peeked his head around the barn door, hesitantly following it inside. "Can I talk to you for a while?"

Gabriel gave him a quick nod and continued stacking the bales of organic hay that Rachel fed her goats. Well, that Simon fed Rachel's goats. "What is it?"

Simon shifted from one foot to the other. "It's about Rachel."

That got his attention. Gabriel stopped and turned to face his son. Hearing her name was like ice and fire. "*Jah?*" He propped one elbow onto the handle of the pitchfork and waited.

"I'm so sorry I made her leave." His voice hitched on a sob.

Gabriel ignored the pang of longing in his gut. "Why would you do such a thing?"

He sniffed. "I was afraid for her to come here. I was afraid that she would take *Mamm's* place and no one would remember her anymore."

"Do you—" Gabriel coughed, unable to continue. He cleared his throat and tried again. "Do you really believe that I could look at you—or any of your *bruders*—and not see your *Mamm* there as plain as day?"

"I did."

"And now?"

Simon shook his head. "*Nay.*"

Rebecca was his everything while she was alive. He could no more forget her than he could forget to pray. Just as the boys would never forget. And Rachel? A sigh escaped him. It would be a great long while before he could wake up and not find her first on his mind. Maybe when the sun fell out of the sky.

"I miss her."

Gabriel gave a nod, not having to ask who Simon was talking about. He knew.

"I know she burned the cookies and the eggs . . . and the biscuits and, well, everything, but she was fun to have around."

A lump of emotion clogged his throat, so Gabriel just grunted, hoping the sound passed for an answer. Rachel was fun to have around, though he never let himself admit it when she was.

"Are you ever going to go after her?" Simon asked.

"What?"

"I overheard Matthew telling John Paul that you should go after her. Are you?"

Maybe he should go after her, make her stand up, not be a coward, tell him to his face why she left by sneaking out in the middle of the afternoon, only leaving him a note.

Then again, he'd thought she'd've returned by now. Only her letters were any indication of what her life was like now. She seemed happy enough. She deserved to be happy. She deserved time spent with her own kin instead of the trials she had faced in Oklahoma.

"*Nay,*" he quietly replied. His heart thumped painfully with the decision. "I'll not be going after her."

Simon's request was still ringing in his ears later that afternoon. As much as he tried to push them aside, the words kept coming back, echoing inside his head. They were still floating around when John Paul pulled his Ford into the driveway and honked the car's horn.

"Good afternoon, *bruder.*"

Gabriel waved in return. He'd be glad when his brother settled down and got rid of the automobile. He was nearing on twenty years old, and soon it'd be time to bow before the church and pledge himself to God and the Amish way of life. Perhaps even in the next couple of months, if Bethany Weaver had anything to say about it.

To Gabriel's surprise, Samuel scrambled out of the passenger's seat and ran toward him, "*Dat! Dat! Dat!*" He threw his little arms around Gabriel as if he hadn't seen him in months instead of only days.

His hand was healing nicely and though it pained Gabriel to look at it, the doctor said he'd be able to do most everything that he had done before the accident. Now when he saw Samuel, saw his maimed hand, all Gabriel could think about was how blessed they were, how fortunate at Rachel's quick thinking.

"I'm taking Samuel in to the doctor. It's time to get the bandages off. You want to ride along?"

He'd almost forgotten, or perhaps he'd pushed the thought from his mind because it, too, reminded him of Rachel.

Samuel raised his right hand still bandaged and growled. "We get to see my alien hand."

The boy was definitely spending too much time with John Paul these days and his younger brother's *rumspringa* seemed to be rubbing off on him.

Gabriel ruffled Samuel's hair, wondering once again why God had blessed him with such a perfect child, maybe not in body and mind, but for sure in spirit. "Do you want me to come with you?"

"Nah," Samuel said, slipping his good hand into John Paul's. "Me and John Paul, we got this."

He'd definitely been spending too much time with his young *onkel*.

Still Gabriel laughed. Samuel staying with family had been good for the *bu*, having his *grossmammi* and *onkel* at his beck and call had kept his missing Rachel to a minimum.

"The *doktah* said I'd be able to do everything I could do before with a little practice."

Gabriel nodded. "He did at that."

"*Gut.*" A huge smile split Samuel's face showing the space

where his two front teeth had been and new ones would grow back. "'Cause I'm ready to go to school."

Gabriel looked up and met John Paul's gaze.

John Paul shrugged.

"Why are you so interested in school all of the sudden?"

Samuel smiled, irresistible and infectious. "Wachel was showing me."

"Showing you?" Gabriel felt strangely like a magpie repeating everything Samuel said. But he had no idea what his son was talking about. It hit him then, that maybe his own child had a life that he knew nothing about.

"My lettews," Samuel danced up on his tiptoes in excitement. "Wachel taught me my lettews."

Gabriel rocked back on his heels. "She did?"

"*Jah*, and how to write my name."

Gabriel looked back to John Paul, who shrugged again.

"So Mary Ann can't say I don't belong at school no more."

"Any more," John Paul immediately corrected, a testament to the amount of time that he'd been spending with the child.

Mary Ann Yutzy had taken over teaching when Katie Rose stepped down to be married. He was so far behind other six-year-olds that poor Samuel hadn't been able to attend, but now, all thanks to Rachel, he might be able to go to school. Just like his brothers.

Gabriel swallowed the lump of emotion in his throat and patted Samuel on the shoulder. "We'll have to see." He would hate for the child to get his hopes up only to have them dashed when school resumed in a couple of weeks.

"*Guck*," Samuel said grabbing a small stick. Despite the bandages still wrapped around his right hand and the missing fingers, he traced his name in the driveway dirt, neat and plain and perfect except for the backward *S*.

He moved back and examined what he'd written. Then he stepped forward again. Tongue sticking out of the corner of his mouth as he erased the first letter and remade it, correctly this time.

Gabriel knew in that moment exactly why the Bible warned against pride. His son had overcome so much. Samuel was a survivor, had been since birth. But where Katie Rose had loved him, raised him, and saw to his every need, it had been Rachel who had drawn him out, pushed him beyond his expected potential.

"We didn't get to weading though," Samuel's voice turned melancholy. "I don't mind the buwnt cookies so much. I miss hew."

"Me too," Gabriel said. He looked up and caught John Paul's gaze intently studying him. "What?"

His youngest brother shrugged and shot him that crooked smile. "Maybe you should go after her."

Gabriel shook his head.

"Why not?"

Samuel looked up. "*Jah, Dat*, why not? You didn't mind the burnt cookies, did you?"

"Samuel, go wait for your *onkel* in the car."

The youngster peered up at each of them in turn, then skipped off to the car, seemingly unaware of the emotions his words had caused.

Nay, he didn't mind the burnt cookies. They weren't always inedible. Rachel was far from perfect, could hardly be considered a proper Amish wife, but she had brought something into his house that he couldn't explain. She'd brought a freshness, a joy . . . she'd brought blessings. Now that the freshness was gone, he sorely missed it. "If she wanted to be here then she wouldn't have left."

"Perhaps she wants you to follow her."

Gabriel shook his head. This just proved what he'd known all along: It was better not to get attached to the things of this world for in a heartbeat they could be taken away. "You haven't read her letters. She loves it in Ohio." The words sent pain tearing through his heart.

John Paul shrugged. "Or maybe that's what she wants you to think."

❧ ❧

"I will now ask Katie Rose Fisher and Zane Carson to come forward."

His sister stood, and Gabriel smiled. She looked beautiful in her crisp blue dress the color of the sky on this fine fall day. Katie Rose made her way to the front of the room where she was met by the fancy *Englisch* reporter who captured her heart.

Gabriel supposed he'd have to find a new way to refer to him now that Zane Carson had joined the church. It had taken two years of studying and living in the community before the bishop finally agreed to it. Rueben Beachy hadn't been as hard on Annie Hamilton when she asked to join. One could only suspect that the bishop had grown concerned about the influences of the outside world when yet another *Englischer* decided to jump the fence to the other side.

"Katie Rose Fisher, I ask you if you will remain with Zane Carson until death. If you will be loyal to him and care for him during adversity, affliction, sickness, and weakness."

Katie Rose nodded. "*Jah.*"

He turned to the groom. "Zane Carson, I ask you if you will remain with Katie Rose Fisher until death. If you will be loyal to her and care for her during adversity, affliction, sickness, and weakness."

Zane nodded. "I will."

The bishop took their hands in his. "I wish you the blessing and mercy of God. Go forth in the Lord's name. You are now man and wife."

A buzz of excitement filled the room. Gabriel stood, and with the rest of the men, flipped the benches into tables for the women to get the feast underway. They were expecting close to six hundred people to come today as the wedding celebration would continue until late in the evening.

The women had prepared the traditional *roasht*, a mixture of bread filling and chicken, along with mashed potatoes, coleslaw, apple sauce, and creamed celery, just to name a few of the dishes available to their guests. There were wedding cakes and pies stacked on top of pies. Puddings, fruits, and sweetbread, enough food to feed their district and the next one over. But such was the way of Amish weddings.

Celery leaves in glass jars decorated tables covered with white cloth. It was a sight to see everyone gathered, enjoying the fellowship and the new union that had been formed. Gabriel couldn't help but wonder—if he had done all this for Rachel, would she still be here?

The thought was ridiculous at best. Rachel was a level-headed woman. She knew what she was doing when she married him. She had no illusions of love.

Or had she?

He looked at his sister who sat in the *eck* with her groom. It was tradition for the bride and groom to sit in the special corner formed by two tables with their attendants on either side of them. However, due to Katie's age and the fact that Zane Carson had not been a member of their community until very recently, friends and family sat beside them.

They could have been surrounded by mules and they wouldn't have noticed. It seemed they had eyes for no one but each other.

The thought fluttered back in. Would it have been different if he had done this for Rachel? If he had insisted on the large wedding, the overabundance of food and company? *Nay*, he thought.

It had been more of a mistake than that. Maybe if he could have loved her like Zane Carson loved Katie Rose, like Gideon loved Annie Hamilton.

He looked over at his brother and sister-in-law. Annie held Baby Michelle in her arms, cuddling her close. She looked like any Amish woman there. So much different from when she had arrived on that snowy spring night almost three years ago. *Jah*, she looked like any of the other women in attendance, but she sat a little closer to her husband than most, her love for him and her *Englisch* upbringing pulling her to his side like a magnet.

The same pull he'd felt toward Rachel at the hotel when he kissed her . . . and the night that Mary Elizabeth had returned.

He felt an arm slip through his. "It's a *gut* day for a wedding, *jah*?"

He patted his *mamm's* hand where it rested near his elbow. "*Jah*." Was that rusty sound his voice?

"Then why do you look so sad, *sohn*?"

Why indeed.

His *mudder* stood beside him, cancer free. His *bruder* and sister were both happily married, something no one in the district thought would ever happen. Samuel had survived the venom of a rattlesnake, and Mary Elizabeth had returned.

"I'm not sad." He said the words, but his heart gave a kick. He had nothing to be sad about. It was all just part of God's plan.

"May be part of God's plan was for you to go after her." He hadn't realized that he'd uttered the words aloud until his *mamm* responded.

"Maybe it was God's plan for her to leave."

His mother laid her hand on his cheek. "You are as stubborn as your *vatter*, Gabriel Fisher. But once you get over that, you'll see."

She turned to go, but not before he asked, "I'll see what?"

"The power of love."

He frowned as she walked away. Whatever was she talking about? It wasn't like he loved Rachel or anything. How could the power of love be involved in a marriage of convenience?

⁂

As custom, the wedding continued on through the afternoon. Friends and neighbors came and went, ate and sang, and wished the couple well. The young people gathered in the barn for a singing. Katie Rose had taught most of them at one time or another, and they turned out in droves to show their love and appreciation to their one-time teacher.

Yet Gabriel couldn't get past his mother's words. Love? When had love become involved?

Nay. He shook his head. This had nothing to do with love.

"Keep that up, *brudder,* and they'll strip you of your position for sure."

Gabriel turned as his brother approached. "Gideon."

"They'll think you're *ab im kopp* if you keep talking to yourself when no one's around."

"If no one's around who will be there to tell them?"

Gideon laughed. "It is almost time for cake."

Gabriel patted his stomach. "I had two pieces of the one they cut after *middawk.*"

"Annie says there's always room for more cake."

"I'll not be able to fit into my pants come Sunday morning. I'd do no good for my standing with the district if'n I turn up at church without britches."

"That is certain."

They stood for a moment and shared the air, then Gideon spoke. "What's troubling you, *bruder*?"

"*Nix,*" Gabriel said, looking out over his parents' land. His property started just beyond the crop of trees, the wooded area between the houses saved for hunting.

"You say nothing, and yet you stand there, looking as forlorn as a lost *kinder.*"

Gabriel shrugged. How could he voice what was bothering him when he wasn't quite sure what it was? "It seems that Rachel has left a legacy."

"Go on."

"She taught Samuel how to make his letters and write his name."

"Sounds like she was busy."

Gabriel nodded. "*Jah,* at that. He can still manage even with his hand."

"That's *gut.*"

"*Jah.*" Gabriel picked up a stick and flung it toward the trees. He wished he could throw his thoughts away just as easily.

"You miss her."

He shook his head then shrugged, thinking he must look like he was having some sort of fit as he tried to figure out his feelings for Rachel. "*Jah,*" he finally admitted. "I miss her."

"Then go after her."

"What?" He met Gideon's gaze, wondering how his brother could say the words so easily when they seemed to stick in his craw.

"Go to Ohio and bring her back."

"If she wanted to be here, then she would not have left." She wouldn't write page after page of how much she enjoyed the children she cared for, the coolness of Ohio, the changes the move had brought to her.

"That's where you are wrong, Gabriel Fisher. I almost lost Annie forever. If she hadn't been strong enough to come back to me and fight for our love, I hate to think what would have happened.

It had nothing to do with me wanting her here or not. It was about stubbornness."

Hadn't his mother just said almost the same thing?

"I sent her away because that's what I thought needed to be done. She wasn't like us. Even though I pushed her away, she came running back. That's what you do when you're in love."

"Love." Gabriel tried to keep the disdain out of his voice. Everyone talked about love. He'd loved Rebecca and look where it had gotten him. After losing the one person who meant the world to him he'd promised himself never to fall into that trap again. It only led to heartache.

"True love is rare. Isn't that what you told me?"

"Maybe."

"And if I'm remembering correctly, you said that it should be snapped up before it had a chance to get away."

Gabriel clamped his mouth shut in an attempt to find a proper response. They had been talking about Gideon and Annie at the time. It was another matter altogether when talking about oneself.

"Right?"

"She doesn't know—" He choked on the last bit, so unaccustomed to saying his feelings out loud. "She doesn't know how I feel about her." Gabriel turned away from the utter disbelief on his *bruder's* face.

"You didn't tell her that you love her?"

He shook his head slowly. "Maybe I didn't know myself. Not until now."

"I had thought you to be a smart man, Gabriel Fisher."

Gideon was right. He'd messed up in a big way. Now his wife was gone. He frowned. "But Rachel . . . she's different from Annie. She's Amish through and through. She won't come back to find love."

"Then you go after her, *bruder*. Go find your wife and tell her that you love her."

"And if she doesn't love me in return?"

Gideon smiled. "I don't think you're going to have to worry about that."

～⁍ ⁌～

Despite Gideon's confidence, Gabriel worried. But worry was useless, wasted energy so he found himself praying. A lot. Praying for God to give him courage. Praying for direction. Praying for it not to be too late, praying that even if his wife didn't love him with the same earth-shattering power that he felt for her that she would still agree to come back to Clover Ridge. He needed her. Samuel needed her. All the *buwe* did. She had become so important to them all.

That was why when the letter came from her cousin in Ohio, his fingers trembled terribly as he struggled to tear it open. He sat down on the bench outside the post office and started to read. His mouth turned to ash as he read the opening paragraph.

Dear Gabriel Fisher and Family,

I hope this letter reaches you in due time and finds all of you well. As her cousin it is my regret to inform you that Rachel has been unwell of late.

She was sick.

And I fear she may be in need of more specific care. I am hoping that you can come and see her. Perhaps seeing your face could bring cheer into her heart to help her recover.

Whatever ailed her sounded serious. She needed him.

Every doubt he had about going to Ohio and bringing her back fled in an instant. He couldn't let her suffer. If she was ill, then she needed to be here, in Clover Ridge, surrounded by the family that loved and supported her. She may not have known it when she left, but she would once he arrived. He would take her hand into his own, kiss the back, and confess his love. He owed her as much.

She had gotten him to live again, not just exist. He'd convinced himself that he'd moved on after Rebecca's death, but that wasn't the truth. He'd just been existing. Until Rachel. Now he would do the same for her.

He had his argument all planned out, all the ways that he could use to talk her into returning with him. He even steeled his backbone to pull the ultimate card. She was his wife and by the laws of God and the church, her place was at his side. Yet he didn't want her to come back for that reason. He wanted her back because she wanted to be with them too.

But if he had to . . . he'd do whatever it took to have her by his side once again.

22

Travel arrangements were difficult. A trip all the way from Oklahoma to Ohio was an undertaking. *How had Rachel managed it all by herself?*

His *mamm* agreed to stay with the *buwe* in order for him to take a week and go fetch his wife. Gabriel contacted the bishop with his reasons for being gone from the church service. Gideon, John Paul, and Matthew volunteered to care for the crops, and Bill Foster agreed to take Gabriel to Holmes County as long as his wife could make the trip with them.

The first day they made it as far as St Louis, Missouri. Gabriel had never seen a town so big. Cars everywhere, streets and highways going every which-a-ways. Although he would have liked to continue on, he was glad to have the chance to stop and rest for a while. That many people in one place was almost more than he could handle.

They spent the night in a hotel and woke the next morning to eat breakfast and get on the road once again. Soon the green hills of Missouri gave way to Illinois, then Indiana, and finally to the golden wheat fields of Ohio. He'd been on the road for two days and he had yet to figure out what he was going to say to Rachel.

The only plan he had was to tell her that he loved her and then go from there. Surely the honesty of his feelings would be enough to sway her into returning with him to Clover Ridge. And least that was his hope and prayer.

But the nearer they got to their destination, the harder his heart pounded in his chest, to the point where he wasn't sure if it was beating right a'tall. He had to bite his tongue to keep from asking Bill Foster to forget the plan altogether and drive him to the nearest hospital.

He didn't remember ever being this nervous when he and Rebecca had been courtin'. Theirs was a gentle love, strong and true, like the rivers that cut through Oklahoma. He had known his entire life that he loved her and one day he would make her his wife. But this love he held for Rachel was something altogether different. He felt like he held electricity in his hands. It burned him, made him tremble, seared him to the core. Dangerous stuff, this kind of love.

Bill Foster pulled into the first store they came to. "We'll stop here for directions."

They all piled out of the van, stretching out the kinks of nearly eight hours on the road. Gabriel wasn't used to being cooped up all day instead of pitching down hay and walking in the field. He'd rather be behind the plow any day of the week as opposed to ridin' around in a car. He didn't know how Bill Foster managed to do it and still maintain the smile on his face.

Gabriel walked around the parking lot of the general store, taking in the sights while stretching his legs.

As far as a town goes, there wasn't much to it, just the store with a Laundromat next door. There were gas pumps out front, but they didn't look like the ones they had stopped at along the way. These were round-topped and a little rusty, but Gabriel supposed there wasn't a great deal of demand for gasoline this close to the famous Holmes County. Off to the side, two buggies were parked, their horses tied to the hitchin' post whilst their owners shopped.

All in all, it looked to be a *gut* place, a little dusty but kind and understanding with many like-minded souls living close to each other and God. A Plain woman watched from the window of the store as Bill Foster came out. He loped down the stairs, unusually spry for a man his age.

"Just a couple more miles east and down another road and we'll be there. They said there was a hotel in town where we can stay."

"*Gut, gut,*" Gabriel said as he climbed back into the minivan and buckled his seatbelt once again.

"Your Rachel's cousin's place is on the other side of town, about three miles to the north."

His Rachel.

He had to admit that he liked the sound of that. Despite the painful thump of his heart and the clench in his gut, he liked the sound of that just fine.

⁂

It was almost dark by the time they reached the hotel and got checked into their rooms. As much as Gabriel wanted to drive right out to Albert Byler's farm and see Rachel with his own eyes, it was best to wait until morning. Going tonight, so close to sundown, would surely mess up the nighttime habits of the Byler household. Plus, one more night would give him a few more hours to think of all the reasons why she needed to return with him to Clover Ridge.

Bill Foster pulled the minivan into the driveway of a rambling two-story house. "This is it." It was well kept with pretty flowers still blooming in the front flower beds. Off to one side a nice-sized garden still had a few squash and what looked to be a very promising pumpkin crop.

The dogs started barking as he and the Mennonite driver got out of the van and made their way to the door.

"*Jah?*" A young woman met them there, her eyes inspecting them as if they could not be trusted.

"I'm Gabriel Fisher. I've come to see Rachel."

The girl's blue eyes grew wide and her mouth rounded into a surprised *oh.* "Just give me a moment, *jah?*"

They didn't have time to answer before she shut the door and effectively kept them outside.

Bill Foster raised his brows. "You want me to wait until she comes back?"

Gabriel shook his head. Bill and his wife had a lot of sightseeing to get to. Either way, Gabriel wasn't leaving until he saw Rachel. "You go ahead."

Bill made his way back to his van, though he seemed reluctant. Gabriel waved to him and sat in one of the large rockers on the front porch to wait.

Ohio was *purtier* country than he would have imagined. He looked out over fields of wheat and corn. Green trees and a few that had already begun to turn into their fall colors. It was colder here than Clover Ridge. This far north the winter would come quicker and last longer than in Oklahoma.

Yet for all of its beauty and bounty, Gabriel couldn't imagine his Rachel here. She belonged to the gentle hills and lush green fields, the endless sky and the red dirt.

His thoughts wandered as he sat there, whiling away the minutes as he waited on his chance to see his wife. He could only hope that she was well enough to travel. *And willing*, that insecure little voice whispered. *Don't forget willing.*

He couldn't allow those doubts to take root. He'd come to get her and take her back to where she belonged. That was his plan, and he was steadfast.

"Gabriel?"

He turned, spying the young woman who had opened the door to him earlier. She smiled hesitantly and motioned him to come on in. "I'm Amanda Byler. Rachel's cousin." She held open the door to allow him inside.

Strange lot these Ohio Amish, leave a man on the porch for nigh on twenty minutes only to invite him in like he was the Lord Himself coming to call.

"You wrote me the letter."

"*Jah.*" She nodded and Gabriel noticed that the strings on her prayer *kapp* were tied tight under her chin. She wore dark, drab gray that did nothing to hide the sparkling light in her sea blue eyes. "I told Rachel that you were here."

"Is she well enough to visit with me?" It was a cryin' shame that a man had to ask to see his own wife, but that was where he found himself.

"*Jah, jah,*" Amanda said, nodding vigorously though she didn't quite meet his gaze. "She's very excited to see you."

Amanda led him into a sitting room of sorts, nothing like he'd ever seen in Clover Ridge. "If you'll wait here . . ." She didn't finish the sentence, just gave a little flip of her hand and disappeared through a doorway covered with a thick dark curtain.

Gabriel wandered around the room, looking out the window that showed the front yard, running his fingers over the backs of the wooden framed furniture, measuring his steps on the large rug that was both humble and beautiful in its simplicity. As far as he could tell the room was used just for sittin' and maybe visitin'. There was no fireplace, no woodstove. It had to be mighty cool in there come the wintertime.

He sat down on the sofa, making himself as comfortable as possible, though his nerves had him perching on the edge of his seat. He just wanted to see his wife. He just wanted to see Rachel.

A small movement stirred at the doorway, and he turned. There she stood. His Rachel. Her hair was smoothed back neatly from her face, so tidy and proper that he almost didn't recognize her. Prayer *kapp* tied tightly beneath her chin. What had Ohio done to his scatterbrained wife that made her so . . . capable and composed? What happened to her *strubbly* hair and infectious smile?

She wore a dress of the ugliest color he had ever seen, something akin to a dried-out prune. But he would have known her eyes anywhere, doe brown and luminous. Her color looked good enough, and he thought that maybe his prayers had been answered and her health restored.

His eyes traveled hungrily down her frame taking in the bulge at her waist, its purpose sending chills though him.

"*Goedemiddag*, Gabriel."

"You're with child." He found himself on his feet even though he didn't remember standing.

She ran a small hand over her large belly, a smile worthy of the Madonna curving her lips. "*Jah*."

"But how?"

Pink flushed her cheeks, but she said not a word.

"I mean, I know *how*, but . . . why didn't you tell me?"

She moved slowly through the room and eased herself down into the chair opposite him. She was so round, her belly big and cumbersome. He belatedly clasped her elbows and supported her as she sat.

He collapsed into the chair behind him, his mind calculating the time since they had first been together and the months since she had been gone. She couldn't be more than five months pregnant, five and a half at most, and yet she looked as if she was ready to give birth there on the spot.

"I—" He shut his mouth and reopened it to try again. "It's been only a few months." He finally managed.

"Go ahead and say it," she chided. "We've been through too much not to be honest with one another."

"Your belly is so big."

She laughed, and he immediately wanted to call the words back.

"It is at that," she said. "You see, I'm having twins."

"We're having twins." He repeated the sentiment, his voice bewildered. "Why didn't you tell me?"

"I didn't know if you wanted one baby, much less two."

"You didn't ask me."

She gave him a sad little smile. "Our marriage was a disaster from the start. I should have never agreed to be your housekeeper. You should have never asked me to marry you."

He shook his head. "I don't think the bishop would agree with you there."

She shrugged. He hated her expression. He couldn't read her. When she had been in Oklahoma with him he'd been able to interpret every nuance of her emotions. Or at least thought he could. Now her features were carefully sculpted into the mask of peace before him.

"How do you think it looks for me to be a deacon? Do you know how hard it is to tell people that you've run off?"

She awkwardly pushed herself to her feet. "I'm sure you'll think of something." Her words were punctuated with another of those plastic smiles.

Gabriel stood on his trembling legs, his thoughts a tangled jumble of unspoken pleas.

She walked to the door as if to see him out. But he wasn't leaving until he had his say.

"Rachel." He followed behind her, stopping close enough to reach out and cup her cheek in the palm of his hand. "I love you. And I want you to return to Clover Ridge with me. I *need* you to come home. We all do."

She opened her mouth to reply, but he cut it short, placing one finger over her lips. "You don't have to say anything now. I'll be back tomorrow. We can talk more then."

She nodded.

He wanted to lean in, kiss those trembling lips, tell her again how much she had come to mean to him. But he needed to give her a little time, a chance to convince herself to come with him. He wanted her home, but he wanted her to believe it was all her idea.

As he stepped out into the cool Ohio afternoon, one thing was certain: He wasn't leaving here without his wife.

⚜

Rachel closed the door behind Gabriel and longed to slip down into the floor and cry her eyes out. Instead she waddled to the couch where her husband had been sitting when she first greeted him and sank down into his warmth. She inhaled deeply, the smell of him surrounding her like a comforting embrace.

He had come looking for her.

She bit back a sob. Oh, how she had messed this one up. Everyday she said prayers asking forgiveness. Her thoughtlessness had almost cost Samuel his life. Despite everyone's assurances that it "could have been worse," and that the accident was God's will, she knew that it was her fault. If only she had told him no, that he couldn't go to the creek with his *bruders*, then he would be safe and whole and not having to learn how to make his numbers and letters with a hand missing two fingers.

"Rachel?" Amanda came into the room. "I thought I heard the door."

She nodded, unable to find her voice amid the threatening tears.

"Did Gabriel leave?"

"*Jah.*"

Amanda sat down on the couch next to her. "He came to get you, *jah*?"

"*Jah*," Rachel whispered.

"Then why did he leave?"

Rachel stood unable to deal with the emotions running through her. Anger, confusion, self-loathing. "I don't know."

Amanda shook her head. "What about the babies?"

Gabriel was nothing if not honorable. Of course he would want her to go with him. Of course he would want his children near.

"If I am here and he is there, how can there be any talk about the babies?"

Why would God give her not one *boppli* but two when it was so painfully obvious that she couldn't be trusted with one that was half grown? How was she going to care for the little ones, feed them, and keep them safe from harm?

"But . . . but how will you live here, Rachel, when your husband is so many miles away?"

It all came down to that. She had known before she came that Albert Byler only wanted her to come to help him with his brood of eleven. Now that she was adding two of her own to the mix, he was less than pleased.

If only she had her goats, she could use them to support herself. She could get a house of her own. Just her and the babies . . . If only she had known before she left. If only, if only, if only . . .

"I think you should consider his offer," Amanda said quietly.

Rachel blinked at her, unsure she heard right. "Accept his offer?"

"You should at least give it some thought."

She didn't know what to say. There was so much that stood in their way. She was no deacon's wife. It took so much of her time just to keep her hair properly covered. She was terrible with the boys. She'd almost let Samuel die and the others had done everything in their power to chase her away. Perhaps they had known from the start what she only learned later: That she was no bride.

"Was he mean to you, Rachel? Did he hurt you? Was he unfaithful? Untrue?"

"*Nay.*"

Amanda took her hand and squeezed it gently, as if the touch alone could impart some faith and strength. "He hasn't turned his back on God. He hasn't turned his back on you. Will you be so selfish to deny your children the life they should have?"

Tears slipped down her cheeks, but Rachel made no move to wipe them away. Her hands inside Amanda's warm ones trembled as they gained the support and love that she needed.

"I wrote Gabriel. I'm the reason he came. I told him you were unwell and needed him. That's why he's here. Not because of the bishop, but because he cares about you. I daresay he even loves you."

Love. There was that word again. But Gabriel had told her long ago that he wasn't looking for love. He'd had that with Rebecca. Like lightning never striking the same place twice, so it was with love. One love per lifetime, and he'd already had his.

"He doesn't love me." Rachel had said the words many times

in her mind, but saying them out loud pained her more than she could say. He might have said that he did, but he didn't mean it. He couldn't.

Could he?

Amanda shook her head. "He does. I could see it in his eyes whenever I mentioned your name."

She wanted to believe that. Oh, how she wanted to believe. "I need some time to think about this."

Amanda released her hands and stood. "*Jah*. I'll go make us some tea."

Rachel gave a little nod, then laid her head back against the couch cushion. There was a lot to consider.

23

The next afternoon, Rachel opened the door and led Gabriel into the sitting room, too tired to battle with words. She hadn't slept much the night before. The babies seemed to sense her turmoil and kicked all night long. No matter what position she switched to, one of them was unhappy and not bashful about letting her know it.

A frown knit Gabriel's brows as he took in her appearance. "Are you feeling okay today?"

She gave a quick nod, still unaccustomed to the feel of her prayer *kapp* tied tightly under her chin.

"I brought these for you." He held out a bunch of flowers tied up with a pretty yellow ribbon. She stared at them, perplexed until he explained. "It's an *Englisch* courtin' custom."

She took the flowers, her hand shaking. "Is that what this is? A courtin'?"

"*Jah.*" He nodded, shifting from one foot to the other, visibly uncomfortable. "I don't have a buggy to take you for a ride. And I reckon we're both too old for a singin'."

She hid her smile, burying her nose in the fragrant blossoms rather than let him see how easy it was to get to her.

"Sit down," she offered, still hiding behind the flowers. "I'll put these in some water."

She made him wait a full five minutes before she returned to the sitting room. Without comment she deposited her ungainly form into the chair across from him and folded her hands across her overlarge belly.

"Did you have a chance to think about my offer?"

She tilted her head to one side, as if thinking about their conversation the day before. "I do not recall an offer."

"Rachel." The one word was something of a growl, uttered in a much more familiar tone.

She sighed, already tired of this game. Or maybe she was simply weary of trying to be what she needed to be. Dark dresses, hair perfect all the time. No goats, heavy with twin babies that seemed to sap all of her energy like nothing else she had ever experienced. "What do you want from me, Gabriel?"

"I want you to return to Clover Ridge with me."

"Why?"

"I know we talked about this yesterday. But I'll say it again, I love you, Rachel."

"And it doesn't look good for a deacon to be without his wife."

"And the boys miss you."

She shook her head before he even finished. "Samuel was the only one who was ever glad I was there and I almost killed him."

"You saved him. Another thirty minutes without medical care and he'd've—" He stopped, unable to finish, but Rachel didn't need the words for the tears to come. They burned at the back of her eyes. Samuel was walking proof of her poor decisions. "He's gotten all the bandages off and has started to school with his alien hand."

"His what?" It was easier by far to focus on the ridiculous

instead of the triumphs that Samuel had accomplished over the summer, knowing that she had almost brought it all to an end.

Gabriel shook his head. "John Paul. You were gone and Annie needed Mary Elizabeth." He shrugged. "Samuel went to stay with *Mamm* and *Dat*. John Paul took care of him while he healed. I think his *rumspringa* has rubbed off on the *bu*."

"He started school?"

"Thanks to you."

She shook her head, though she was proud of all that he had learned and overcome this year. Oh, how she missed him.

"Simon is sorry for all the mischief he put you through. He misses you too."

She couldn't find the words to reply.

"He's been taking care of your goats. Though you should know, he's got Sundae so spoiled she will barely eat the grass in the pasture."

Rachel stood suddenly unable to hear any more. "Gabriel, I . . . I don't know what to say."

He stood as well.

Just standing in his shadow made her feel protected and safe, as if no harm could come to her as long as she was by his side. She had to do it. She had to return with him to Clover Ridge. For the babies.

For herself.

She took a steadying breath gathering courage. "Okay."

"Okay?"

She nodded. "I'll go . . . home with you."

She thought she saw the flash of tears in his eyes before he pulled her close. But that couldn't be. Her eyes fluttered closed as he pressed a sweet, sweet kiss to her lips. By then the tears that wet her cheeks could have just as easily been her own.

The trip back to Oklahoma was even more tedious than her original journey to Ohio. Of course, the first time she had traveled the *bopplin* were so tiny that she didn't even know they existed. She had been nauseous and light-headed, not knowing that both afflictions were from the babies she carried. She had figured heartsickness was her ailment and that only time could cure that. Despite the fact that she had gotten sick in every bathroom at every rest stop along the way, she had pressed on till she reached her destination.

After she arrived and still couldn't shake the sickness, her cousin Amanda had talked her into going to the doctor in Millersburg. After a series of tests the results came back: She was pregnant. She wasn't sure if she should laugh or cry, so she did a little of both. But it didn't soften the blow when the doctor examined her and found not one, but two heartbeats.

Amanda had tried to talk her into returning to Oklahoma then, but for Rachel there was no going back. How could she live in a place knowing her husband hated her, didn't need her, would blame her every day for not being a good enough parent to watch Samuel? How could she look at that sweet, freckled face knowing that he would be whole if not for her poor decision making?

But now she had to put her feelings aside and do what was right for the *bopplin* she carried.

The return trip took three days. Bill Foster, the kindly Mennonite driver and his wife, Linda, were solicitous in making sure that she was comfortable.

But it was staying in a hotel each night that about did her in. He told her that he would give her time, but her wounded heart knew it was just a way to cover for him. It gave him an excuse to secure a double room and keep to himself. But all Rachel could think about was the night they'd spent together, intimate and close, the night Mary Elizabeth had returned.

Surely when they arrived back in Clover Ridge she'd be able to put all that behind her and go on as if nothing had ever happened.

Like that would be possible.

She pressed a hand to her growing stomach. She would have a constant reminder of the "what might have been" between her and Gabriel. But she knew deep down that Amanda was right: Gabriel had not turned his back on God, and he had not hurt her in any manner. Truly her heartbreak was her fault and hers alone. She had so many reasons to continue on with their agreed marriage. Many an Amish woman had made a worse match than she had with Gabriel Fisher.

"Are you okay?" he asked, nodding toward her hand still curved around the mound of her stomach.

"*Jah*." She removed her hand, dropping it back onto the seat next to her. "The babies are quiet when we're in the car."

"*Jah*?" His mossy green gaze was so intense she had to look away.

She turned to look out the window. The close quarters were getting to her. Two nights in a hotel and endless hours in the car sitting side by side with not much to do but count the license plates from other states and the number of dogs as they passed through the towns. And think.

It'd be *gut* to get back home to Clover Ridge. *Gut* to try and get things back to normal. Though she wasn't sure normal was ever something she would be able to achieve.

"Can I—" Gabriel reached out a hand almost, but not quite touching the dark cloth covering her stomach.

How could she deny the earnest look on his face?

She gave a nod, and the warmth of his hand pressed against her. She wasn't sure how much he could feel, but he sat that way for a moment or two before one of the babies started to kick.

"Here," she said, moving his hand down to the spot where the twin was acting out his own version of hopscotch.

Gabriel's eyes grew wide. "Are there really two of them?"

Rachel nodded. "I was as surprised as you."

"I doubt that," he replied. "When you came into the room . . ." He shook his head, but didn't continue.

"What?"

He sat back, pulling his hand away from her. "It was a shock, to be sure."

"I suppose it was."

Gabriel turned and looked out the window.

Rachel wasn't sure what he found so interesting on the other side of the glass. She herself had a great deal of trouble looking out at the blur of the landscape as they whizzed past.

In no time at all, they'd be back in Clover Ridge and able to put some distance between each other. She would be glad of that. She needed a break from being so close to her husband and unable to tell him how she really felt. That, despite the fact that she had so many regrets where the two of them were concerned, she loved him more than anything—and always would.

~§ §~

It was just before dark when Bill Foster pulled the minivan onto the dirt lane leading to Gabriel's house. A more welcome sight, Rachel was sure she had never seen.

As she pushed herself from the van, the front door opened and the Fisher boys spilled out followed by Ruth.

"Wachel, Wachel!"

Samuel was the first one to her, throwing his arms around her and holding her tight as if he never wanted to let go.

Then he pulled back and pointed to her belly. "Is that a *boppli*?"

She nodded. "*Jah.* Two, as a matter of fact."

Samuel's big green eyes grew round as did those of everyone in earshot.

"Two?" Simon seemed mesmerized.

Just then, Ruth reached her, wrapping an arm around her and walking her toward the house. "Twins," she breathed, as if it was the most special thing in the world.

"Two babies!" Samuel danced around like he had ants in his britches.

"But it's a secret." Ruth placed one finger over her lips.

A confused frown puckered his brow. Rachel laughed. With a belly the size of hers, keeping their news secret was going to be a miracle indeed.

"I got an alien hand." Samuel held up his right hand to show her. "But it ain't a secret."

"It's not a secret," Rachel corrected, doing her best not to break down at the sight of Samuel's hand. If she was going to make this work, she had to forgive herself for the mistakes she had made.

Ruth pulled her close as they neared the house and whispered in her ear, "One day at a time, sweet Rachel. One day at a time."

One day slipped into the next, and they fell into a sort of pattern. Gabriel was up and gone before she got out of bed and got the *kinder* ready for school. Exactly how early he got up, she didn't know.

He would stay away all day, not even coming in to eat at noon, but managing to get back to the house just in time for supper.

Afterwards, he read to them from the Bible, then headed off to bed while she and Simon cleaned the kitchen and helped Samuel with his homework. Then the rest of the household retired for the night only to get up and start the configuration all over again.

But the stress of the day in and day out was beginning to take its toll.

Rachel rolled over in her bed and stared at the moonlit ceiling. How much longer could they keep this up, this polite existence that they had embroiled themselves in? Not much longer she was certain, before it extracted its price on them all.

She pushed herself out of bed and eased across the cold floor and down the stairs.

Maybe it had been a bad idea to come back. Maybe it would have been better for them all if she had stayed in Ohio. Better for her and Gabriel maybe, but surely not better for all the *kinder*, the ones living with them and the ones to come next.

She pressed a hand to her large belly, just now fully understanding how much her life was about to change.

Her knees hit the floor under the weight of her realization. She was about to bring forth not one life, but two. What more of a testament to God's will did she need? She and Gabriel had only spent one night together and here was the result, the babies growing within her. God knew that Gabriel Fisher was an honorable man, devout and true and would not let her go through this alone. But was it so much to ask that he love her in return?

She bowed her head despite her lack of head covering and started to pray.

"Rachel, *mei liewe*, what's wrong?" Suddenly he was at her side, warm calloused hands rubbing her shoulders, solicitous and true. "The babies? Are they *allrecht*? Is it time?"

She shook her head, unable to find her voice among her tears.

He hooked his arms under her elbows and lifted her to her feet. In one efficient move, he spun her to face him, wiping her tears and smoothing back her hair. "*Was iss letz, mei liewe? Was iss letz?*" he crooned over and over as she continued to cry.

How did she explain that it was just so much? This love that she carried for him, his *kinder*, his family, and the babies she carried. It was a *gut* love, but overwhelming, filling her up and spilling out around her. But that he couldn't love her in return . . .

"Why did you come after me?" she whispered, her voice thick with emotion.

"I've already told you that." He brushed the tears from her cheeks, planting a small kiss in each spot where his thumbs had been.

"Because it doesn't look good for a deacon to have a wayward wife?"

"Because I love you."

Oh, how she wanted to believe that. "But you said—"

He shook his head. "Forget what I said. That was before I knew you, before you let your goats eat my hybrid wheat, before you burned the cookies, and taught my *sohn* to write."

"I don't know."

"I do."

She shook her head. "I've prayed and prayed for direction and my prayers have gone unanswered."

"A prayer cannot be answered twice."

"I—" she stopped unable to finish the thought.

"You've prayed for understanding of God's will, a family of your own . . ."

"And the love of a husband."

"*Jah*," he said, and kissed her then.

She moved closer to him, as close as her new girth would allow. Her belly pressed between them, and she laughed despite the tears that rolled down her cheeks.

"I've tried so hard, Rachel, to give you time, let you adjust. But I am only a man. I am weak. I'm tired of you sleeping a world away. I want to wake up in the night and hear you breathing beside me. Knowing that you are mine and you will always be there. I love you, Rachel, but more than that, I *need* you."

"You love me?"

"*Jah*," he said, his thumbs still caressing her cheeks though her crying had subsided. "*Ich liebe dich*. And I think I have always."

Rachel laid her head on his shoulder, content for the first time in a long while. Gabriel loved her, truly loved her.

"I love you too, you know."

"I didn't." His chin bumped against the top of her head as he spoke the words. "But I am very glad to know it now."

Somehow he drew her closer still, enveloping her in his warmth and love.

What had she done to deserve such goodness in her life? She might never know, but she'd spend her lifetime trying to figure it out, all the while knowing that she was as loved and as blessed as one woman could be.

Epilogue

She had thought that having two more *buwe* around the house would be a challenge, but she was way off. Tuesday was her normal pie baking day, but she had barely got the dough rolled out when the ruckus started. Any pans that happened to be within reach were pulled onto the floor, resulting in a clatter Rachel was sure could be heard all the way to the General Store.

She washed her hands, then gathered the pans, placing them back where they belonged. Fast as she could, she waddled to the toy chest and fetched them each a wooden pull toy in hopes it would keep them occupied long enough to roll out the dough for at least two pies. She wanted to get them over to the Old Esh place for Zane Carson and Katie Rose. Katie had just given birth to a beautiful baby girl they had named after Ruth. Baby Ruthie was just now two months old and the apple of her *dat's* eye. Zane Carson had turned out to be a quite *gut* Amish man, contributing regularly to *Die Botschaft* while taking on the business with Rachel of raising goats for milk and cheese. Between the two properties they had nigh on one hundred goats, each one carefully named by Samuel.

Zane Carson's help with her business had benefited them both, though Rachel thought she got the better of the deal. She was able to keep her favorites close and still maintain her high standards of cheese making and organic feeding. *And* she was able to contribute to the household monies and still have plenty of time to spend with the *kinder*.

"Now stay out of there before I nail your *frack* to the floor."

Micah sat down on his diapered bottom and chewed on the wheels of the toy, babbling and grinning, showing her his pearly teeth.

Yes, the Lord must have a sense of humor for making them identical. Truth be known, no one could tell them apart. Rachel hoped that one day they would grow a little differently, gain a freckle or a mole or some type of distinguishing mark, but for now she had tied a strip of leather around Micah's ankle so she'd know him from Adam.

At eighteen months old, they gave double trouble a whole new meaning.

Satisfied that they would play for a few more minutes, Rachel went back to her pies. She really wanted to do this for them, to pay them back for all their help after the twins were born. Katie Rose had sewed quilts for them, helped make clothes for them, and Zane Carson had given assistance with the goats.

A couple more weeks and she would be giving birth herself. She pressed a hand to the mound of her belly and smiled. Every day she prayed for a girl. A healthy girl, she amended, lest the Lord think her too demanding. But after watching Baby Michelle grow into a toddler she knew that girls were easier to raise than boys. Right now, she would be mighty grateful for any break she could get.

She swung Adam down from the kitchen table. "Oh, no you don't." Last time he'd climbed up there he had taken a bite out of every peach in the basket. She had definitely learned from that mistake.

"*Mamm, guck. Guck!*" Samuel came bursting through the front door holding a bunny by its hind legs. At least it wasn't a garter snake or a frog.

She stifled a shudder at the thought of the reptiles. "Samuel Fisher, take that bunny outside right now."

"Okey-dokey."

She shook her head as he skipped from the room, rabbit in hand.

She was going to have to speak to John Paul about the things he was teaching the *bu*. Samuel was too impressionable by far. But her talk with John Paul would have to wait until another day. She still had pies to bake. She'd like to have them in the oven before the rest of the boys finished their chores. Then maybe she could sit for a minute and rest her aching back.

A clatter from behind alerted her that her rest might be a fading dream.

"That's it," she said scooping up the twins and depositing them in their highchairs. She gave them each a hard toast biscuit and a smear of honey goat cheese. Maybe if she kept them busy eating she could get her work done.

She went back to the pie crust, turning it over on the counter and rolling out the dough quickly and efficiently. It might be a bit boastful to say, but her cooking had improved. At least these days she properly cooked more than she burned. But either way, her husband didn't seem to mind.

She knew that he had more on his mind than cookies.

Mary Elizabeth had set off for the *Englisch* world again, but she stayed close, taking a job at a vet's office in Pryor. It was the perfect job for her, requiring less schooling than that of a veterinarian and still allowing her to be around her beloved animals. She came by every Saturday afternoon for supper. Bishop Beachy turned a blind eye to her visits, knowing firsthand how hard it was to let *kinder* out into the world of the *Englisch*.

If that wasn't enough for Gabriel to spend more time on his knees prayin' than half the men in the settlement put together, Matthew had entered his *rumspringa* and was taking his lead from John Paul. Whatever his young *onkel* did, Matthew was right behind.

It wouldn't be so bad if John Paul wasn't heartbroken himself. Bethany Weaver got tired of waiting around for him to join the church and up and married Danny Detweiler. It was a *gut* match. Danny worked in construction with his father and grandfather roofing houses as far away as Claremore. When John Paul found out, he just shrugged it off, but Rachel recognized the pain in his eyes. To the outside she was certain he appeared like any other Amish young man, nearing twenty-one and taking his sweet time about joining the church. But she knew there was more to it than that.

Rachel brushed her hair back from her forehead and ignored the pain in her belly. Practice contractions were not going to get the best of her today. She had a mission and she intended to see it through.

Adam babbled something that sounded like *puppy*, then began squealing. Not about to be outdone, Micah started in as well.

That's when she saw the puppy biting at Adam's toes.

"Who let the dog in?" Like it mattered. It was probably Samuel when he brought in the rabbit.

When no one answered she went to the back door, using her elbow to push it open instead of her flour-covered hands. She had not yet managed the art of *neat* baking.

She looked down at herself. Flour covered her front as far as she could see. Chances were it was smeared across her lower belly as well. She opened her mouth to call one of the boys to come get the dog when another pain hit, this one far worse than the last.

She stumbled, placing one hand on her stomach and one on the door frame to steady herself. Yet the pain was intense, and she found herself on her knees.

"Rachel, *was iss letz*?" Simon came running from the direction of the goat pen. It was his afternoon chore to milk the creatures using the fancy gas-powered milking machine that Rachel had bought when they expanded.

"The *boppli*," she gasped, feeling the wet stain of her water. "It's time."

"It's time?" He hopped up and down, whipping his hat in the air.

She pushed herself to her feet. Pie making would have to wait.

By then Simon's antics had gained the attention of the other boys. Joseph and David rounded the corner of the house with Samuel close behind. "*Was iss letz*?"

"It's the *boppli*," Simon said proudly.

"Simon," Rachel called. "Go get your father. He's in the north field of corn."

"*Jah.*" Simon sprinted away, his hat flying off. He back tracked, picked it up, and with a grin, was back on the way to get his *vatter*.

"David, you run over to your *grossmammi's* house. Tell her it's time for the baby."

Wide-eyed, David nodded and trotted off to the road, one hand holding his hat in place as he ran.

"What can I do, *mamm*?" Samuel ran a hand over her distended belly.

"Go get the dog out of the house," Rachel instructed.

She led them back inside, each step growing more painful as the baby prepared to make its way into the world.

The twins were still seated in their highchairs though they had managed to smear soggy biscuit and cheese through their soft blond hair. They both needed a bath, but that would have to wait until their father came into the house. If Gabriel acted anything like he had when she was delivering the twins, he'd need a diversion for sure.

"What can I do? What can I do?" Joseph asked, jumping up on his tiptoes in excitement.

"Pray," Rachel said with a smile. Another contraction hit and she knew the *boppli* would be here soon. "Pray that this time it's a girl."

Glossary

ab im kopp	off in the head (crazy)
Ach	oh
Aeamen	Amen
aenti	aunt
allrecht	all right
boppli	baby, babies
bruder	brother
bu, buwe	boy, boys
dabbich	clumsy person
danki	thanks
Dat	Dad
Deutsch	Pennsylvania Dutch
dochder / dochdern	daughter / daughters
dumm	dumb
dunnerwetter	thunderweather (used like dang)
eck-	special place for the bride and groom at the corner of the wedding table
Englisch	non-Amish person

ei, yi, yi	my, oh, my
elder	parents
der fisch	a fish
fraa	wife
frack	dress
freind / freinden	friend / friends
froh	happy
gern gschehne	You're welcome
goedemiddag	Good afternoon
grossdaadi / daadi	grandfather
grossmammi / mammi	grandmother
guck datt hie	Look there
guder mariye	Good morning
gut himmel	Good heavens
gut nacht	Good night
halt	stop
haus	house
ich liebe dich	I love you
jah	yes
kapp	prayer covering, prayer cap
en katzfisch	a catfish
kind, kinder	children
kshpassich	strange
kumm dummel	Come hurry
liebschdi	Dear child
liebschen	Dearest
mach schnell	Hurry up (make quickly)
mamm, mammi	Mom
middawk	noon meal
mudder	Mother
naerfich	nervous
narrisch	crazy

nachtess	supper
nay	no
nix	nothing
onkle	uncle
Ordnung	book of rules
outen the light	Turn out the light
redd-up	Clean up
roasht	traditional wedding dish made of cut up chicken and stuffing
rumspringa	running around time (at 16)
shveshtah	sister
sohn	son
Vatter	Father
verhuddelt	confused
Was iss letz?	What's wrong?
Wie geht?	How are things?

Dear Reader—

Alfred, Lord Tennyson once said, "I am a part of all that I have met." *Gabriel's Bride* is truly a little piece of all that I am, as well as many people who are close to me.

I have a kinship with Rachel Yoder that I've never had with any other of my characters. No, I'm not an orphan. I'm not being forced to get married. And I'm not a stepmother to six reluctant children. But I've been known to wander away from the oven and burn the cookies. Or the potatoes. And the bread. Especially the bread. I love my "hobbies" more than housecleaning, and I'm easily distracted. Yes, Rachel Yoder is a bit ADD. But she's got a big heart full of love, a kind soul, and she's a bit of a dreamer. Not bad qualities if you ask me, and perfect for a man like Gabriel Fisher.

When I started the Clover Ridge Series, I knew that Gabriel needed someone special to bring him to love again. But Rachel was a surprise. Her spunk, her energy, and the chaos that seems to follow her hit a little close to home. In Rachel, I found a common bond, a soul sister, and I am so happy to give her a story.

Gabriel's Bride is fiction . . . mostly. And the rest is a bit of family stories and inspirations from conversations with friends. Truth can be stranger than fiction. But love is bigger than both.

Blessings to you and all those you love—

Amy

Discussion Questions

1. When Gabriel discovers that Mary Elizabeth has gone to live with the English, he tells his sons, then says they will not speak of it again. Have you ever known anyone like Gabriel? A person who hides their feelings instead of talking about them? How has their suppressing their emotions affected your relationship with them?

2. Rachel Yoder came to live in Oklahoma after her parents and brothers were killed in an accident. Have you ever had to move quickly, leaving friends and family behind? How did you handle it? How did your response differ from Rachel's?

3. Gabriel denies Deacon Ezekiel Esh's claim that he is the right man to be the district's new deacon. Gabriel resists. Have you ever denied something that you knew was for you, that perhaps suspected God wanted for you? What finally changed your mind?

4. Gabriel's middle sons are none too happy about his marriage to Rachel. In today's blended families this is a concern for a great many people. What are some ways two families can live as one and how do they survive their many differences?

5. What does Ruth mean when she tells Rachel there is only one kind of marriage? Do you agree with her statement?

6. Ezekiel Esh tells Gabriel, "The Lord sees a need, and He provides for it. It is a sin to waste opportunities as surely as it is to defy God Himself." What does he mean by this statement? Do you agree?

7. Ruth tells Rachel that if the cancer is back then it was God's will all along. Have you ever experienced something such as this in your life or perhaps to a loved one? How did you discern God's will from mere circumstance?

8. Ruth makes Rachel promise not to tell anyone that she has found another lump. Rachel feels that this is an unfair promise. Do you agree with Rachel? What of Ruth's feelings? Is she justified in her decision not to go for further testing?

9. In *Gabriel's Bride*, a new deacon is chosen for the district and the process of choosing a leader by lot is outlined. What are some of the benefits of choosing church leaders this way? What about drawbacks?

10. When Mary Elizabeth returns, she is saddened that she wasn't able to fit into the world of the English. Most of us, at one time or another, have felt like we weren't accepted or didn't fit in.

How did you handle this? How important is it to be welcomed? Discuss ways to handle this problem.

11. When Samuel gets bitten by the snake, Rachel believes that it's her fault. Is she correct in her thinking? Have you ever blamed yourself for something beyond your control? How did you learn to forgive yourself?

12. Rachel grows up quite a bit in *Gabriel's Bride*. Some of her experiences are good and some are bad. How have certain happenings in your life caused you to "grow up"? Were most of these good or bad experiences?

13. At the end, does Rachel have a boy or a girl? What are the reasons behind your choice?

If you enjoyed *Gabriel's Bride*, you can read more about the wonderful people of Clover Ridge in *Saving Gideon* and *Katie's Choice*.

Saving Gideon
9781433677526

Katie's Choice
9781433677533